W9-AKU-112

CLAN NOVEL:
Tzimisce

ERIC GRIFFIN

author	eric griffin
cover artist	john van fleet
series editors	john h. steele and
	stewart wieck
copyeditor	anna branscome
graphic designer	kathleen ryan
art director	richard thomas

More information and previews available at
white-wolf.com/clannovels

Copyright © 1999 by White Wolf, Inc.
All rights reserved.

No part of this book may be reproduced or transmitted in any form
or by any means, electronic or mechanical — including photocopy,
recording, Internet posting, electronic bulletin board — or any other
information storage and retrieval system, except for the purpose of
reviews, without permission from the publisher.
White Wolf is committed to reducing waste in publishing. For this
reason, we do not permit our covers to be "stripped" for returns, but
instead require that the whole book be returned, allowing us to resell
it.

All persons, places, and organizations in this book — except
those clearly in the public domain — are fictitious, and any
resemblance that may seem to exist to actual persons, places, or
organizations living, dead, or defunct is purely coincidental. The
mention of or reference to any companies or products in these pages
is not a challenge to the trademarks or copyrights concerned.

White Wolf Publishing
735 Park North Boulevard, Suite 128
Clarkston, GA 30021
www.white-wolf.com

First Edition: May 1999

10 9 8 7 6 5 4 3 2 1

Printed in Canada.

To Victoria—

*For all she has endured
at the hands of the undying.*

Tzimisce

part one:
the war
council

My Dearest Vykos,

How can I describe to you my feelings upon hearing from you again after so many years? Words are rough clay vessels that tend to crack when filled with such emotions—emotions that run deep and span lifetimes. I had thought you lost to me for all time.

To learn that you are not only alive, but here! It is altogether too much to hope for. It is almost better to believe this all some cruel joke or perhaps a cunning trap. Between Truth and Treachery, the latter is much the more constant mistress. She never strays far from my side these nights.

But your letter gives me cause to hope. I had almost forgotten what a fierce and terrible thing it is to hope. This is another debt I will have to repay you when we meet.

Ah, but what am I saying? We both know that such a meeting is impossible. As you have pointed out, your mere proximity places me in a rather precarious position. I cannot leave the city without attracting enough unwanted attention to destroy the both of us. You cannot venture so deeply into hostile territory. If you were to attempt it, all of my influence would not be enough to shield you from the consequences.

No, for the present you must lock away all thought of me in the secret places of your heart and make fast the door. If you will only keep faith a while longer, I will contrive to come to you, whatever the price. You may rely upon it.

I am not so vain, however, as to believe you have come all this way—across the intervening oceans and centuries—merely to look up an old friend. I fear your very presence bodes ill for the doves among us.

Have no fear, your secrets are safe with me. I mention this only in the foolish and sentimental hope that perhaps once you have loosed your hawks, we might arrange a rendezvous under the flag of a parley. You see how eagerly I embrace any pretense that might bring you to me once more. I am almost shamed by the fierceness of my desire to hold your delicate throat within my hands.

Ah, soon my dearest. Keep your secrets safe a little while longer. What are a mere few weeks to us, who have measured our loss and longing in centuries? With each passing day, the anticipation of our reunion consumes me.

I remain, yours in undying devotion,
—Lucius

Saturday, 19 June 1999, 9:12 PM
Chandler Room, Omni Hotel at CNN Center
Atlanta, Georgia

Polonia surveyed the conference room with a critical eye. *Perfect.*

Still, he seemed somewhat preoccupied as he went about his ritual—shifting a placecard here, removing a piece of chipped crystal there, plucking out an ill-concealed listening device. Absently, he corrected for a half-dozen subtle but potentially disastrous breaches of etiquette and precedence. He was painfully aware of just how little it would take to transform a Sabbat war council into an uncontrollable raging maelstrom.

He completed one full circuit of the prodigious conference table and began again. The fingertips of his right hand trailed along the surface of the rough-hewn table as he went. The touch was reassuring.

The blackened oak table was a presence in the room. Polonia approvingly ticked off its virtues. To begin with, it was massive. Its sheer size made it unlikely that even the most hulking Tzimisce monstrosity would be able to smash it or (as they were so wont to do) smash someone else *with* it. This alone would prove a telling advantage when the discussion grew heated, as it inevitably would.

The great circular table had the additional weight of tradition and history about it. The piece had been brought in, at considerable expense, from a private collection in England's Lake Country. It was undoubtedly a forgery, but it was a forgery with a history. And that made all the difference. Like its legendary predecessor, this round table was intended to forestall

TZIMISCE

the endless posturings and power plays that might otherwise arise in such an assembly of proud and temperamental warlords as each vied for a place of honor near the table's head.

Polonia smiled at the thought. It was not only the table that had no head. It was the whole damnable assembly. He was all too aware that there was nothing to compel the factious Sabbat packleaders to follow his lead. He had spent a good deal of his effort in planning this event simply to ensure that he would not be among those torn to pieces during the opening arguments.

As the Sabbat Archbishop of New York, Francisco Domingo de Polonia was undeniably one of the foremost Cainite leaders in North America. New York was, after all, one of the first Sabbat footholds in the New World and it remained the jewel in its crown, despite a nagging Camarilla presence there. Polonia suspected that the fact that he still thought of America as the "New World" was perhaps a bit too revealing of his age. It was precisely this patient nurturing, however, that had grown New York from the mere stuff of pre-industrial nightmare into the full-blown playground of Gehenna that it was today.

It was only fitting that, even here in Atlanta, far from his sphere of control, the responsibility for hosting this little get-together should fall to Polonia.

In the geography of the undying, only Miami dared put itself forward as a rival to New York's preeminence. Between these two cities lay only an unbroken stretch of enemy territory covering nearly the entire Eastern Seaboard. Polonia knew his power and influence were dulled and muted here in Atlanta. The city had been a Camarilla stronghold since its founding. There was little he could depend upon here. Certainly he could be sure of the loyalty of those hand-picked forces he had brought with him to the council—assuming of course that no more compelling opportunity arose for them. He would ensure that no compelling opportunity developed. It was an arena in which he had some experience.

The gathered Sabbat warlords, however, were an even greater uncertainty. Drawn from marauding bands that ravaged the length and breadth of the American countryside, these autonomous mercenary groups gave allegiance to none and respect only to a select few—those who had earned such through trials of fire and sword.

In less than an hour, Polonia realized, this conference room would be filled with a clamoring throng of the most ruthless tyrants, predators, fanatics, mafiosi, serial killers, highwaymen, ganglords, and anarchists that had been gathered in one place since—well, probably since the onset of the First Crusade.

Polonia's thoughts only reluctantly returned to the present century. This modern assemblage would be the pride of the Sabbat—the elite of the elite— the packleaders, the prelates, the warlords. All those who could command a following of at least a dozen Cainites would be on hand to strike a blow against the hated Camarilla.

Polonia had come around full circuit again to his own seat and to the body that swung gently behind it, like a tapestry. It was intended as a visible sign of the proximity of the Camarilla—a young Toreador, prim, effete, immaculate. He did not seem in the least inconvenienced by the coarse noose or by the improbable angle of his neck. Like the rest of the room, he was perfect.

Polonia wanted to keep attention focused on the Camarilla—on its posturing, its weakness, its vulnerability. He could not have been more pleased with his hunters' catch. The victim's hands were clasped before him in an attitude of supplication. They clenched a viscous-looking black candle. Polonia lit the wick and long shadows stretched away from him in all directions.

By the light of the candle, Polonia further scrutinized the victim's features. Priceless. Even the Toreador's fangs were vestigial, unthreatening—a fact that, no doubt, explained the curious artifact Polonia had found earlier.

He again drew out the carefully folded and slightly perfumed silk handkerchief. Opening it, he revealed an intricately etched silver bauble—a long thimble of exquisite workmanship with a wicked lancet protruding from the tip. Swiftly, Polonia tapped the underside of the victim's chin, withdrawing the lancet before the first droplet of blood could fall. He carefully rewrapped the delicate silver needle to the sound of the first drops hissing and spluttering onto the oily candle below.

He was now irrevocably committed to the ritual at hand. It was only with great reluctance that he turned his back upon the conference room. His fingers ached for the tactile assurance of the great table, to make one last circuit of the room, to order the uncertainties of the coming night carefully.

Enough. There was nothing more he could do here. Resignedly, Polonia gave the corpse a gentle shove, setting it swinging in a slow pendular arc.

Blood and wax splattered an intricate spiral pattern on the tile floor.

He wondered what signs and omens might be read in the curious pattern of fallen droplets. Here in a gentle spray of trailing blood, an influential warlord lay dead, slumped over his cups. There, in a notable clot of wax, he saw a seal affixed to a compact that would bring feuding packleaders together and give the entire Camarilla cause to tremble.

The answer was here somewhere, hidden in the riddle of falling droplets. But which images were glimpses of things to come and which were mere phantasms conjured from a desire, or its converse, a fear? Polonia, faced only with further uncertainties, abandoned his musings.

He could not resist taking one last long look over the room. Then, with mingled satisfaction and resignation, he reached out a sure hand toward the swinging corpse and took a single step sideways into shadow.

Polonia pushed through the barrier and into the tenebrous realm known only to the most accomplished shadow warriors of his clan. The room beyond looked very much like the one he had just quit. A rough-hewn circular conference table dominated the hall. In the uncertain half-light, each of the wormholes that riddled the oaken surface was clearly visible, thrown into sharp relief.

The play of the light and shadow worked further mischief over the carefully ordered feasthall, seeming somehow to exaggerate Polonia's chair. It now resembled nothing so much as an empty throne draped languidly with the trappings of the grave. This funerary seat presided over a great banquet of tarnished silver, goblets brimming with dust, delicately woven cobweb linens. Polonia surveyed the board with a hint of satisfaction. A vibrant red apple atop a decorative fruit bowl immediately arrested his gaze. Aside from the candle flame, it was the only spot of color in the room. All else was decked in subtle and varied shades of gray.

"Missed that one," Polonia mused aloud.

"Poisoned, perhaps," came the reply. "Very romantic, but not quite so effective. Surely it will not be necessary for your guests to keep up the appearance of eating on such a grand occasion."

No matter how many times it happened, Polonia always found himself somewhat startled at the transitionless appearance of the envoys. One moment they were not there, the next they were—speaking, or taking, or touching.

Polonia turned quickly, but not so quickly that the other had not already taken his elbow to usher him to his chair. The sensation was not unlike sawing through bone. He disengaged as politely as he could manage and took his place at table. "No, more likely the apple conceals some weapon or perhaps even an incendiary device."

"Ah…" the envoy replied with escalating interest. There was a flutter of a breeze and a shadow seemed to break away and stretch toward the apple. Suddenly, a brilliant flash illuminated the room. Tatters of shadow streaked in all directions and then fell to the floor in a gentle rain of scorched confetti. The explosion of light and its aftermath were accompanied by a complete and unsettling silence.

Polonia settled back in his chair. There were no

further stirrings, no further signs of color, of vibrancy. He resigned himself to wait.

"A most excellent incendiary. Yes, quite satisfactory. Borges?"

Polonia had expected the voice to come from one of the corners of the room, where the shadows had fled. He was disappointed as the form materialized directly before him, standing atop the table. It made a low bow.

"In all likelihood. It bears his mark," Polonia replied, trying to appear unruffled. "I understand that in Miami such modern contrivances are all the rage—firearms, grenades, flame-throwers...."

The shape before him fluttered excitedly at the very mention of flame-throwers. "Will Borges be in attendance, then?"

"Yes, of course. You will see him yourself. He will be seated directly opposite me. There." Polonia gestured to the far end of the table where a crude wooden stool half leaned against the table leg. There was a truncheon of stale bread and a tin cup sitting before the stool.

Polonia smiled at this further contrivance of the shadow realm. He was well acquainted with the subtle alterations these environs worked upon the eye of the beholder, images carefully arranged to flatter, to tempt, to cajole.

He found himself once again thinking of the strange omens worked in blood and candlewax at the threshold of this twilit realm—reflections of desires and of fears made manifest. Visible emanations of things that were hidden or, more accurately, concealed.

"I was under the impression that Borges had

sworn never to set foot in Atlanta."

Polonia smiled. "He made a great show, of course, of not coming. I believe my fellow archbishop took it as something of a slight that the honor of conducting the siege did not fall to him."

"He may well have more to say about that issue before your gathering is concluded."

"Yes, I am much of the same opinion," Polonia replied. "Atlanta is, after all, veritably right in his backyard."

"And quite some distance from your own territory. I believe I understand you. He had, no doubt, extended his ambition, if not his actual hand, over the city already?"

Polonia laughed aloud. "Yes, his agents were among the very first sent in to reconnoiter the city and, later, to disrupt the operations and posturings of the Camarilla. But there was never any real possibility of Borges passing up this war council. The Siege of Atlanta will be something talked about for generations to come. It is simply too great an event to be missed."

"If they don't all kill each other first," the shade replied.

"If they don't all kill each other first."

An uncomfortable silence fell in the shadowy throne room. It was the envoy that broke the silence.

"And what of the regent? Does she send no representative to the council?"

"The regent?" Polonia lowered his voice. "Our Most Distinguished Excellency is content to remain unavoidably engaged in Mexico City. No, she has made it quite clear that she is taking no hand whatsoever in such 'regional squabblings.'"

"Ah, but she could not remain uninterested in anyone who could bring the feuding warbands together and drive the Camarilla from Atlanta…. Such a one would certainly be well on his way to winning a cardinal's throne."

Polonia could feel the seat shift beneath him, expanding, bearing him upward. He made a dismissive gesture with the flat of his hand and the motion ceased. "The Vicar of Caine merely exercises her uncanny sense of when there is likely to be any contention among her archbishops. She is shrewd enough to remain conspicuously absent on such occasions. No regent, no legate to argue her cause, not even a nuncio to proclaim her will."

Polonia broke off. It was always a somewhat delicate matter as to how much one could or could not say before the envoys. It would be foolish to believe that the regent's mastery of the shadow was not as great as Polonia's own. It was quite possible that the regent might be just as adept at extracting damaging testimony from the shadowy envoys as she was from the Cainites that fell under her power.

The envoy interrupted these musings. "You fear that they will not put aside their differences, that they will not follow your lead."

"I fear," said Polonia, "that we shall bring down upon ourselves the bloodiest internecine war that has ever ravaged the Sabbat."

"Ah, but you have gone to such great pains to ensure that this does not happen," the envoy soothed. "Look around you. All is in order. Everything in its proper place."

The envoy cast an admiring eye over the precise arrangements. It paused, its shadowy hand eclipsing the placecard to Polonia's left. "Vykos? I do not believe we are familiar with…"

"No, you would not be. A Tzimisce. From the Old Country. She is the special emissary from Cardinal Monçada of Madrid." Polonia's tone betrayed his resentment of what many would see as a foreign intrusion in a purely domestic matter.

"Ah, now Monçada, that is a name that I do know. But what interest can the great cardinal have in this undertaking? It has been quite some time since he last turned his attention to these far shores."

"Monçada is a dangerous and cunning strategist," Polonia mused. He toyed absently with a rusted chalice. "It is less than a year now since the newest member of the College of Cardinals secured his office by putting an end to the ravenous Blood Curse. The pestilence had utterly decimated Sabbat packs on both sides of the Atlantic.

"In New York, no fewer than one in every three pack members fell victim—a loss from which we will not soon recover. Madrid was rumored to have been even more savaged by the epidemic, some reports placing the level of attrition as high as three in four."

"Death by pestilence," the envoy commented ruefully. "Such a needless and wasteful final emanation." There was a sudden dank chill in the air, which might have been a sigh.

"Given such desperate odds, some would say that it is no coincidence that Monçada should have been the one to make the critical breakthrough. If he had failed to do so, he and all of his line would certainly be dead and forgotten by now.

"There are those, however," Polonia's voice fell to a conspiratorial whisper, "who go so far as to say that Monçada's discovery was not merely an act of Providence. I have heard it told that it was Monçada's own agents that engineered the plague in the first place, although for what possible advantage I could not imagine. Not that I would count myself among these rumormongers, you understand."

Polonia paused significantly before continuing. "At any rate, none would contest the fact that Monçada has set his ambitions very high indeed—and that he is not adverse to resorting to extreme measures to accomplish his ends. It would not be unreasonable to think that he is positioning himself to contend for the regency itself."

"And what price would be too high to pay for such a lofty prize?" the envoy replied excitedly, borne along by this train of thought. "The lives of a few hand-picked followers? He certainly would not scruple at so meager a cost."

"It is not the lives of his own followers that concern me," Polonia replied coldly, picking at the nearest of the coffin nails that pierced the arm of his throne. "Merely having forces present at a victory in Atlanta will not bring Monçada a single step closer to the regency."

"Yes, but…oh, I see. You fear that perhaps it is not only his own followers that he is willing to sacrifice. What, after all, are the lives of a few dozen upstart New World Sabbat to the great cardinal?"

"What worries me more," Polonia replied, "is that Monçada might be willing to sacrifice all—his followers, his allies, victory in Atlanta itself—for some greater advantage. The cardinal weighs out his gains and losses very carefully, but I cannot see his shadowy scales and I mistrust them greatly." He pressed on. "How does a victory in Atlanta measure up against the possibility of destabilizing the North American Sabbat? Of weakening the regent's New World power base? Of depriving her of her nearest allies? It is quite possible that Monçada's emissary comes not to bolster but to betray our war effort."

If Polonia had hoped to startle some reaction from his shadowy companion, he was disappointed. The envoy merely nodded, accepting this new information without comment or censure. After a pause, the shade asked somewhat distractedly, "But why would he send a Tzimisce as his representative?"

Polonia had been troubled by this choice of ambassador as well. Monçada was a Lasombra, a shadowmancer like Polonia himself, and the regent, and most of the other highly placed leaders of the Sabbat for that matter. It would have been natural for Monçada to send one of his attendants, a fellow Lasombra, to the gathering.

A Tzimisce was another matter entirely. Although the Tzimisce had always proved steadfastly loyal to the Sabbat and formidable allies to their brethren Lasombra, they made for notoriously poor politicians, negotiators, and councilors. Few would think to stand against a Tzimisce in head-on conflict—for they were fearsome foes, with a flair for inspiring awe and terror. But sending a Tzimisce to represent you in council was paramount to throwing down the gauntlet.

"Perhaps he hopes to strengthen his position and support among the New World Sabbat," Polonia said. "After fighting side-by-side against the Camarilla, Monçada might well hold up the Siege of Atlanta as an example of how his forces had stood with Borges and myself—up to the waist in the blood of the enemy, or some such romantic notion—while the regent, whose forces were close at hand, could not be bothered to lift a finger to come to our aid."

"Ah, and if some new cardinal should emerge from the struggle," the envoy chimed in with honeyed words, "he would naturally be well-disposed toward his new sword-brother."

"A more pleasant thought, certainly, than the possibility that he might be sending a Tzimisce because no one is more capable of disrupting a fragile peace than a ravening, short-fused, shape-shifting monstrosity.

"I can't help but feel that Monçada's involvement bodes ill for our best-laid plans." Polonia fixed the envoy with a gaze that allowed for no argument. "I will be relying upon you to neutralize this threat."

"How may I assist you in this matter?"

Polonia unwrapped a small, tattered piece of cloth. Until recently, it had been a delicate, perfumed silk handkerchief. Now it resembled nothing more than a scrap of hooded mask a leper might use to cover his deformity.

Inside the folds of burlap shone a brilliant glare of silver light. The envoy shrank back instinctively.

Polonia held out his hand, his face half-averted from the newborn star in his palm. Reluctantly, the envoy took the proffered parcel and hastily rewrapped it.

"You will position yourself here." Polonia pushed himself up and moved one place to his left. His hands rested on the chairback before the place marked *Vykos*. The frame of the chair seemed to be crafted entirely of gleaming white bones, cracked off sharply at the top. Polonia unheedingly wrapped his hands around the jagged edges. His knuckles showed white with the intensity of his concentration.

"The silver will strike true—even through the barrier that separates the two rooms." He brought one hand down and around in a leisurely arc and tapped at the empty space where the guest's throat would be.

"Do not hesitate to strike should I signal you. The touch of the silver will do you no lasting harm. Nothing, certainly, compared to my anger should you fail me."

"We shall not fail you," the envoy replied, still holding the deadly parcel at arm's length.

"You never have done so before. Please send my respects to your lord and master and tell him that Polonia has the honor to remain his good and faithful servant."

With that, Polonia turned and reached up to touch the corpse, which still swayed gently behind the throne. One brief sideward step and he was back through the barrier and in his own world once again. A world filled with shadow and with moonlight and with the trappings of the grave.

Saturday, 19 June 1999, 11:35 PM
Chandler Room, Omni Hotel at CNN Center
Atlanta, Georgia

"And another thing. I don't really care *how* things are done back in New York. We ain't in New York. We don't want to be in New York. And I'm getting just a little bit tired of hearing about New York. If I wanted things to run just like they do in New York, you'd be the first to know."

Caldwell punctuated each point by jabbing a finger in the face of the man opposite him. He leaned far out over the conference table to do so, as if it were the only thing holding him back from physically assaulting his counterpart. Seeing that his antagonist was losing composure, Caldwell pressed on more aggressively.

"I'd call you up myself. I'd say, 'Costello! I've been thinking. What we really need around here is a little more, you know, New York. Would you mind terribly coming down here to Atlanta and straightening all of us backwards bumpkins out? You will? That's swell! You're a regular guy.'

"So in the meantime, why don't you just take your sorry old mostly dead and starting-to-stink wormy carcass back to LaGuardia, and just park it right there next to your telephone—at the very center of the known universe—and wait for my call, all right?"

Costello fumed. Liquid darkness seeped from his fists, which were balled tightly around the arms of his chair. From over his shoulder, his shadow unfurled silently like a bird of prey and perched menacingly atop his seatback.

"Why, you misbegotten and ungrateful cur," he began, rising from his seat.

"Gentlemen!" Borges's voice cut through the building tension. "We are not here to give vent to our differences, but rather to lay them aside. There is important work at hand. Glorious work!"

At his first word, all eyes turned toward Borges. He held their attention, not with his gaze, but with his immaculate and predatory smile. His was the face of an ancient and well-loved mastiff. The upper part of that face was hidden in perpetual shadow. Light could not prevail across the barrier in either direction. Below, however, the lines of cheek and jowl were yet visible, and these clearly showed the wear of passing years. Slowly and not without apparent effort, the Archbishop of Miami rose, gesturing for everyone else to be seated. He trailed one hand along the edge of the table, feeling his way around its circumference. "There will be ample opportunity to demonstrate your prowess upon our common enemies."

Reluctantly, both Caldwell and Costello settled back into their chairs.

"Yes, that's better. Sit. Drink. Be of good cheer," Borges soothed. "We are gathered on the threshold of a glorious victory. Before we have parted company, we will strike a mighty blow—a blow from which neither the Camarilla, nor their Antediluvian puppetmasters, shall soon recover.

"However," Borges raised a cautionary finger, "we are still poised upon that threshold. There can be little doubt of what awaits you beyond the doorway." He gestured toward the room's sole exit, but all eyes fell rather upon the corpse of the hanged Toreador youth that swung gently next to it. "This is Camarilla territory, gentlemen. Have no uncertainty as to what fate would befall you if it were *you* caught on the wrong side of that door.

"The game, gentlemen, is called Blood Siege. The stakes, nothing less than uncontested ownership of the city of Atlanta."

A howl of enthusiasm went up from a Tzimisce war ghoul seated much further down the table. Perhaps "seated" was not the proper word. The ghoul *loomed*. The hulking form was easily nine feet tall at the shoulder and gave the impression of being stooped nearly double under its own weight. It shuffled unsettlingly from side to side, giving rise to a sound like a whetstone biting into a pair of shears. The crystal goblets upon the vast conference table trembled and sang slightly in response to each of the beast's movements.

A very slight man, who looked like no more than a child beside the hulking war machine, craned upwards and spoke to it in hushed tones. The booming reverberations fell silent.

Others around the table made a point of not noticing this timely intervention. In fact, the other Sabbat leaders and councilors maintained a healthy distance from the pair. If the truth were known, their aversion to the towering aberration did not even approach the unease they felt in the presence of its prim, bespectacled companion, the man they called the Little Tailor of Prague.

Two seats on either side of the Tzimisce and his attendant war ghoul remained vacant. No one among the company made the least attempt to conceal a distaste that was rooted in more than mere xenophobia. Only Caldwell was so incautious, however, as to remark upon this fact. "Does that—Christ, I don't even know what to call it—that *thing* have to be here? I can't even think with it sitting right on top of me like this." He pushed back his chair and made to rise.

The man seated on his left placed a restraining hand on Caldwell's arm. "Hold your ground, *Capitán*." His voice was low, with just a rumbling hint of threat in it.

"Jeez-us H…" Caldwell turned his head away with a snort of disgust. His commander did not release his grip on Caldwell's forearm until he felt the resistance go out of it. Caldwell, did not, however, pull his chair back up to rejoin the conversation. Instead, he propped first one foot and then the other noisily upon the table, crossing them.

Averros chose to ignore this slight show of defiance. He pitched his voice so that it carried across the entire room. "But my associate raises a good point. We have answered this urgent 'summons' to council. Not because we acknowledge that this assembly has any authority to 'summon' anyone—because it doesn't; let's get that straight from the outset. And not because our esteemed (if conspicuously absent) host, Polonia—and the rest of his New York syndicate—has any jurisdiction here at all, because they don't. And not because any one of you has any claim upon us, or even any reason to expect our support— because you don't.

"The Nomad Coalition is here, gentlemen, because the word is out that Atlanta is spoiling for a fight, and you guys don't have the experience, the firepower, or the balls to carry that fight without us."

A roar and a riot went up from the gathered Nomad warchiefs and even Caldwell was on his feet. A man to Averros's left brandished a fist in which danced no fewer than three wicked and vitriolic-looking butterfly knives, each blade as long as the man's forearm.

The venerable Borges raised a hand for silence and the crowd gradually began to quiet back down enough so that individual voices could be heard once more. Even some of the Nomads seemed inclined to return to the table, gathering whatever chairs remained in serviceable condition after the outburst of exuberance.

It was a new voice that cut through the clamor. "Honorable Borges—" the sound of the woman's voice had an appreciable effect upon the burgeoning mob. Attention turned toward her. "Honorable Borges, we are pleased to be invited here as a guest of this council. Know that Montreal stands firmly behind the decisions and actions of this assembly. We would further like to express our apologies that the archbishop could not personally be in attendance, but we are confident that you appreciate the weighty demands of his office."

Encouraged by a gracious nod of acknowledgement from the Archbishop of Miami, the representative from Montreal continued. "We have come at your behest, to offer what good council we might. We have come in good faith and in accordance with the terms set forth by Archbishop Polonia in his invitation. We have come with the clear understanding that there were to be no weapons of any sort allowed within the Council chambers."

A Tzimisce some distance around the table performed a particularly life-like, if ill-mannered, transformation of its middle finger—a gesture intended, no doubt, to express his opinion of the feasibility of such a ban given the present company. The representative from Montreal pretended not to have observed this commentary.

"Yes, the sound of drawn steel. I heard it quite unmistakably," Borges mused aloud. "If any here have weapons about their persons," his Cheshire-cat grin was the only thing visible beneath the cowl of purest shadow, "let him put them aside now."

Nobody moved.

"Hardin…" Averros prompted.

"No way. No fucking way. I'm not giving my blades to some—"

"Do it."

"No. That's it. I am out of here. As far as I'm concerned the whole lot of you can just kiss my cold white…"

Averros rose.

Hardin cursed under his breath. "So is this how it's gonna be?" Hardin tried to push past, but Averros put a hand on his chest.

Hardin's hands were at his sides, but an unmistakable ring of metal told Averros that they were no longer empty. Hardin spoke very slowly and softly. "Why don't you do everyone here a favor and just get the hell out of my way?"

"Can't do that, buddy. Too many packmates have gone to the Final Death so that you can be standing here, mouthing off and making an ass out of yourself. That contract's been written in blood. Nobody walks out on the Coalition. One in blood, one in body. Now, put the blades on the table."

"You talk a good game about this Coalition."

Knives began to flicker open and shut in nervous agitation. "But when it comes to the show...well, we all see how it is, don't we? It's all brotherhood and all-for-one crap as long as it's all going your way. But what happens when they turn up the pressure? What happens when it comes to sticking up for your own?"

All around them, other leaders of the Coalition were getting cautiously to their feet and beginning to form a cordon around the two antagonists. Averros didn't even glance aside to weigh where the support was lining up. He just smiled and reached out a hand. "The blades."

Hardin seemed nervous and distracted. He glanced around for encouragement and must have found at least a few friendly faces in the throng. He turned upon Averros with renewed determination.

"This is the big time, tough guy. Whatcha gonna do? These bastards here," he gestured to the conference table where the rest of the assembly looked on with alternating distaste, detached curiosity, and ill-concealed blood hunger. "You think these guys are gonna stand with you when they see how you pay back the folks who put you where you are now? Come off it. These guys are the real deal. Hell, these guys *are* the Sabbat, I mean the real Sabbat. The folks that make things happen. You're not dealing with a bunch of low-life drifters and clansmen; fugitives and survivalists, weirdoes and cultists, anymore. You think these guys are sitting around waiting for someone to come along and tell them what to do and who to do it to?

"Look at that guy," Hardin gestured angrily in the direction of the Little Tailor. "You think that guy gives a damn about your Coalition? That guy is one weird mother. And I'm willing to bet that he's been doing that same twisted shit since before, well, since before Dr. Frankenstein was a glimmer in Mary Shelley's eye. And he'll *still* be doing it long after you and I have bought a worm farm—*really* bought it, I mean. For keeps, this time."

"For keeps," Averros agreed ominously.

Hardin circled warily, positioning himself so that the wall was behind him and Averros had to turn his back on the entire treacherous assembly in order to face him. The knives were spinning freely now, flipping through a complex series of patterns, too fast for the eye to follow.

"Don't be an idiot," Hardin's menacing whisper cut through the barrier of whirling blades between the two. "You're unarmed. I'll cut you down where you stand, before you can even lay a hand on me."

"Look, I don't want to kill you and my guess is that you don't want to die," Averros said in a tone one might take in addressing an idiot child. "Although I wouldn't want to have to prove it with only the evidence of the last few minutes. If you want to do this thing, take your shot. Otherwise, give me the blades and sit down, 'cause I've got a city to storm and some Camarilla bastards to hunt down and make plead for their pitiful unlives, and you are holding up the show.

"So what's it gonna be, Ripper? You take a cut at me and you won't walk out of here. You know it. Look at these bastards. Go ahead, look at them. These guys will eat your sorry carcass for lunch—would have eaten it already if I weren't standing here between you and them. You think they're playing around? This is for keeps, Ripper. This is the show. So let's do it like you mean it. One blood…"

Hardin's right arm shot out, unleashing a screaming arc of steel at point-blank range.

Averros made no effort to sidestep the oncoming blade. He held Hardin's eyes unflinchingly.

The swirling knife cut hard, banking out and down. It slammed home into the table with a resounding *chunk* and stood there trembling.

"One body." Hardin snapped the remaining blades shut and purposefully turned his back on Averros. He took three steps toward the table. With each step, he could feel the muscles between his shoulderblades tense in anticipation of the retaliatory strike. Once. Twice. Thrice.

Nothing.

He let out a long slow breath as he slid the blades noisily, disdainfully, across the great circular table. They clattered to rest near its center, well out of reach of any of the councilors seated around the perimeter. Without a sideward glance, Hardin took his seat. "Your pardon, venerable Borges. I believe the gracious lady from Canada had the floor."

Averros held his ground as if lost in deep thought. His gaze never wavered from the space Hardin had so recently occupied. He could not help but feel glad for the respite offered by the other's theatrics.

He let his eyes fall closed for a moment as he collected himself. With one part of his mind, he summoned up the power of the blood to staunch the new wound in his left side, just beneath his arm. With another, he reached for a loose strand of shadow and lashed it in place to mask the cut where the blade had sliced neatly through his leather jacket—without even slowing—and then glanced away sharply to impact the table.

Snatching up another trailing end of shadow, Averros turned toward the assembly. He flashed a disarming smile for the benefit of those who were still watching him expectantly, and took hold of the high seatback with both hands. He leaned into it, feeling its weight, its solidity. It steadied him.

His side still burned like hell, but he couldn't spare it much attention as yet. As the eyes around the table turned once again to the Montreal delegate, Averros took advantage of the opportunity to send the thread of shadow snaking toward the knife that still thrummed in the tabletop. The twist of darkness coiled tightly around the blade, concealing any telltale trace of blood that might yet be clinging to it. Only then did Averros allow himself to relax a fraction.

Hardin would pay later, of course. And keep paying, the smug bastard. Averros had seen the gleam of triumph in Hardin's eyes just before he had turned his back. Averros would make a point of remembering that look, so that he could arrange Hardin's face in just that same expression after the body had been laid out.

No, there was no doubting it. Hardin had scored first blood and he *knew* he had done so. There would be no working with him until he had been put back in his place.

But to his credit, Hardin had kept his little show of defiance private, just between the two of them. To the rest of the council, it must have appeared as if Hardin had backed down—backed down in a rather flamboyant manner, but backed down nonetheless. That counted for something.

He had allowed his commander, and thus the Coalition, to save face. Lord knew the Coalition had little enough clout here as it was—only what shred Averros could personally wrest from the voracious lords of the Damned seated all around them. It was something of an unwritten rule among the Sabbat. A law of conservation of respect. Among this company, esteem could neither be created nor destroyed. It had to be taken from someone else who already had it.

Yes, Hardin deserved some credit. He had pushed the matter to the brink, but had drawn back from the edge before blowing their one shot at the big time. Maybe he only did it because it was the only way he could think of to save his own miserable undead hide. But he took the fall.

Hell, Hardin knew what was at stake here. A victory in Atlanta would give the Coalition the clout it needed to play with the big boys. But they wouldn't get a juicy piece of the action in Atlanta unless Averros could convince the council that he had what they desperately needed—a bloodthirsty horde of seasoned killers poised (as far as such a mob might be said to demonstrate any degree of poise) to descend upon the unsuspecting Camarilla.

Averros was a fair, if unforgiving leader. Hardin, he decided, would pay. But he would be punished in a manner that suited his transgression—he would suffer personally and privately.

"We are satisfied," the Montreal representative waved dismissively toward the blades in the center of the table, as if she would brush them from sight.

"But we," Averros countered, "are not yet satisfied."

Dozens of wary eyes regarded him once again.

"The point I was making, gentlemen, the point that *Capitán* Caldwell had expressed so frankly in his earlier comments, is that all weapons have not been removed from this council chamber." He turned pointedly upon the Little Tailor of Prague.

His meaning was not lost upon his audience. Even the war ghoul began to growl menacingly in protest.

The gentleman so accused did not meet Averros's gaze. Instead, he very slowly removed his eyeglasses and held them up to the light. Taking a tattered and obviously bloodstained handkerchief from his pocket, he proceeded to polish the lenses. Periodically, he paused in order to hold the frames up to the light again. It was not long before it became clear to all assembled that the lenses had become evenly coated with a clinging red film. Satisfied, the Tailor replaced the glasses on the bridge of his nose and addressed the group.

"Gentlemen, it is to me no great surprise that many of you should remain somewhat apprehensive, even distrustful of my presence here today. I knew that, as a visitor from the Old Country, I could expect something of a cool reception from my New World cousins. No, do not deny it. I know this to be so."

The Little Tailor held up a finger to forestall an argument that was not forthcoming. All eyes were immediately drawn to that wickedly tapering finger. Like many of his Tzimisce brethren, the Little Tailor was not easy to look at. Each of his fingers had apparently been stripped of all flesh and sharpened into long, delicate needles of bone. He wagged his finger knowingly at them, revealing long viscous-looking lines of blackened catgut threaded through his needles. These strands ran along the inside of his palm, over the hump of his wrist and away down his forearm into the recesses of his sleeve. Averros's first disturbing impression was that the Little Tailor's hands and arms had been flayed open, revealing the taut lines of vein and artery beneath. He quickly saw that this was not so. The moist black catgut simply wound over and about his arms, like thread on a spindle.

"You are jealous of your hard-won freedoms," the Tailor continued. "This is good. And for many of you present at this assembly, perhaps, the excesses—even the cruelties—of Europe's ancient ones is not the stuff of distant legend, but rather of all-too-recent memory, yes?"

There were a few mutterings of assent from around the table, but the rumbling undertone was dangerous rather than affirming.

"It is nothing with which you need concern yourself, Master Tailor." The voice was icy. It belonged to an ambitious young Lasombra of Borges's camp. Perhaps even one of his kin, the Tailor thought. It was always difficult to tell among the Lasombra. They had an unsettling habit of fawning all over their elders, even when they had no right to expect that such attentions would be received. They were like puppies in that respect, squirming over one another, shouldering their way toward the center of their master's attention and affection. It was, well, it was just not quite proper. It was enough to make any self-respecting Tzimisce somewhat queasy.

The Tailor remembered the youth's name from

an earlier examination of the golden placecards—
Sebastian. Such a lovely name. It always reminded
him of beautiful young boys pierced through with
barbed arrows.

"The fact of the matter is," Sebastian was continuing, "that we are justifiably wary of the
convoluted games of dominance and empire played
by our old-school 'cousins' across the Atlantic. How
can we hope to make any progress in tearing down
the deadly web of intrigue cast by the Antediluvians,
if in so doing we blunder into a no less formidable
trap laid for us by our European counterparts?"

There were scattered words of assent and one
loud "amen" from the New York faction. Perhaps
there was some story there, the Tailor thought, but it
would come out in time, no doubt. He knew from his
decades of experience among the dungeons of the
most notable houses of Europe—it would all come
out in time.

"The one fact that you are overlooking," a commanding voice cut through the commotion with
military precision, "is that the gentleman of Prague
is no powermonger. So far as I have been able to determine, he himself has little, if anything, to gain from
this undertaking."

"Except of course, the favor of your master!"
Sebastian retorted, turning angrily upon the speaker.
"You will not deceive us so easily, Vallejo. Do you
deny that the Butcher of Prague is here at the specific request of your beloved cardinal?"

All around the table, faces that had not seen the
sun in generations suddenly went a full shade paler.
Only the very incautious even dared to look in the
direction of the Little Tailor to observe the full ef-

fect these words had upon him. A number of those present had spent the entire assembly thus far very pointedly avoiding that particular ancient and derisive epithet. Sebastian surely realized his mistake as soon as the words had left his lips. But he stuck to his guns and did not turn from his confrontation with Vallejo.

"The butcher," the gentleman of Prague repeated the words as if searching for some meaning in them. Sebastian winced, hearing the syllables parroted back at him. He tensed, expecting a blow.

"The baker. The candlestick maker," the Little Tailor mused aloud. "Now there's a moral there somewhere. No, that's a fable." He seemed lost in thought. He drummed the tips of his fingers together distractedly. The bone needles clacking together sounded like the rattle of machine-gun fire in the silent chamber.

The entire assembly seemed to hold its breath.

"Do any of you know the one that goes…" the Little Tailor began. "No, never mind, you wouldn't know."

Sebastian was perspiring openly now. Tiny beads of shadow and blood seeped from his pores and stood out in bold relief on his forehead.

"Be easy now, grandfather," another Tzimisce soothed, perhaps the representative from Detroit. "You have much work to do still this evening and we mustn't keep you from it." He took the ancient one by the arm to help him to his feet.

The war ghoul bellowed a challenge, shattering the uneasy hush that had fallen over the room. The other quickly loosed his grip upon the Tailor's arm and retreated a few quick paces.

"All right," the Tailor chuckled indulgently.

"One more, but then it's off to bed with all of you. Let's see now. This is one of my favorites. Humpty Dumpty. Humpty Dumpty sat on a…" His voice trailed off into a quiet murmuring that, after a while, might have been the beginnings of a snore.

As one, the group seemed to exhale. But soon a low chuckling was heard. It began deep in the Tailor's chest, but it rose in pitch and intensity until it swallowed the room.

"No, that's right. They couldn't put him back together, could they?" His eyes remained closed as he spoke and he smiled contentedly. "Well, it was like a jigsaw puzzle, really. Yes, a life-size jigsaw puzzle. First, they had to gather up all the little pieces. And they weren't likely to find all the little pieces, now were they? No, not if you've hidden them well. They'll never find the pieces. Never find the pieces. Never find…" his voice trailed off into a taunting childish singsong.

Very soon, the unmistakable sound of snoring echoed across the conference table.

"I believe," said the venerable Borges, "that we should adjourn for the evening. If any of you would like to pursue further some of the issues raised here, I will be more than happy to receive any and all of you in my suite on the upper floor of this hotel. For the rest of our honored guests, I will bid you good night and look forward to seeing you here again at the same time tomorrow evening."

The company did not quite tiptoe out of the room, but they did retire in short order, leaving the old one and his attendant war ghoul in possession of the field.

Sunday, 20 June 1999, 2:37 AM
Penthouse suite, Omni Hotel at CNN Center
Atlanta, Georgia

"I tell you, I don't like it," Sebastian stormed. He hung languidly on the heavy blackout curtains that ringed the lavish penthouse suite. They served a function much like tapestries in the great castles of Europe—to keep out the worst excesses of an unfriendly clime. In the wind-swept North Atlantic, the unwanted extremes were those of cold and draft, while here the obvious concern was to keep out the deadly rays of the unforgiving Atlanta sun.

Borges raised a quieting hand. "Enough. You made your point in council. And in doing so, you managed to avoid the primary threat—which was, incidentally, the very real possibility of your being gutted where you stood by Vallejo. But, as they say, tomorrow is another day."

"Vallejo? Who had time to worry about Vallejo? You threw me upon the mercy of the Butcher!"

"I?" Borges settled back deeper into the plush, throne-like chair facing the fireplace.

The flickering flames made Sebastian distinctly uneasy. It was not only that the evening was oppressively warm already. Nor was it merely the instinctive fear of fire that was deeply ingrained in all the Children of Caine. It was that, well, even when his master faced directly into the firelight (as he was doing at this very moment) Sebastian still could make out no hint of Borges's features save that gleaming, predatory smile.

It reminded him that although he and Borges were of one blood, they were not of a kind. "Your pardon, Borges. I am not myself. The very thought of that monstrosity! I feel quite unwell."

"Nonsense. It was a calculated risk. The exact probability of your being torn apart right there in the council chamber, although difficult to calculate precisely with all those Tzimisce wildcards in the equation, was actually quite slight."

"That is very reassuring," Sebastian replied. He picked up the poker and, holding it up to one eye, sighted along it. He tested its heft and struck up the *en garde* position. Borges continued to stare fixedly toward the fire.

"You might have told me," Sebastian continued, "that 'Butcher of Prague' was more than just a passing slight, a play on an occupational title." He resumed a more casual stance and, taking the poker between both hands, flexed it one or two times experimentally. "I actually thought for a moment there that he was going to lose it. I mean, *really* lose it. What would you have done if that thing had just gone berserk?"

Borges waved a hand dismissively. "Now, it did not come to that. And in this, at least, we have cause to be grateful. Yes, overall, I must admit to being quite satisfied with the evening's events."

"You did not answer my question," Sebastian brooded. Then, with a sudden theatrical twirl of the poker, he planted it like a cane and began to walk jauntily across the room. He stopped, trying to seem casual about it, directly behind Borges's chair. "But I did not think the council such a decisive victory. The Nomads, for instance, monopolized far more than their share of the proceedings. I was well prepared to shout down a disorganized rabble of thin-blooded ruffians. But I thought they put in quite an impressive showing."

Borges did not turn from contemplation of the flames. "Far too few casualties for the opening session. It bodes ill for the morrow."

"An astute point." Sebastian raised the tip of the poker and regarded it critically. "But a moment ago, you were claiming a clear victory for our party."

"Well then, consider our gains." Without turning, Borges ticked off his points on immaculately manicured nails. "One. With Polonia absent, we were uncontested in our assumption of the role and powers of council chairman. I cannot overstress the importance of this preeminence. The privileges of this position have allowed us to set the agenda, guide the discussion, define the terms of the confrontation with the Camarilla, bring pressing decisions to a head, or table them indefinitely. The game will be played by our rules."

"Well played," quipped Sebastian, taking an experimental swing with the fireplace iron. "Point two?"

"Two. All parties present, including both the Coalition and the Old Worlders, acknowledged our precedence in these proceedings and the superiority of our claim—Miami's claim—in these contested territories. Did you note how they railed against our absent 'host while deferring to my authority? Our battle line is firm. The entire Southeast is our backyard, period. Never mind the fact that some of these renegade bands of Nomads have been operating in this region for years now. The home-field advantage, as they say, is ours."

"Bravo. I shall especially keep this point in mind as I would like to further discuss our plans for the conquered Atlanta. But do not allow me to distract you; point three?"

"Three. This Averros desperately wants to be a major player in this theatre. And he's way out of his league. We can use that. Give him a bit of encouragement. Point out to him that there may well be another archbishopric to carve out of the Eastern seaboard. A great triumvirate! Polonia in the North, Borges in the South and Averros—at the head of his glorious Nomad Coalition—in the Mid-Atlantic. A formidable line of battle from which the Sabbat could smash the territories in the soft Camarilla underbelly. But perhaps I get ahead of myself."

"Not at all. You, sir, are a visionary. And visionaries must be given their full head of steam. Is there a point four?"

"Four. Neither of us is dead yet."

Sebastian brought the poker down across the top of the armchair. He leaned his elbows upon it and spoke directly over his master's head. "There are those who might quibble, but I shall cede the point. Very good then. Tonight we celebrate. But tell me first, what we must do on the morrow to press our hard-won advantage? That Tzimisce monster won't be on hand again, will he? I must admit that he has me quite flustered. Doesn't he have some battle ghouls to, if you will excuse the indelicacy, stitch together?"

"That, my child, remains to be seen. But pull up that stool and sit here at my feet awhile and we shall lay out our plans for tomorrow's council. Your pacing will drive me to distraction."

"My thoughts exactly," said Sebastian. He walked back around to the front of the chair and slammed the poker noisily home into its rack. He obediently retrieved the stool near the fire. "Now let me see. The first order of battle, suppose, is to settle upon some plan to push the siege into its final stages. To hasten the death throes of the Camarilla. Now let me see. If memory serves me correctly, as the Siege of Miami drew to its glorious climax…"

"Slowly, my son. You are so impatient. The first step is to finish driving the wedge between the New World Cainites—our party, of course, is already firm on this point but the followers of Polonia and the Coalition must be brought into the light as well—to drive the wedge between us and Monçada's interlopers from Madrid."

"Ah, I stand corrected. Or rather I sit corrected, but it is much the same thing. You are right, of course. Let's see. That means the Butcher and his slavering horde of war ghouls. And Vallejo and his damnable legion of the cardinal's household troops. And isn't there a Koldunic sorceress somewhere in the lot?" Sebastian continued. "I don't recall hearing from her today, but I picked her out easily enough. She is quite unmistakable. All tribal tattoos and blood bodypaint and bone piercings. Ghastly, really. And then, of course, there is this Vykos. Monçada's handpicked emissary. That's another thing I'm not in the least bit happy about. Vykos.

"I don't really know anything about her of course." Sebastian pressed on, pulling a large opaque hookah toward him. "Nothing, of course except what the other councilors are whispering."

He took a long slow pull from the mouthpiece and blew out a perfect ring of purest shadow. There was a long pause, but Borges did not seem eager to supply further information.

"She's a Tzimisce, of course," Sebastian hinted, still getting no reply. "And a particularly hoary old

TZIMISCE

fiend if what they say is true—hailing from Byzantium or Constantinople or some such. An authentic Old World nightmare. You haven't had the opportunity to meet the lady in question, have you, Borges?"

"Make yourself easy on that point," Borges said. "They don't let her kind out much. Like to keep them where they can keep a good eye on them, no doubt. You know the old saying, 'always keep your enemies close at hand.'"

"I know the saying." Sebastian shot Borges a look. "I have heard you cite it on numerous occasions. And I believe it is 'always keep your enemies and your childer close at hand.'"

"Why so it is," Borges absently stroked Sebastian's hair, and none too gently. "And I thought you weren't paying any attention to the words of a doddering old man."

Sebastian instinctively shrank from the mastiff grin, pulling free from the old man's grip.

"Do not worry yourself over this Vykos," Borges said flatly. "If you carry out your appointed task, if you drive your wedge skillfully, she will have no firm ground on which to stand."

"But what if she is another ravening lunatic?"

"What if she is?" Borges repeated. "Ravening Tzimisce we have in great abundance. One more will certainly not threaten our position. What worries me more is, what if she is *not* a ravening lunatic?

"Now attend to me, and I shall describe how we are to proceed."

And Sebastian stared intently into the dark cowl of shadow where the master's eyes should have been, and committed to memory each word that passed those lips.

Sunday, 20 June 1999, 11:18 PM
Chandler Room, Omni Hotel at CNN Center
Atlanta, Georgia

"And will you also deny," Sebastian railed, "that your precious cardinal has taken an all-too-personal interest in the future of the city of Atlanta?"

Vallejo weathered these accusations, as well as the outburst of barking laughter from the Coalition side of the table that accompanied them, but his veneer of aloof composure was wearing thin.

"His Eminence the Cardinal, has made no secret of the fact that he is gravely concerned with the events unfolding in and around the city of Atlanta."

"Secret? I should think not," Sebastian retorted. "By now, surely even the Camarilla has learned of the presence of you and your 'legion'—as I believe you are calling that mob of worm-ridden, somnambulant refugees that accompanied you from Madrid. Honestly, I don't know what it is about the state of Georgia that so inspires Europe to throw wide the doors of her prisons at the slightest provocation...."

"I think," replied Vallejo through clenched teeth, "that you overstep yourself, sir."

"Perhaps you are right," Sebastian calmed himself and began pacing the room. A dramatic affectation, perhaps, or it may have been intended to cover the fact that those seated nearest him had begun to edge away warily.

"Perhaps I should rather say what is foremost in the minds of all those here assembled. I shall speak plainly, sir. As even you must be aware by now, your very presence here compromises our position."

Vallejo snorted dismissively into the silence that followed this proclamation. "Although I am willing to grant that yours is the more intimate knowledge of compromising positions," he began, warming to the challenge at hand and encouraged by a new round of catcalls from the Nomads, "you must in return admit that, of the two of us, I have a few more seasons of campaigning to my credit. And I, for one, have yet to see the army that was lost on account of its receiving timely reinforcements."

"It is not the reinforcements that worry me," Sebastian was nearly shouting to be heard above the throng. "It is the cost of that reinforcement. We are not so green as you would have it. Do you think that the significance of your ambitious cardinal's 'interest' is lost on this astute assembly?"

The pitched argument was interrupted by the resounding of three great blows upon the chamber door.

"Open!" cried a commanding voice from outside, "in the name of His Eminence de Polonia, Archbishop of New York, Gatekeeper of the New World, Guardian of the Paths of Shadow."

The herald did not wait for the effect of his words to sink in. Before anyone could make a move toward the door, it burst inward. Revealed in the doorway was a broken and misshapen figure, wielding a gleaming silver-headed pickaxe. The implement had obviously seen some rough usage. It was weathered and battered and had an unmistakable weight of ages about it. The wooden handle had been sharpened to a wicked point and blackened in fire. The sinister purpose of this makeshift wooden stake was lost on no one—especially in light of the fact that the lower three feet of the handle were stained dark with ancient blood.

The figure brandishing the pickaxe was no less disturbing. Its body was cumbersome and bloated, giving the distinct impression of a drowned corpse. Its facial features seemed mushy, like a porous fungus that might well collapse into scattered spores if even brushed with the fingertips. The creature's head was shaped something like a moldy apple which had begun to fall in under its own weight.

The herald came forward into the room dragging one leg, obviously no longer fit for bearing him up, behind him. He inverted the axe and banged its head straight down on the floor three more times.

The room fell silent.

A worm, easily as big around as a delicate lady's wrist, burst from the herald's cheek. His head sagged further and seemed about to collapse entirely. The worm twisted as if to regard the assembly, revealing no less than five segments of its slimy black body, before disdainfully withdrawing again from sight.

The herald gave no sign of being aware, much less discomforted, by this interruption.

"All rise!" he commanded.

All around the table, councilors began to stand—some of them much more quickly than others. Costello and the New York contingent leapt to attention. The visiting dignitaries from distant Sabbat cities who had little personal stake in the power struggle for Atlanta, notably Montreal and Detroit, also rose promptly to honor their host.

Even the Old World representatives—including the minions of Cardinal Monçada—were seen to be standing. To be sure, most of them, like Vallejo, were already on their feet in the midst of the heated confrontation with Sebastian. But none among them was so ungracious as actually to return to his seat.

The Coalition side of the table, however, was another matter entirely. Some of the Nomad warchiefs could be seen to shift uncomfortably in their chairs, but no one seemed anxious to make any move that might be interpreted as acknowledging Polonia's authority. Many watched Averros circumspectly— some clearly looking for his lead, others watching patiently for any sign of weakness.

In the midst of the uncertainty and tension, Caldwell slowly and deliberately propped first one foot and then the other upon the table. He crossed them with an exaggerated sigh.

Averros, who had settled back comfortably in his chair, now sat forward. He said something sharply to Caldwell, pitched low to keep it from the ears of those around them. Caldwell snorted.

With a mutter of disgust, Averros stood and grabbing Caldwell by one foot, swung his legs violently from the table.

"What the hell!" Caldwell protested. Spun around and out of his chair, he found himself on his feet facing his leader.

"Not worth it," Averros cautioned, seeing the anger and challenge in Caldwell's face. Instinctively gravitating toward the confrontation, the other Nomads rose and pressed closer, encircling the pair.

"Yeah, you're not," Caldwell turned away, but he was hot and could not resist another parting shot. "But if you're a real good boy and do just what master tells you, maybe the nice archbishop will let you lead us all in the national anthem, or the pledge of allegiance. Hell, you could even make hall monitor."

Caldwell felt a tightening in his throat as his collar was grabbed from behind. He twisted in the grasp, launching a blow that would drive the claws of his right hand deep within his opponent's chest cavity and tear out his black heart.

Shattered claws cascaded to the floor. Caldwell cursed and jerked back a bleeding and probably broken hand. He staggered back a few paces, but Averros did not seem inclined to pursue him and finish the job.

"The next time you pull a stunt like that," Averros hissed just loud enough for the ears of his followers, who were crowding close around the two, "you're dead. You understand? So you'd better just get used to the idea of being the best damn hall monitor in the whole Coalition, because the next time you step out of line, it's over. The next time you mouth off, it's over. The next time I have to remind you who's running this show, it's just over. Now straighten up your act, *Capitán*. Understood?

"Sir," Caldwell acknowledged somewhat grudgingly, without looking up. He occupied himself in pulling the bones of his fingers noisily back into their proper places.

Fortunately for Averros, he had not come to today's council session as unprepared as he had yesterday. After the incident with Hardin, Averros was not about to be caught by surprise in a similar show of bravado today. He gingerly rubbed at the tender spot on his side where Hardin had blooded him. The damn thing hadn't closed right. There had been fresh blood on the sheets this evening and even now the jagged pink seam still burned.

He had stitched it up hurriedly at last night's council with a loose strand of shadow that was ready-to-hand. Earlier this evening, he had spent a considerable amount of time gathering up similar strands, testing their strength, weaving them tightly together into thick cables of shadow, and binding them about his person. The result was a protective vest much more formidable than mail, much more resistant than Kevlar—an armor that might well withstand just about any force he was likely to run into within the confines of the council chambers, short of the first gentle touch of the morning sun.

Unnoticed among the commotion caused by the Coalition power struggle, the only figure who kept to his seat throughout the entire proceeding was the venerable Borges. The rest of the Miami faction had risen to pay their respects to Polonia, but their own archbishop was under no such compulsion.

Polonia entered decked in all the formal regalia of his office—the traditional ermine robe, miter and crosier of an archbishop. It may have been a trick of the uncertain light streaming in from the corridor behind him, but he seemed to cast not one, but two distinct shadows before him.

As he crossed the threshold, these two attendant shadows grew more distinct, seeming to take on substance and dimension. Where previously both had stretched out flat on the floor before the archbishop, they now seemed to ascend, as if climbing a flight of stairs. First their heads emerged, breaking the plane of the floor at right angles. Then their shoulders rose into view. Soon it could be seen that each of the shadowy attendants bore aloft a small black velvet cushion. Upon each of these cushions rested a precious artifact that was easily recognizable to the assembly. Upon the right hand was the golden apple of New York, and on the left, the orb of dominion over shadow.

The bearers deposited their charges with stately grace before Polonia's place at the vast circular table. They then turned and descended into the floor in the same curious manner in which they had emerged.

Polonia paused to survey the gathering before taking his seat. Everyone else was forced to remain standing as well. Receiving the homage of the gathered Sabbat leaders, framed by the spectacle of the young Toreador hanged from the ceiling behind him, Polonia was clearly in his element.

He addressed the gathering. "Thank you for coming, ladies, gentlemen, friends, honored guests. I sense a certain exhilarating expectancy in the air of this room—a premonition, if you will, that greatness and glory are close at hand.

"I appreciate the sacrifices that many of you have had to make in order to be with us on this momentous occasion. You have crossed vast distances and braved great danger to reach this meeting place, isolated deep behind enemy lines."

He reached out and gently started the body of the dangling Toreador swinging in a slow, circular arc.

"Let me assure you, therefore, that the decisions we reach here, and the challenges that we are called upon to meet in these coming nights, will give the Camarilla cause to tremble."

Polonia paused to allow the roar of the assembly to quiet itself.

"As you are no doubt aware, Atlanta has been a

TZIMISCE

Camarilla stronghold almost since its founding. It is, perhaps, no great wonder that a city which was originally named Terminus should attract the attention of our rivals. It is the very sort of thing that would appeal to their affectations."

Polonia jabbed an accusing finger at the unresisting body of the young Toreador and was rewarded with a trickle of blood running down the victim's chest. The tantalizing aroma of it wafted across the room.

"You should also know that Atlanta is a city ripe for Sabbat conquest." He raised a hand in an effort to restrain their enthusiasms and began again. "For some time now, we have been engaged in laying the groundwork for the Siege of Atlanta. The Camarilla is reeling, gentlemen, and tearing itself apart in its flailing attempts to prevent its inevitable fall.

"It began with the Blood Curse. The Red Death savaged the Camarilla's numbers. Losses among the most vulnerable fringe elements of their society— the neonates, the clanless Caitiff and the Anarchs—are rumored to have reached as high as forty percent attrition within the opening weeks of the epidemic. And the pestilence raged unchecked for nearly six months.

"In a desperate attempt to halt the wildfire spread of the curse, the city's ruler, Prince Benison, laid down strict decrees aimed at quarantining these high-risk groups. Naturally, those who were subjected to the harsh dictates were resentful of being stripped of their liberties. The exact course of events and reprisals that followed from this point is a bit difficult to reconstruct.

"We know that, incited by the meddling Brujah,

the Anarchs revolted. Soon open conflict raged in the streets of Atlanta. It is further said that the Brujah made an attempt on the life of the Prince himself, an unfortunate occurrence which only hastened their exile from the city."

Polonia waited patiently for this news to sink in. Borges and his faction were, no doubt, already appraised of the situation. They had had forces on the ground in the city for months now—running reconnaissance, rousing the Anarchs, picking at the seam of the Camarilla's cherished Masquerade.

For the others present, however, the fact that the Brujah had been ousted from the city would be welcome news indeed. Polonia was pleased at the effect his words had produced. The assembly seemed in high spirits and there was much side discussion.

"The Brujah," Caldwell could be heard to snort dismissively.

"They are a hard-fighting clan," Vallejo admitted, in animate discussion with the delegate from Detroit. "Always the toughest knot of resistance in the Camarilla battle lines."

"Nah, the it's those damned Gangrel that you have to watch for. Maybe you don't have them so bad in Madrid, but up on the border, you can't swing a dead cat without startling up a whole nest of them."

"Certainly, we have Gangrel in Madrid. Well, not in Madrid, but in España, yes? In open terrain, I grant you, there is no fiercer opponent that the bestial Gangrel. But in the close fighting of city combat? No, here the Brujah are the more dangerous opponents."

"The Gangrel?" Hardin chimed in from across the table. "You're not from around here are you?

Where you gonna find Gangrel around here? Sure there's bound to be a few scattered packs holed up in the north Georgia mountains or something. But there's just no way a bunch of Gangrel are going to rush down here to Atlanta to defend the city. Believe me, there is no love lost between Atlanta and the rest of this state. And the Gangrel are going to be especially unsociable about the state's primary source of pollution and industrial ravages."

"Well, fewer Gangrel are fine by me." There were scattered words of assent from around the room.

"That only leaves the Tremere."

This bombshell brought the conversation crashing to a halt. It was an overstatement of course. There were actually seven clans that made up the Camarilla. Whenever discussion turned toward pure firepower, however, the three major threats in the Camarilla arsenal were almost universally acknowledged to be the Brujah, the Gangrel, and the Tremere.

The Tremere weren't a militant faction. Not in the same way as the Brujah and Gangrel were anyway. They were however, feared for their prowess and the threat they represented. The Tremere were masters of Thaumaturgy. Their powerful enchantments had been the downfall of many Sabbat offensives.

"How strong is the Atlanta chantry?" Madame Paula, the Koldun sorceress, had perked up at the mention of the dread Tremere.

"Strong enough," replied one of the Nomads, who boasted an especially chalky complexion (even for one of the damned) and unsettlingly pink eyes. *Such beautiful pink eyes*, Madame Paula thought. She could not recall ever seeing such a perfect hue in a Cainite before, but perhaps this was another New

World novelty. She resolved to try it out herself at her earliest opportunity.

She emerged from her reverie as the albino explained further. "It's old—well, old by American standards—over a century. That means we can expect some pretty complex arcane defenses. And it houses at least a dozen warlocks."

"I think that estimate may be a bit inflated," interrupted Sebastian authoritatively.

"Okay then, say a half dozen, although I think it's pretty foolish not to expect worse. Does that make it any better? We're looking at some serious casualties here."

"And a siege does little to weaken the resolve of a well-established chantry," Madame Paula mused. "You can't starve them out, you know. And while you're occupied with slowly squeezing the city into submission, they will be picking away at the besiegers. Oh yes, every night. One here, a few there. It all adds up. Quite disheartening."

"If I may be allowed?" Vallejo's voice, tuned to the pitch of command by a lifetime of military service—many lifetimes in fact—cut through the room. "On this very point I have been instructed to deliver a message from my liege."

Polonia was suddenly wary. He glanced briefly to the opposite end of the table to where Borges sat, but his counterpart's face was as inscrutable as ever behind its omnipresent cowl of shadow.

The eyes of the assembly were on Polonia and he had no choice but to acknowledge the self-proclaimed messenger. "Yes, yes," he waved dismissively. "Hand it here."

"My cardinal thought it unwise to commit the

message to paper. I can, however, recite it verbatim. It is only this:

"The council need have no anxiety over the Tremere. The cardinal's ambassador, the Lady Sascha Vykos, will neutralize the Tremere threat."

There were coarse barks of derisive laughter from the Nomads. Color rose in Vallejo's face.

"Desist at once," he ordered. "These are the words of His Eminence the Cardinal Monçada. You mock them at your peril."

His tone quieted the worst of the offenders, but from beside the Archbishop Borges, Sebastian rose to his feet to confront the Spaniard.

"Perhaps then you could illuminate us as to how this Vykos will singlehandedly defeat the assembled might of the Tremere chantry. You must admit, on the surface of it, it seems quite…ridiculous."

"I am not given to know my lord's instructions to his legate," Vallejo replied coolly. "Nor would I be likely to reveal them if I did. I know only that it will be done. Monçada has given his pledge. It will be done."

"And where, exactly, is this ambassador? The council has been in session for two full nights now and has she even appeared to present her credentials? No. We are well aware of your master's 'interest' in this affair and I am of the opinion that we would be far better off without his meddling and yours."

"Why, you ungrateful lapdog," Vallejo began, his hand straying to his side where a sword might well have once hung, centuries ago. "I have warned you once and shall not do so again. If you persist in these ludicrous pronouncements, you must be prepared to defend them with your honor."

"*Ungrateful?*" Sebastian parroted in disbelief. "Do you think that we should be grateful for this intrusion? Your cardinal is a ruthless and cunning man. This is not an insult, it is merely a statement of fact. There is no denying it. I am familiar with his type. For him, a 'personal interest' is just of a polite way of saying that he has drawn up a deed of ownership, but the ink on the contract is not quite dry yet."

Sebastian knew that there were others, of course, who would do everything within their power to see that the Cardinal Maledictus Sanguine—the Cardinal of the Blood Curse, as Monçada was known by his detractors—did not extend his hand out over Atlanta. Perhaps the foremost among those who opposed Monçada's intervention in Atlanta was Borges himself who, as it was said in the parlance of the Lasombra powerbrokers, remained 'deeply concerned' over the present state of affairs in the city. By 'deep concern' it was understood to mean that he had moved his forces into position to exert leverage directly upon the city.

Such concern, of course, was paramount to throwing down the gauntlet. Monçada had countered in turn by 'extending his sympathies' to the people of Atlanta. Which was to say, he'd escalated the conflict further by committing forces of his own—in particular, his elite legion of household troops, the unsavory war-ghoulist from Prague, a Koldun sorceress, and his personal representative, this Vykos.

It was an unorthodox and ragtag army, no doubt cobbled together on short notice. But as Sebastian systematically tested the mettle of each finger of the cardinal's four-clawed reach, each was proving a power to be reckoned with. Collectively, they would be formidable indeed. But surely, not even Monçada could effectively wield this strange and unpredictable weapon across intervening oceans.

Sebastian heard his name mentioned and turned to his master. "I believe Sebastian was only expressing his admiration and perhaps envy of the cardinal's ruthlessness and cunning. It would be very thin-skinned of you to take mortal offense at such innocuous comments. It was my impression that you were made of sterner stuff." Borges flashed his mastiff grin at Vallejo.

Sizing up the situation, Sebastian was quick to chime in, "Of course, of course. Do sit down, my excitable friend. I have only the utmost respect for your dear Cardinal Maledi... Did I ever tell you," he recovered seamlessly, "what my master always says about him? No? Well, Borges has always maintained that there is not a Cainite in all of Europe with such an unjustifiable—"

"Humility about his person," Borges finished with a sharp glance at his young protègè. "Now, if we might return to the subject of pushing forward our preparations for the siege?"

"But that is exactly what I have been attempting to relate to you, gentlemen." It was Polonia's voice raised in polite disagreement. "There is not going to be any siege."

Monday, 21 June 1999, 2:41 AM
A subterranean grotto

A small, tarnished chain dangled from the desk lamp. Above it, the bulb flickered. A sharp blow to the lamp set the matter right, though the insular patch of light was considerably dimmed. Darkness crowded the seated figure. Taloned fingers turned a page, and then another. A raspy, discontented sigh accompanied the rattle of paper.

Silence. Stillness.

Then the gnarled talons reached for the red pen on the desk and, with surprising deftness, began to scribble notes on the page.

20 June 1999

FILE COPY

Re: Investigation

Spoke briefly with Rolph via SchreckNET
link——reports raid on Toreador party
in Atlanta will fall at midnight 6/22.
Some Sabbat activity in city, verified
by multiple sources, consistent with
report. — *some movement from Miami*

Raid should provide opportunity for
Rolph interaction w/Hesha's man —
(re: EoH). Emmett also planning *Vegel*
accordingly——reports arrangements
finalized; investigation matters to be
resolved, pursuance pending arrival at
Solstice engagement; hostess V. Ash.

Note: Julius to attend; likely result
Julius-JBH interaction obvious; cross-
reference also interaction matrix,
re: Julius-Victoria Ash;

    Julius-Eleanor Hodge;

    V. Ash-E. Hodge;

    V. Ash-Thelonious/Kantabi.

file action update: Hazimel
file action update: Petrodon
Note: query Rolph re: General (Mal.)

Monday, 21 June 1999, 4:43 AM
Thirteenth floor, Buckhead Ritz-Carlton Hotel
Atlanta, Georgia

Three sharp knocks. At the sound, Sascha Vykos checked her pacing and looked up with more than a slight hint of annoyance. She carefully refolded the letter. It vanished into an inside pocket of the immaculate Chanel suit.

The door opened just far enough to allow Ravenna to slip through. He did not shut the door behind him but put his back against it, as if to keep it from opening further.

"I am sorry, Vykos. There is a...*gentleman* here who insists he must see you without delay." The ghoul managed to maintain just the proper tone of distaste, but his anxiety was obvious.

Vykos smiled at his discomfort. "And what is this gentleman's name?"

A look close to terror flitted across the ghoul's carefully controlled features. "My lady! I did not...one does not... What I mean to say is..."

It was apparent Vykos was not going to help him out of his predicament. Ravenna's voice fell to a conspiratorial whisper.

"He is an Assa..."

There was a sharp crack and Ravenna fell to the floor.

"*Assassin* is such an uncouth word," said the visitor, stepping over the inert body of the ghoul. "A thousand blessings upon you and your house. You may account this the first."

Vykos held her ground and studied the stranger.

His motions were like dripping honey—fluid, tantalizing. His form was almost entirely concealed in a draping robe of unbleached linen. *An unusual garment for an assassin.* She had come to think that there must be some sort of unspoken dress code among those hired predators. All seemed to favor close-fitting garments that would not interfere with the necessities of combat or flight. She had already run through four or five ways her visitor's flowing garment might be turned to his disadvantage should it come to close fighting. It was quite likely, however, that those folds concealed a number of lethal ranged weapons which might render such speculation moot.

It was also her understanding that dressing entirely in black was something of a badge of office among practitioners of the second-oldest profession. This garment would shine even in dim moonlight, frustrating all efforts at stealth. Surely, not even an amateur would make such a mistake. No, it stood to reason that her guest was utterly unconcerned with concealing his approach. His words, his actions, even his dress, spoke of a healthy confidence in his own prowess. Vykos found this slightly irritating.

"Was that strictly necessary?" Vykos's tone betrayed only a businesslike displeasure—enough to make clear that she would not account the ghoul's death a service rendered.

Her guest turned up the palms of his hands and bowed his head slightly. His hands were long and elegant—the hands of a pianist, an artist, a surgeon. Their languid grace spoke of a barely suppressed energy. They fluttered gently like the wings of a delicate bird.

Vykos's eyes never left those hands.

"You might at least return him to the front room so that we will not have to look at him as we talk," Vykos continued. "I find it hard to believe that you are always so casual about disposal of bodies and the like. And bring in another chair as you come. My servants have hardly had a chance to unpack yet."

An ice-white smile stole across the visitor's chiseled ebony features. "I am not in the habit of concealing my handiwork. Unless, of course, you count the removal of witnesses. And you need not concern yourself for my comfort. I will stand. We are quite alone? You spoke of servants."

"Yes, we are *now*. I have, of course, sent my most valued associates away for the evening. Some of my guests have a reputation for being somewhat…excitable."

The stranger's voice became low and menacing, "And you do not fear for your safety? There are many in this city who would see you come to harm."

"Tonight, I am the safest person in all of Atlanta." Vykos purposefully turned her back to him and crossed to the cluttered desk. "Your masters are not so careless as to dispatch an agent to kill me when we still have unfulfilled business. Very unprofessional. Nor could they allow me to come to harm from a third party when suspicion would be sure to fall squarely upon themselves."

Vykos turned upon him and pressed on before he could interrupt. "No, I do not fear you, although you bring death into my house. Tonight, you are my guardian angel, my knight-protector. You will fight and even die to prevent me from coming to harm before you can conclude our business. Is it not so?"

"Tonight," again the Assamite flashed a predatory smile, "I am your insurance policy. But for tonight only, Lady."

From beneath his robes, he produced a burlap sack. With a sweep of his free arm, he cleared the clutter from the center of the desk and deposited his parcel with a thud.

Dramatic bastards, thought Vykos. But there was no choice but to play along at this point. She couldn't very well bring this business to completion otherwise. With a sigh of resignation, she opened the sack.

She recognized the familiar features immediately, from the reconnaissance photos. It was Hannah, the Tremere chantry leader. More precisely, it was her head. Hannah's hands had also been severed and were folded neatly beneath her chin. *Nice touch*, Vykos thought. Just the right blend of superstition and tradition. She was well aware that the Assamites' hatred of the warlocks was as ancient as that of her own clan.

Of course, she did not give him the satisfaction of expressing that admiration aloud.

"She's dead all right."

The Assamite tried his best not to look crestfallen at her matter-of-fact reaction.

Before he could respond however, she continued, with perhaps a hint of malice, "Are you certain it's her?"

His pride pricked, he seemed about to make a retort. Then he checked visibly and composed himself. "Ah, now I see you are having a small jest at my expense. Surely, you are more than casually acquainted with…the deceased." The Assamite's tone was soft and formal, like that of a funeral director —

couching an indelicate concept in the gentlest terms possible.

"I have never seen her before," Vykos answered coolly, pronouncing each word separately and distinctly. "And if I understand you correctly, I did not even arrive in this country until after her death."

"Have no concern on that account. All has been carried out in exactly the manner you have specified. As to the matter of the witch's identity, there can be no doubt. If you will allow me…"

The Assamite absently knotted a fist in the hair of the severed head to steady it as he slid one of the lily-white hands from beneath its chin. He turned it over, palm up on the desk.

"The witch's magic is still in her hands. The knife cannot sever it, the scythe cannot gather it in." He recited the words with reverence, as if quoting some ancient scripture.

He caressed the hand gently, like a lover.

Under his touch, the network of delicate lines that crisscrossed the palm darkened, deepened. As he continued to brush the hand with his fingertips, the lines seemed to writhe and then curl up at the edges as if shrinking back from a flame.

As Vykos watched, the snaking lines knotted themselves into a series of complex and subtly unsettling sigils.

The Assamite drew back with a satisfied smile. The glyphs continued to twist and slide gratingly across one another. "Do you know these signs?"

Vykos said nothing, but her eyes never left the dance of arcane symbols.

"It is not given to me to interpret the sigils," the Assamite continued. "But an adept could give them their proper names. Each sign is a unique magical signature – a lingering reminder of some foul enchantment that occupied the witch's final days. Do you have need of such knowledge?"

Still staring at the hand, Vykos shook her head slowly. Then, as if coming back from a great distance, she replied, "No. No, it doesn't matter now. With Hannah dead, the entire chantry will be…"

She changed gears suddenly, but without pause. "But where are my manners? I must not bore you with details of such trifling and personal difficulties. Really, you are much too indulgent of me. Now, what were you telling me about indisputable proof of Hannah's identity?"

With a slight upward curl of his hand, the Assamite gestured toward the sigils.

"A fascinating exercise," Vykos countered, "and let us assume for the moment that I believe unquestioningly your account of what I have just seen." She held up a hand to forestall any protestations.

"But this still tells me only that the hand belonged to a Tremere witch. It does not tell me that it belonged specifically to Hannah.

"Appearances," Vykos intoned, "can be fatally deceiving." She sat down at the desk. As she spoke, her hands absently brushed aside a few wayward strands of Hannah's hair that had drifted down over the pallid face. She ran both of her hands slowly downward, stroking the unresponsive flesh of cheek and throat.

When she again addressed her guest, her gaze never lifted from the death mask before her. "I have seen her, of course, but only in photographs." Her fingertips came together at the nape of the neck. "Do you think her beautiful?"

The question seemed to take her guest by surprise. He snorted dismissively before regaining his composure. "Lady, these considerations, they have no place in my work."

Vykos smiled. Her thumbs swung up, tenderly smoothing closed the eyelids.

"No, of course not." Her voice was soft, her eyes lowered. Her thumbs lingered upon Hannah's sealed eyes, pressing slightly as if to ensure they did not flutter open again. "But I was not asking a professional opinion. You surely had ample opportunity to see her, to study her. Would you say that she was beautiful?"

The assassin wheeled away from her and muttered a few syllables in a harsh and foreign tongue. "You will, perhaps, forgive me if I say that you are the most exasperating of clients. Of course, I observed the movements of the witch. How could I not do so? There is room neither for error, nor hesitation, nor mercy when dealing with her kind. She is there before you now. Judge for yourself whether she is beautiful!"

Vykos, apparently unmoved by his outburst, regarded the unmoving face before her with a critical eye. After some deliberation, she opened a desk drawer, extracted a silver hairbrush and began to brush Hannah's long auburn hair.

"Yes, but you saw her in the full flush of the blood—when she was yet 'alive'—when there was still movement and gesture, expression, emotion. These are the things that the photographs—and this little keepsake—cannot tell me."

He paced the room briskly and was a long while before answering. "Yes, I saw the witch living. I was, as you well know, the last person who might make such a claim." His gaze fixed on some imaginary point in the middle distance as if seeing, not for the first time, people and things that were no more.

"I felt the arch of her back as my hand closed around her waist. I saw the delicate throb in the line of her throat as the flowing hair pulled taut. I saw the lips part to form words of power that they would never complete. Yes, she was as beautiful in dying as she is in death."

Vykos smiled and continued her brushing, counting softly under her breath.

Her guest stirred uncomfortably but did not resume his pacing.

An uneasy silence ensued, filled only by the regular stroke of the brush. As if suddenly struck by a thought, Vykos looked up and fixed her gaze upon him. From beneath half-closed lids, she asked, "What then shall I call you, my sentimental assassin? You have not yet told me your name."

He cocked his head to one side and regarded her for a moment as if to determine whether she really expected an answer or if she were simply goading him further. There was a peculiar undertone to her question. Something subvocal, almost feline, certainly dangerous. It belied the innocent allure of her gaze. Without willing it, he slipped into a more defensive stance.

"Nor am I likely to. You may call me Parmenides."

"Ah, a philosopher then. I had nearly mistaken you for a poet." She continued to muse aloud. "You do not appear to be a Greek and you surely are not so wizened as to have walked among the luminaries of the School of Athens. You are, then, something of a classicist, a scholar...a romantic."

He almost visibly shrank from this last epithet and began to protest.

"No. Say nothing more of it. The conclusion follows inevitably from the premises. But have no fear, your secret shall remain safe with me." She picked up her brush and resumed her task, apparently forgetting him entirely.

He stared at her in open disbelief, but she seemed completely absorbed. Under her unrelenting brush, Hannah's hair came away in great tangled clumps. Soon the surface of the desk was covered, but still she did not pause.

"My lady, I believe we yet have business to discuss."

Vykos still did not look up from her labor. The brush began to scrape gratingly across the exposed stretches of scalp now visible through the remaining patches of hair. The sound seemed to play directly upon the nerves without first traversing the intermediary of the ear.

The flesh began to blacken and bruise. After a long while, Vykos said absently, "You were endeavoring to prove that this is indeed Hannah, the Tremere witch and the leader of the Atlanta chantry. The more I subject this specimen to scrutiny, however, the less resemblance I see between the two."

She set down her brush and pushed her chair back to study the results of her efforts. She nodded, satisfied.

"There is a certain...luster missing." Vykos pinched the cheeks gently as if to bring up the color in them, but seemed disappointed at the result. "A certain defiance no longer apparent in this delicate line of jaw." She illustrated with a slow caress of the index finger.

"And the eyes. Even in the photographs one could see that the witch's eyes were set deep—as if shrinking from the things she had witnessed in the dark hours. These eyes bulge noticeably, and without any of the fire that is the legacy of the Tremere devilry."

Vykos ground her thumbs into the sockets as if to set things aright. Parmenides made a noise of disapproval or disgust and turned away. "Enough. You know these signs for what they are, my Lady. They are the marks of the grave, of the Final Death, nothing more. If you continue along these lines, however, you will certainly mar the remains beyond all recognition."

Vykos pushed back her chair and stood. Her voice was conciliatory. "Now you have gotten your feelings hurt again. Come here my young romantic, my *philosophe*. If you tell me that this is the witch, I will accept your pledge." There was a scraping noise as she rotated the head on the desk to face him.

"Look upon her. Do you not find her beautiful?"

Almost against his will, he looked. The flowing auburn hair was gone entirely. The flesh of face and scalp was bruised to a uniform blackness. The line of jaw was set proudly, powerful and masculine. The cheeks had lost their full feminine roundness and drawn taut so that a hint of the skull was discernible beneath. The eyes had become wary—small, dark, recessed.

None of these individual changes, however, made the slightest impression upon the stunned Parmenides. He had fallen victim, instantly and completely, to the sum of these alarming alterations. The face that stared back at him was unmistakably his own.

Vykos's voice, when it broke in upon him, came from directly behind him and very close. He could feel her breath upon his neck and ear. "…The reason I do not place my trust in photographs. Images may be altered."

He felt her lips upon his throat and let his eyes fall closed.

If anything, Polonia's announcement in the previous night's council meeting had only increased the intensity of the infighting among the Sabbat war councilors. There had already been no fewer than three casualties during the evening's proceedings and the pace did not appear to be slackening noticeably.

The grave news that Polonia had brought to the council was that all their plans had suddenly and irrevocably changed. Months of effort and sums of money that would have put many nations' gross national products to shame had been expended on positioning the Sabbat for a Blood Siege. Forces from as far afield as Miami, New York and, most startlingly, Madrid had moved stealthily into position. The forward agents had whittled away at the Camarilla's infrastructure, fueling the Anarch revolt and jeopardizing the Masquerade. They had summoned the leading powers, advisors and specialists of two continents to attend this council of war. They had argued and threatened and eventually forged a strategy that would bring the city of Atlanta slowly and inexorably to her knees.

And now all of that effort was overturned in a single evening, in a single utterance. There would be no siege.

It had taken some time to quell the initial commotion (which bordered on total riot) that accompanied this pronouncement. Only then had Polonia been able to explain his enigmatic declaration.

"There will be no siege, gentlemen, because the battle for Atlanta will be decided by one single, irresistible assault. We will sack the city, smashing every last shard of resistance in an all-out offensive. That offensive, gentlemen, will take place tomorrow evening at precisely midnight."

The stunned silence that had met that pronouncement was a marked contrast to the unbridled chaos that reigned in the council chambers tonight. The news had had its chance to sink in, to work its transformations. Where last night's gathering had been a somber council of war, this night's assembly was a whooping war party waiting to be loosed that it might massacre its unsuspecting victims.

Polonia was not entirely pleased by this turn of events. For one thing, the unruly crowd was *rearranging* things, and not entirely to his satisfaction.

He had gone to some effort to ensure that everything was just so for this momentous meeting. He noticed the first of the glaring changes immediately upon entering the council chambers this evening. It seemed that for some inexplicable reason, someone or -ones must have broken into the hall for some early-morning mischief. The stolid circular conference table that had dominated the room—which he had brought in at considerable expense—was gone. Missing. A seven-hundred-pound table.

It had been replaced with a much more contemporary conference table. In Polonia's eyes, the immediate disadvantage of this arrangement was that the long rectangular table had a distinct head and foot—a small fact that radically altered the rules of precedence for seating the assembled dignitaries. A small fact to which Polonia attributed at least one of the three—now four, he corrected himself—untimely deaths this evening.

To make matters worse, the table itself was made of an opaque black glass, polished to a mirror-like shine. This last property was causing not a few of the Lasombra some measure of ill-concealed discomfort. More than once, Polonia noted, his lieutenant Costello jerked back sharply as if stung, when his forearms accidentally came into contact with the table.

Polonia could see the already strained tempers beginning to grind together. Fortunately, the foul mood of his fellow Lasombra was somewhat offset by the capering of the Tzimisce. The fiends were in their element. Foraging parties burst in upon the assembly at odd intervals, bearing grisly trophies of their excursions into the city. These they hung up about the room until there were no fewer than a score of corpses dangling from the ceiling.

Some, like the young Toreador, were hanged by the neck. Others were inverted and slit to the sternum, their blood spilling into commandeered ice buckets. Others still were bent double and hauled up by ropes bound about their waists

The rest of the room was in a similar state of utter disarray. Carefully drafted and numbered plans for the assault were strewn haphazardly about the table. Photo dossiers on important Camarilla targets had grown hopelessly mingled and many of the pictures had been pinned to the wall and then slashed into tatters. The carefully arranged placecards were swept to the floor to clear the way for impromptu bouts of arm-wrestling.

Presiding over this reign of chaos, the heady scent of blood filled the room. The guests poured generously, sloppily from cut-glass decanters brimming with that most common of all red wines. They passed silver trays of jellied candies that gave every sign of only recently having coagulated.

Polonia's nerves, however, were on edge and he did not give in to the temptations of these delicacies. Tonight it would be very easy to indulge himself, to drink deeply of the blood until it sang in his ears and formed a crimson film before his eyes. To allow the Beast within to test its tether.

But tonight he must remain vigilant—not only against the desperate Camarilla who would be fighting for their very unlives, but also against his brothers in the Sabbat who would be looking to improve their lot through any means at their disposal.

For many, this would mean a grab for glory on the field of battle. Polonia did not doubt that many hunting trophies and keepsakes would be harvested this night—mementos that could be brought out as a diversion to while away some cruel and brutally short winter evening, decades hence.

For others, the assault would mark the culmination of their intrigues and plays for political power. In the unfolding of the final act, these powerbrokers would be bringing to bear all of their resources. And very few would scruple at crushing anyone so foolish as to stumble in upon their dark compacts.

And then there were always the opportunists, who knew full well that the assault would provide the perfect cover for the disappearance of a careless rival, or the entertaining of any of a host of other vices that even the Sabbat normally frowned upon.

Polonia found himself hoping that enough of the council would survive the remaining two hours before the assault to carry the project through to its completion. Fortunately, the captains of the pivotal forces spearheading the attack were already dispatched and taking up their positions in the field around the High Museum of Art.

There had been a good deal of argument, of course, over which forces should have the honor of leading the attack and incidentally securing the lion's share of the glory—discussions to which Polonia attributed two more of the evening's fatalities.

Tonight's high-society gathering at the High would bring together all of the notable Camarilla leaders in the city under one roof. All the Sabbat had to do was bring down that roof.

Polonia was reflecting upon how this might be best accomplished, and watching an altercation that was probably casualty number five developing, when his attention was caught by the sound of the chamber's door opening. He was perhaps overly sensitive to this occurrence as he was presently seated with his back toward it.

The choice was his own, of course. This option was far preferable to the only other alternative: to have at least one of his fellow councilors seated between himself and the only means of egress from the chamber. Given the nature and disposition of his guests, Polonia had decided he would be better off at the mercy of whoever might be lurking *outside* the room.

The figure who entered was Polonia's own herald, who had been stationed directly outside the door. Polonia was not such a fool, after all, as to leave his back unguarded.

The herald bowed to his master and then, in

answer to a questioning look, rolled his eyes upward. The gesture nearly dislodged one of the orbs that clung precariously to its sunken socket.

Inverting his axe, the herald rapped once sharply upon the floor. "The Lady Vykos, legate, nuncio and ambassador extraordinaire of His Eminence, the Cardinal Monçada."

He stepped aside as the elegantly attired figure swept forward. She was dressed in the style of a sixteenth-century noblewoman—the long flowing gown, the puffed sleeves cuffed midway up the forearm, the rigid tombstone-shaped collar that stood out well above her shoulders, razor-straight in the front and gently curving around to meet behind the nape of her neck.

Her looks were unexceptional. Her mouth was terse, slightly lined perhaps, with the telltale hint of cruelty barely discernible at the corners. Her large dark eyes were half closed in an affected languor, but they missed nothing. Her hair was piled high upon her head and bound in place with perfumed ribbons.

As the unremarkable lady entered the room, the assembled Tzimisce went absolutely berserk. A chorus of cries went up from the capering mob.

"The Blood Countess!"

"It is she, I tell you. Bathory!"

"The coat of arms. There! Embroidered on her collar."

"Yes, the dragon swallowing its own tail. It is she!"

"What are those maniacs going on about?" Sebastian leaned over to ask his master.

"Carefully," the venerable Borges exhaled the word rather than spoke it. "Tread lightly. I think they say that there is a serpent loosed among us."

"No, master, what they said was…" Sebastian suddenly fell silent. He knew full well that Borges's hearing far surpassed his own. Decades of living without the benefit of eyesight had fine-tuned his master's hearing to a level far beyond even what a Cainite might expect.

No, Borges had not misheard. He was, rather, supplying his protègè with additional information that might well prove necessary to Sebastian's well-being. If Borges said their was a viper in their midst, Sebastian was not about to leave his feet dangling within easy reach of the floor.

Borges was not unaware, of course, of the legendary and sadistic exploits of the Blood Countess. The name of Bathory itself was like a familiar and not altogether pleasant exhalation from the Old Country. The syllables were inexorably linked with dark tales of the methodical torture, maiming and murder of countless young women. What had begun with the taking out of a furious temper upon the serving maids of her estate, was then nourished by the devising of elaborate and ingenious punishments, and eventually culminated in a predilection for bathing in the rejuvenative blood of young maidens. By the time Bathory was finally brought to trial in 1610, her accusers had conservatively placed the total number of her victims at just about 650 souls.

It was much more likely that Vykos was deliberately exploiting this myth to her advantage rather than the alternative—that she was, in fact, the Tzimisce patron saint in the flesh.

Either way, this Vykos seemed intent on pushing the number of deaths attributable to the countess even higher. In her hand, she held a delicate silk handkerchief, which she used to carry a distasteful burden—the severed head of an Assamite.

With a casual shrug, she heaved the head onto the table, where it rolled some distance before coming to rest.

"Your pardon, my lords and ladies, for the lateness of my arrival. As you can see, I have been engaged in proving that there is no force—neither among the living nor the dead—that can deny us our victory here tonight. The head of the assassin that was sent against me is only the first gift I lay before you this night." Vykos unfastened the curious necklace she wore. It was shaped to resemble a pair of folded hands. The smallest finger of each hand was grossly elongated and stretched all the way back around to the nape of her neck, clasping to hold the necklace in place. Vykos tossed the necklace after the head. As all eyes turned to these dismembered offerings, no one failed to note the disturbing dance of arcane symbols upon the palm.

"The hands belong to Hannah," Vykos announced, "the Tremere chantry leader. As I said, no one will deny us."

Cries of "Bathory!" and "Death to the warlocks!" erupted from all around the table. Foremost among the company of gibbering Tzimisce, the Butcher of Prague viciously tore into the dangling corpses nearest him. His wicked claws, as sharp and efficient as shears, reaped a bountiful harvest of alabaster limbs. These he laid at the feet of the Lady like an offering.

Spurred on by his example, the fiends laid into the bodies surrounding them with reckless abandon. Most of their victims had been previously rendered inanimate and well beyond the reach of pain by the efforts of the hunting parties. No small portion of their grisly harvest, however, was commandeered from the fiends' fellow councilors in the excitement of the moment. The Tzimisce lined the path before her with dismembered arms and legs that had been slashed, sawed, torn and, in some cases, bitten off cleanly from their owners. She glided forward, never once losing her footing among the tangle of limbs and never once having to condescend to set her foot upon the floor.

The pathway thus created ran to a place of honor that had been cleared at the center of one of the long sides of the table. There, one enraptured Tzimisce had already crafted his body into the frame of an imposing throne. His fellows were throwing large, wet clumps of flesh upon this framework, much as a potter might throw clay onto the wheel.

The throne swelled in size, looming ever larger under their efforts.

Vykos ascended to the still-living throne amidst a scene of pandemonium that would have put to shame the best efforts of seven of the nine hells.

She raised her hand for silence, but it was not forthcoming.

She attempted to raise her voice above the clamor but her words were carried away by the enthusiasm of her devotees.

With a flutter of skirts, she stepped down from the rapidly ascending throne onto the conference table and strode boldly out into its center. This curious displacement of a person walking atop the table seemed to startle the cavorting fiends as no amount of shrieking or bloodletting ever could. All eyes were upon her.

"Thank you. Thank you all for your…affectionate welcome."

She pressed on quickly as the clamor began to rise once again. "You are no doubt aware that only the space of a few short hours stands between us and the utter and devastating conquest of the city of Atlanta. Two nights ago you heard the venerable Borges relate to you tales of the glory of the pending Blood Siege. Last night, Polonia came to you with a compelling plan for launching a daring and decisive assault.

"But I say to you, that the conquest of Atlanta will be accomplished by neither siege nor assault." She paused to let her words sink in. "Tonight, gentlemen, our forces will totally overrun the unsuspecting Camarilla. We have the advantage of them in numbers, tactics, power and surprise. Our single-minded devotion to the cause allows no room for failure.

"The Camarilla is weakened by attrition, civil disorder, Anarch revolt, the exile of the Brujah, the absence of the Gangrel, and the unfortunate demise of the leader of the Tremere chantry." Her lip curled into a grimace of a smile as she swept Hannah's hands from the table with the side of one slippered foot.

"But it will not be a battle, gentlemen. It will be a rout, a glorious Firedance. It is one of the most ancient and glorious traditions of our people—it is party, ritual and wild bacchic revel. It is a time of steeling our courage and casting our prowess into the very faces of God, Cainite and man."

Polonia sat well back in his chair in shocked silence. This shameful display was already well out of hand. He had hopelessly lost track of the current body count among the raging mayhem. He firmed his resolve. This Vykos must be stopped and stopped quickly, before her fanatic converts brought the entire council chamber crashing down around them.

Polonia knew that even his voice, from which many present were accustomed to receive commands in the midst of pitched conflict, was unlikely to shout down this frenzied mob of zealous Tzimisce. Doubtless, debate and negotiation were not what was called for here. This situation required a more brutal and decisive solution.

Fortunately, Polonia had prepared for just such an eventuality. Deliberately, he folded his hands before him on the table. He noted with mild distaste that its surface sent an uncomfortable crawling and stinging sensation up his arms, much as if he had unknowingly brushed a nest of fire ants.

Slowly, he twisted his episcopal ring around in one full circuit anti-clockwise.

Even Polonia had some difficulty following the exact sequence of events set into motion at this prearranged signal.

Vykos was caught up in the fervor of her own exhortations. "And it will not end here, gentlemen. Already, our advance forces are on the move. By week's end we shall smash the Camarilla forces in…"

She was brought up short by the appearance of the hilt of a delicate silver knife protruding from between her shoulderblades. There was an audible gasp from the assembly, followed by cries of dismay and, almost immediately, of fury.

Vykos took one staggering step forward, and nearly pitched from the table into the press of her followers. Many nearby Lasombra cautiously edged away toward the shadowed recesses of the chamber.

A voice whispered in Polonia's ear, the voice of the envoy from the shadow-walking ritual he had enacted only two short nights ago. "It is done, master. I am bidden to ask you to come among us again at your earliest convenience. We have much news to discuss and we now have a boon to ask of you in return."

When Polonia did not object, the envoy pressed on. "Think upon your wretched servant and have pity. It would be callous indeed for you to stay away longer than it takes for this wound—which I have received in your service this night—to heal. I have suffered the touch of silver for your sake. Come to us soon."

Polonia rubbed his temples and nodded. The voice was gone as quickly as it had come. He knew that no one else had overheard, that no one else could have overheard. What concerned him more at this moment was Vykos.

As he watched, Vykos slowly, painfully, turned to face her assailant. Her eye immediately fell upon Averros. Averros glanced quickly to one side and then the other. Finding himself alone, the sole source of her scrutiny, he raised a hand in protest.

"No, my lady. You are mistaken," he began. The nearly crazed mob of Tzimisce surged toward him, drowning out his denials. It was as if the wave of fiends had fused into a vast entity animated by a single will. The amorphous horror seemed to fill the room. It boasted no fewer than twenty heads and some fifty arms. Some of these flailing appendages terminated in vicious claws, others in slimed tentacles, others still in gaping maws. Averros saw numerous weapons borne aloft by the churning waters. Among the flotsam and jetsam, jagged shards of shattered crystal decanters threatened. Numerous bludgeoning limbs that had lined Vykos's path now loomed over him. Not a few chairs in various states of ruin rode the flood tide.

The irresistible wall of flesh and debris crashed over him. He felt himself going under, drawn down by a riptide that left him with the distinct impression of dozens of hands clutching at his legs and ankles, dragging him to his death. He may have screamed in horror as the surge of shapeless flesh closed over his head. But the insignificant sound was lost in the eternal roar of the surf.

Vox populi, vox dei. The voice of the people is the voice of God.

Vykos bent nearly double as if under a great burden. Seemingly, the additional weight of the delicate dagger upon her back was simply too much for her to bear. She staggered beneath her load and fell heavily to one knee.

The Tzimisce wave surged again, this time toward the table and their fallen lady. But it drew back hesitatingly from that shoreline, reluctant to touch their patron—as if by doing so they might undo the magic of her incarnation, dispel the vision. They could not endure the possibility that their salvation might prove as fleeting and insubstantial as a morning fog upon the beach.

As the tide withdrew, it deposited its latest victim upon the rocky shore. Vykos did not even look at the mangled body.

With a cry of undiluted agony, she rolled her shoulders as if to work some terrible kink out of them. As she did so, the haft of the silver knife also rolled. It crested her shoulder like the mast of a tall ship coming over the horizon. The blade's course was jarringly arrested as it ran painfully aground upon her collarbone. But it was enough. The fingers of her right hand closed over the finely wrought hilt and drew forth the blade. A fountain of blood arced toward the ceiling as Vykos slumped.

Polonia could no longer see her slight form over the swirling maelstrom of fanatics that pressed in upon her. He was aware that he was standing now, craning forward, although he could not remember rising to his feet.

Something was happening. There was some commotion there, but he could make out no details amidst the throng. Suddenly, from the very edge of the table nearest the fallen Vykos, a Tzimisce screamed. Polonia instinctively shrank from the hideous sound. The pitiful victim had been crushed, no doubt, between the weight of its fellows and the unyielding surface of the table.

But there was an undertone of uncertainty to Polonia's conjecture. He could not say with confidence that the howl was one of pain. Perhaps it was one of grief. It might well be that the mournful cry heralded the death of Vykos, the Lord have mercy upon her black heart.

It was all such a great waste, Polonia reflected. This Vykos had traveled thousands of miles to make her bid for power here at the most significant Sabbat gathering on this continent in over a century. She had played her hand boldly and with great dramatic flair. And she had very nearly pulled it off.

Polonia could not help thinking of what a fearsome adversary the dread Monçada must truly be to command the loyalties of such potent and unpredictable minions. He resolved to steer well clear of the machinations of the Cardinal Maledictus Sanguine for the foreseeable future. Perhaps a decade or so hence, Polonia might attempt to reestablish relations by inviting the cardinal to follow the fine precedent he had set here in Atlanta—to commit some forces to the siege of Buffalo or Atlantic City or some other logical extension of Polonia's domain.

Another shriek shattered the solemn silence of the council chamber. This time, Polonia was even less certain of the signs and omens present in the pregnant outcry. If he was not greatly mistaken, it sounded like a howl of shuddering ecstasy.

Surely not! They would not dare. Polonia fumed and began to shoulder his way forward through the throng, swinging his crosier before him in an attempt to clear the path. The shifting mob unconsciously resisted his efforts. It was like swimming through tar, or molasses, or quicksand.

"Halt! Desist immediately or suffer my extreme disfavor! You will not defile this council with your unclean hungers—with your foul diablerie. Stop, I command it!"

Suddenly the crowd seemed to part before him and he stumbled forward. The sight that greeted his eyes stopped him cold.

The body of Averros was there, on the floor. But it was not the body of Averros. It was twisted, contorted, torn from its original God-given shape. Now it resembled nothing more than a low marble altar.

The sickly pink marble was veined through with lines of palest blue. It was no stone that occurred naturally. More disturbingly, it seemed to pulse slowly and rhythmically. Crouched over a natural basin in the top of the altar was Vykos. The blood still seeped from the wound above her collarbone and plished softly into the nearly full basin below.

As Polonia watched, a Tzimisce staggered forward toward the basin. He picked up the delicate silver knife that rested beside the recessed basin, and made a deep, cross-shaped incision in his palm. Then, steadily meeting Vykos's eyes, he squeezed his fist over the basin.

A small stream of blood ran from his hand and down his wrist before abandoning itself to the fall. Vykos cupped her hands and dipped them into the font, drawing up a double handful of the mingled blood. She extended her hands before the young Tzimisce's enrapt face. "One blood," she recited softly, affectionately.

He was hers utterly. "One body," he replied solemnly. He drank deeply with closed eyes, in reverence and rapture. Taking her wrists gently, he licked her palm clean of blood.

The communicant bowed and withdrew, only to be immediately replaced by another.

Polonia got quickly to his feet, leaning heavily upon his crosier as he did so. The crowd did not seem to resist him at all on his journey back outward from the center of the mystery rite. He swung his crosier before him a few times, nonetheless, just for effect. He was anxious to escape any further pandemonium that was in store this night—the unbridled carnage that was now clearly beyond his meager power to prevent or even redirect.

As he none-too-gently brushed past his herald, he ordered, "Have my commanders attend upon me in my chambers. *All* of them," he added firmly, with a significant glance back over his shoulder.

As the doors of the council chamber thudded closed behind him, he could already pick out the first wild, bacchic strains of the Firedance.

part two:
the firedance

"This isn't right!" Caldwell sputtered through clenched teeth.

Antonio Vallejo barely suppressed his rage. "The attack must go forward, Señor Commander."

On the other side of Peachtree Street, the main thoroughfare of downtown Atlanta, stood the High Museum of Art, a distinctive rounded structure built around the circular well of the interior lobby. Aside from the handful of cars that had arrived earlier, including two limousines and a Rolls Royce, there was no evidence of the gathering that Vallejo knew to be occurring there on the fourth floor—a gathering of the Camarilla vampires of the city, come together to fawn and gawk over mortal sculpture, come together to deceive themselves, to pretend that they were somehow still human. Come together, unknowingly, to die in a hellish conflagration of violence.

If Commander Caldwell, that was, would pull his head out of his ass and give the preliminary orders so the attack could go forward.

"It is a simple order, Señor Commander."

Commander Caldwell obviously felt otherwise. In his agitation, he paced among the preternatural shadows that concealed the two from view; he ran his fingertips along his scalp, up and down, a thumb above each ear, pinkies together along the crest of his bald head. As he rubbed his stark, white scalp, his fingers left furrows in their wake—slight furrows of skin, barely noticeable at first, but as Vallejo watched and as Caldwell's agitation increased, the furrows deepened until they became gullies that must have, of necessity from their depth, delved into the substance of the commander's cranium itself. Yet he continued his pacing and his stroking, seemingly unconcerned by, in fact unaware of, the deformity he wrought upon himself.

Tzimisce, thought Vallejo. He was reminded again—as if he could ever forget!—why the mere mention of the clan evoked such unease in his heart. They at least, unlike the Camarilla pretenders, retained few pretensions to humanity. But perhaps the fiends had taken their transformation, their transcendence, many of them would claim, a bit too far.

Not that Vallejo had any doubts about where his own eternal soul was eventually headed. But these Tzimisce, these fiends…

May the Virgin help us if they ever gain control of the Sabbat, Vallejo thought, then cringed at the inadvertent piety. Ostensibly, he had left behind the religious trappings that had so bound his mortal life, but like a penitent having allowed his confession to have lapsed for quite some time—two and a half centuries, to be precise—he didn't like to press his luck by drawing the attention of the Holy Mother. Such a misstep was as sure an indication of Vallejo's own agitation as was the self-disfigurement of the Tzimisce's.

Vallejo chastised himself for such laxity. A time of battle was the most important instance for discipline. Thus Caldwell's recalcitrance was that much more galling.

"The attack cannot go forward until you draw in your patrols, Señor Commander," Vallejo said.

Caldwell abruptly ceased his pacing, shoved a stubby finger toward Vallejo, and bared his obvious fangs as he spoke: "Somebody has screwed up the orders. This *can't* be right."

Vallejo was dumbfounded, so foreign to his frame of reference was this assertion—an order not acceptable to a subordinate? Nothing of Vallejo's centuries of training at the hand of Cardinal Monçada in Madrid had prepared him for this. As a squadron leader of the cardinal's hand-chosen legionnaires, the most elite, highly trained military force the Sabbat possessed, Vallejo *knew* that a soldier's job was to execute his orders, not to question them.

But this New Worlder, this American, was unwilling or unable to see that basic truth. It was more than the predictable and natural resentment of a Tzimisce against the more astute and politically dominant Clan Lasombra, Vallejo realized, since the "objectionable" orders had come from another Tzimisce, Councilor Vykos. No, this insubordination rose from Old-World efficiency trampling on New-World sensibilities. The offensive about to be launched had been conceived of by Cardinal Monçada and was to be implemented by Councilor Vykos. Certainly Caldwell and others, in seeing designs they had bungled for decades carried out by perceived interlopers from across the sea, suffered from wounded pride. But to endanger the entire operation, to place at risk the ascendancy of the Sabbat on this continent, was unthinkable, unconscionable!

And yet it was happening.

Caldwell recommenced his pacing. His aide, a slightly built, not overly defaced Tzimisce, who appeared quite unhappy to find himself near the epicenter of a burgeoning dispute, skulked farther into the shadows. The attack was to have gone ahead at midnight. It was already unnecessarily delayed and seemed likely to be delayed additionally, judging from Caldwell's manner.

"This ain't *right*," Caldwell said again. "I'm not letting all the credit for this attack go to damned…" he stopped suddenly, seeming to remember Vallejo's presence.

"…To damned foreigners?" Vallejo offered, allowing a certain level of menace to creep into his voice.

The American glared at his fellow commander and groped for perhaps a less inflammatory choice of terms than he'd started to utter: "To…to *others*," he spit out at last.

"Sir," said Vallejo, forcing the use of a formal, clipped tone so as not to vent his growing ire, "your patrols ensure that our victory will be complete. None of those people will escape us, and no one from the outside will be able to interfere."

"I want a piece of the action!" bellowed Caldwell.

Vallejo flinched. Now, incredibly, beyond becoming an obstacle to the mission by his refusal to carry out simple orders, Caldwell was, by way of his fulminations, risking discovery of two of the three point-of-contact commanders for the assault.

"*Lower your voice!*" Vallejo barked forcefully, but without imprudent volume. In dealing with the American, Vallejo felt compelled to revise his estimation of his fellow commander. There might be a touch of Old World-New World rivalry at work, but the root of the conflict was a lack of professionalism on the westerner's part. Vallejo had dealt with bores on both sides of the Atlantic, any of whom might have balked as Caldwell did now. Caldwell happened to have the added impediment of being an idiot. All of this led Vallejo to one unavoidable conclusion.

If he shouts again, I will kill him.

It would be well deserved. Failing another outburst, however, Vallejo believed that the political situation, with which he tried to keep respectfully uninvolved, was too fragile for him to take direct action against this pompous fool.

"My patrols should be part of the attack," Caldwell insisted, slamming his fist against his other palm.

"Give the order, or step aside for someone who will…someone who *can*," said Vallejo.

Caldwell bristled at the suggestion that he was not up to the task at hand. Again, he pointed at Vallejo. The Tzimisce's finger, trembling with rage, almost touched the Spaniard's nose. Vallejo, for his part, resisted the temptation to grab that finger, to bend it back until it snapped, and to keep bending until it came completely free of the hand. Caldwell's aide did his best to slink even farther into the shadows.

"I won't take that from you," Caldwell threatened, his voice rising very close to the level that Vallejo had decided would require drastic action.

Vallejo, however, stood at perfect attention. Only his steeled nerves kept him from striking out. He was in the awkward position of trying to convince a Tzimisce commander to carry out an order from a Tzimisce superior, and while Vallejo was by far the most seasoned combat veteran on the scene, the Council had made clear that all three commanders—

Vallejo, Caldwell, and Bolon—were considered equal in rank. All this was running through Vallejo's mind as he stared at the quivering finger of this incompetent windbag.

"I won't take that from you," Caldwell repeated more quietly.

"Take?" asked an icy-calm voice from behind Caldwell.

He turned to see, less than a foot away, Councilor Sascha Vykos. Caldwell involuntarily took a step back.

Vykos was tall and slender. As was the custom of the Tzimisce, Vykos had altered her appearance, the very formation of her bones and skin, although not so much as the battalion of battle ghouls, those walking masses of destructive musculature, that she directed through Commander Bolon. Her high forehead was folded upward and back, a symmetrical feathering of flesh. At least it was tonight, at this moment.

Over the years, Vallejo had seen Vykos on numerous occasions back in Madrid. Though physical appearance was fairly malleable for the Tzimisce fiends, she more so than most of her clan reinvented herself as often as a mortal woman might change hairstyles. Yet this ever-variable appearance, as Vallejo well knew, though definitely disconcerting, was less disturbing than the casual air of cruelty that clung to her no matter what twisted guise she chose, and whether she was knee-deep in dismembered corpses or sipping vitae from fluted crystal.

This was the woman, the creature, that Caldwell faced. This was the will he had flouted in his refusal to set into motion the first phase of the night's attack.

"There's nothing for you to take, Commander," said Vykos. "Your job is to give—to give the orders that were entrusted to you."

"Councilor Vykos," he said with a short, jerky bow. "I didn't expect to see you here."

"Indeed," she purred like a large predatory cat as she edged even closer to the disgruntled and increasingly uncomfortable commander. "I had not planned to venture so close to what I presumed, in my ignorance, would be a field of battle."

Caldwell flinched at the rebuke. The lion's share of his indignation seemed to have deserted him, or at least to have been tempered, now that he stood face to face with the superior to whose orders he took such exception. Her gentle tones and tight, insincere smile took the starch from him.

"Something's wrong. There's been some…misunderstanding," Caldwell told her. "What I got can't be the orders you gave. Somebody screwed 'em up, didn't tell us right."

Vykos stared fixedly at the commander. She responded neither in word nor expression to what he said.

"My patrols are ordered to stand by," he continued, "to sit back and just watch the assault." His dander rose again somewhat as he reminded himself of the indignities that had been heaped upon him. "My boys can kill as good as anybody. A lot of them are *Tzimisce*," he emphasized to his clanmate. "They deserve a piece of the action. And some of the others…some of them are here to fight against their own clans."

Vallejo casually spat at this mention of the *antitribu*, those Cainites who had indeed broken with their clans, disavowed their blood and defied their elders. Vallejo could summon no respect for them. *Cannon fodder. Nothing more.*

His spittle striking the pavement sounded like a thunderclap in the tense silence of the shadows. The insult was not lost upon Commander Caldwell, but he had more urgent problems at the moment.

"I know you couldn't have ordered us just to sit and watch," Caldwell said. "You wouldn't do that. My boys deserve a piece of the action. So do I. This is all a trick.... Somebody changed the orders."

"Hmm." Vykos leaned forward and sniffed near Caldwell's left ear, then his right. The commander seemed totally unsure of what to make of this, but he held his ground and persisted in making his case with only minimal stuttering. "My patrols...*our* Tzimisce, and the others...are...I mean, you know, they deserve a piece...."

Vallejo, completely ignored for the moment, watched this peculiar exchange that was so far beyond his perception of the relationship between officers of differing rank. The two fiends, only centimeters apart yet not making contact, now impressed him as serpents engaged in some elaborate mating ritual.

But then Vykos did touch her clanmate. "Shh," she cooed to him, a mother to her babe, as she placed her palms gently on his cheeks. "You are very much mistaken, Commander." Her voice was soothing now, but only in the way that ice brings numbness.

Even amidst the dense shadows that Vallejo maintained, he thought he saw her eyes glowing, not the bestial red which many Cainites might achieve, but a piercing, cold blue. Caldwell tried to protest, but she shushed him again, and with a tender finger upon his lips silenced him. She returned her hand to his cheek.

"No active part in the assault?" she asked. "How could you believe such a thing, my dear Commander?"

Vykos shook her head sadly. "When the patrols are ordered forward, they will form a seal around that museum. You see the museum?" She turned his face slightly so that he faced the High. Then she nodded his head, once, twice, in the affirmative.

"No one will escape—because of the patrols," she explained patiently. "And do you know who is inside, Commander?" This time she gave him no time to reply, but herself continued. "The prince of this city is there, which means that it is likely that others will try to help him—mortal police, perhaps. But do you know what they will find?"

A light was dawning in Caldwell's eyes as well, a light of realization—not realization of strategy, which Vallejo thought should have been obvious from the start. Caldwell, as Vykos soothed and stroked him, was realizing his own fear.

"They will find their way blocked," she answered her own question. "There will be no help for the prince. Nor for any of the others."

The absence of sound rivaled the absence of light on that dark street. Caldwell and Vykos stood practically eye to eye, his white face in her white hands. Vallejo, feeling very much the spectator, looked on in detached amazement, while Caldwell's unobtrusive aide seemed to ooze into the cracks of the sidewalk—surely a trick that not even the Tzimisce had perfected.

"So you see how important the patrols are?" asked Vykos. She allowed Caldwell to nod his own head this time.

"Good. I wanted to be sure." Then she began to press her hands together, steadily, forcefully. An expression of consternation crossed Caldwell's face but quickly gave way to fear. He grabbed her wrists, tried to pull her hands away, but to no effect.

Vykos's eyes shone more brightly. Caldwell's face began to give way beneath the steady pressure of her palms. Slowly, her hands compressed the bone structure of his cheeks and jaw. His face suddenly took on an elongated manner, exaggerating further the furrows along his scalp. A garbled moan arose in his throat.

Vallejo watched in horrified fascination. He could not force himself to turn away.

· *Like warm butter*, he thought. Shortly her hands would meet in the center. *Squeezing him like…*

But just as Vallejo managed to form those thoughts, Vykos plunged her thumbs into Caldwell's eyes, *through* his eyes—for she didn't stop at that jellied matter, which dribbled down his face. Caldwell jerked spasmodically as her thumbs, like hot knives, dug into his brain.

Vallejo did not remember seeing the body fall or slump to the ground, but there it was, Vykos standing over it. She flicked her fingers, and a splatter of bodily juices struck the ground like the first raindrops of an approaching storm.

Vykos turned to Caldwell's aide, the slight Tzimisce, whose every ounce of determination was barely preventing him from fleeing into the night.

"Give the order," she said. "The attack will go forward."

She turned and walked away, secure in the knowledge that her directive would be carried out promptly.

Vallejo, watching the councilor, thought he could hear her humming faintly as she left.

"Shut your mouth before I rip it off your face,"
Marcus said to either or both of the dark, lithe figures, Delona and Delora, beside him atop the parking
garage. They, along with "Fingers" Jorge, who was
obediently quiet and wrapped up in his cloak, had
been in position for nearly two hours. Marcus had
expected orders before now, and the waiting was playing on his nerves.

Playing on his nerves almost as much as the
twittery laughter between Delona and Delora. The
two had a jittery sort of language they spoke to each
other that Marcus couldn't understand, and he always felt that they were talking about, and *laughing
at*, him. He realized, after making his threat, that it
would be difficult to rip someone's mouth actually
off her face—the mouth being just a hole—but he
decided to let it slide.

"Shut up, you little turds."

They were dark and small—of course, everyone
was small next to him—so turds they were, as far as
he was concerned. But they looked more like spiders,
with long spindly limbs that they folded up near their
body. And their skin, not only dark, looked as if it
had been singed all over. Marcus, unable quite to rec-
oncile his own analogies, wasn't sure why a spider
would be burnt, or why a turd would be either, for
that matter.

Worse than the fact that they were ignoring his
order for silence—and Caldwell had put *him* in

charge—Marcus was afraid their constant blabbering would give away the patrol's position. They were within sight of the museum, after all, just around the corner. Couldn't they see that this was an assignment of such importance that the little turds should shut up? The burdens of command weighed heavily on Marcus.

"If I've gotta tell you one more—"

But they all fell silent at once. Delona's and Delora's tufted black ears tensed and quivered. Marcus heard it too—a door opening below them; a door *being* opened, and that meant *somebody* was opening it. Marcus, his blood fairly boiling from the endless waiting and the trials of leadership, rushed to the edge of the parking deck to peer down. The turds flanked him on either side.

A lone figure had, indeed, exited the garage and was moving toward the street corner. Marcus had been told to allow no one to pass the parking deck in either direction, toward or away from the museum. The figure below was moving away from the museum, and he was being sneaky about it. Only the slight creak of the door opening had given him away.

As Marcus debated what commands to give, Jorge tore past him over the railing and dropped onto the figure in the street.

Marcus was astounded. Jorge had preempted his first *real* order of command. Worse still was the lack of success that Jorge met with. Maybe it was the fluttering of his cape that gave him away, or maybe the victim just possessed incredible reflexes. Either way, as Jorge made contact, the stranger fell backward and rolled, coming to his feet even as Jorge crashed to the ground.

Marcus roared in disbelief. Delona and Delora, as if amused that their leader had just unwittingly and completely relinquished whatever remained of the element of surprise, giggled hysterically.

The astonishingly agile stranger, with his light brown skin, expensive haircut, and formal attire, looked up at Marcus and the others. Jorge moved closer. He threw back his cloak and unfurled his fingers, each several feet long, which bobbed and weaved like restless serpents. Simultaneously, like a constrictor consuming big game, he unhinged his jaw and laughed as his mouth stretched wide enough to ingest a small child.

Again surprisingly, the stranger did not flee. Instead he took a combative stance and his voice echoed off the cement walls of the parking deck: "Come on then, you bastards! I'll take one of you with me. Which one wishes to accompany me to the hellish pits of Set?"

Set! Marcus couldn't believe his luck. Of course, only another creature of the night would've been able to elude Jorge's lunge. More importantly, Caldwell would be very pleased when Marcus brought him the trampled husk of a Setite!

Delona and Delora, without waiting for orders, were already crawling down the face of the building, and the Setite was backing away. Marcus had no intention of being left out of the fun. He hoisted a leg over the railing and then launched himself into the air. His legs, powerful enough to crush a bowling ball or mangle a parking meter with only slight exertion, sent him well beyond the retreating Setite, who was obviously dismayed—as well as cut off from a route of escape. Two new potholes marked the point of Marcus's landing.

"So good of you to come to us," hissed Delora in her rarely used and strangely accented English.

Marcus leapt again, this time straight at the Setite. Despite the distracting approach of the other three Sabbat, however, his victim saw him coming and dove off the sidewalk, again rolling and jumping to his feet, leaving Marcus with only an armful of air as he grasped for a crushing blow at the space the Setite had vacated.

Now the Setite did run, but Delona and Delora were incredibly agile and quick. They bounded ahead of him, cutting him off again, and when he paused, Jorge struck. His fingers flashed through the air like long-starved vipers. They lashed the Setite and wrapped around his body, pinning one arm to his side.

From his vantage point, Marcus saw what Jorge probably could not. With his free hand, the Setite produced a small knife from somewhere. He'd bent low; maybe an ankle sheath hidden beneath his dress trousers.

Such a cute little knife, Marcus thought, as he approached from the Setite's blind side, wanting to finish off their prey before the dancing turds had a chance to beat him to it. That would show them who was in charge. Marcus kept an eye on the knife, though there was little chance that such a tiny blade would even penetrate his inhumanly thick skin, much less do him any serious harm.

I like this Setite, thought Marcus, seeing their victim still struggling, even down to one arm and surrounded. *He's got guts*. At least he would until Marcus squeezed them out of him.

Just then, the Setite whipped his hand and his blade through the air, not throwing the knife, but—

Something struck Marcus across the face. Burning, searing pain in his eyes. Darkness. Pain spreading deeper.

He clawed at his face, at his eyes, not caring that his fingers, too, began to burn. Denied sight, Marcus lurched from one side to another, stabbing with his massive feet whichever way he felt he was falling at that moment. The pavement crumbled beneath him, making footing that much trickier. And still his eyes burned.

Acid, or something like it.

Marcus dug his fingernails into his own face and ripped away some of the surface flesh around his eyes. That helped only a little. He tried to force open his eyes, squinting and blinking in the harsh light of the nearby street lamp.

He was still closer to the fight than he'd realized in his blindness. The Setite had struck again. Only a few steps away, Jorge was down, the little knife impaling his hand. His movements were jerky, twitchy, as if control of his limbs had left him, and he wailed piteously, like a dying cat. The Setite, his back turned to Marcus and Jorge, was squared off against Delona and Delora.

Marcus lashed out with a sledgehammer fist and caught the unsuspecting Setite solidly between the shoulder blades, propelling him into the air. He landed hard on the pavement several yards away. No cushioning roll this time.

Delona and Delora were on him at once, raining blows upon his head and shoulders, knocking his legs and arms from beneath him as he tried to regain his feet. Marcus brushed them aside and lifted the Setite by the collar, then spun him around so the two were face to face.

And Marcus smiled.

Despite his burning and watering eyes, despite the blurred vision, Marcus smiled as he wrapped his arms around the Setite and squeezed. Ribs snapped. Such a beautiful sound—almost as pleasing as the anguished scream that now came from the Setite.

Die, little man. Die! Marcus's smile broadened at the sound of his helpless victim choking on the blood that welled up in his throat as broken ribs punctured and sliced through his innards. The hulking Tzimisce even took pleasure from the blood the Setite coughed into his face. It was the blood of victory.

Marcus roared with triumph as the last resistance of the Setite's body gave way before the incontestable vise of his bulging arms. Joints popped. The Setite's carcass was crushed almost beyond existence, no doubt liquefied by the nearly geologic force Marcus exerted. Marcus hugged the remains to his chest. He could smell the rich blood soiling the once-exquisite evening wear. Then Marcus held at arm's length the remains—

Except there were no remains. At least no body. There was blood, yes, but not enough. No ruptured entrails, no liquefied flesh dripping to the pavement. The last strains of Marcus's triumphant roar curdled in his throat and were reborn as a cry of frustration.

Delona and Delora seemed to realize what had happened—the Setite had somehow slipped out of Marcus's grasp, leaving behind only clothing like shed skin. But the blackened twins had no more idea where the Setite had gotten to than did Marcus. They hurried about in different directions—up the street, down the street, around the corner, into the parking garage—but clearly the Setite had escaped.

"Gone," said Delona, as if explanation were necessary.

"Gone," echoed Delora.

Marcus let the empty clothing drop. After hours of waiting and having his orders ignored, the one intruder his patrol had spotted had eluded them. Jorge lay convulsing on the ground, and Marcus himself was half blinded by what must have been some type of poison on that puny little knife. It was all more than he could bear. Marcus's already blurred vision clouded red with rage. Without warning, he opened his powerful jaws and struck at the surprised Delora. He caught her on the neck, which snapped. In fact, her head remained attached to her torso by only a few cords of tendon or muscle or something. Denied his proper feast on the Setite, Marcus sucked what vitae there was in her tiny frame, then discarded the desiccated husk onto the street like so much garbage.

"Get rid of *that*," he said to Delona, indicating her former mate, "then carry Jorge back upstairs. Now!"

Delona, he noticed, rushed to obey him this time. While she carried out his orders, and Marcus blinked repeatedly and rubbed at his eyes, the tiny radio in his pocket began to beep at him. The device looked like a child's toy in his colossal hand. He labored briefly to press the correct button.

"Patrol five," he said.

"Tighten perimeter," said the voice that sounded much farther away than it really was. "Close to fifty yards."

The voice was not Caldwell's, Marcus noticed.

It was one of his aides', the skittery one. But that of itself was not unusual.

"Gotcha," said Marcus, then remembered that there was something more formal he was supposed to say, but with all the waiting and the ruckus and the frustration, the specific wording escaped him. "Moving in," he said, and stuffed the radio back into his pocket.

"Come on, you turd," Marcus called to Delona. Jorge wouldn't be ready to move yet, if ever—who knew what Setite poison might do to a little fellow like him?—so Marcus's patrol now consisted of himself and Delona. At least she wasn't giggling any more.

Thankfully, Caldwell's body had been removed. Not that Vallejo couldn't stomach proximity to a mangled corpse—in fact, his job generally involved actions that produced mangled corpses, often in large numbers—but he needed to concentrate on the attack he was about to launch without being distracted by that grim reminder of what Councilor Vykos had done to the former commander.

That obstacle quite removed, the patrols were pulled in forming a tight perimeter around the museum, and official-looking roadblocks were set up all around to discourage casual passersby, though midweek downtown Atlanta was fairly deserted at this hour. The possibility of a few civilian casualties didn't worry Vallejo, but there was the danger that the police might take an interest in the roadblocks or the museum itself. In an effort to ward off that eventuality, a series of drive-by shootings were taking place many miles north of downtown. Vykos had ordered that at least two dozen mortals be killed. An attack of that magnitude in a sleeping city, she believed, would keep emergency crews and police busy for hours.

Vallejo did not expect to need that long.

Silently, he gave the signal for the attack to commence. A casual observer might have wondered at the lack of response to Vallejo's signal, but that observer would have overlooked the sprawling swath of blackness that crept from near where Vallejo stood and spread slowly across the street. The streetlamps seemed to flicker as the light they shed was sucked into the blackness. The shadow kept advancing, until the entire street was shrouded in darkness and the streetlamps were little more than distant beacons, miles and miles away. The three-quarter moon was conspicuously obscured.

Vallejo was filled with pride at the skillful advance of his squadron of legionnaires. The inky blackness crept forward, wrapped tightly around the base of the museum, then oozed up the long ramp and stairs to the main entrance. The other exits were being secured as well, Vallejo knew, most notably the parking area attached to the museum where intelligence reported at least a half dozen drivers and servants—ghouls fed on Camarilla blood, most likely—awaited their masters.

As if in response to Vallejo's thoughts, a figure of pure shadow took shape beside him where before there'd been nothing. It rose from the pavement and took on human form, but it was darkness through and through. Then the darkness coalesced, taking on more identifiable hues and substance, and Vallejo stood next to Legionnaire Alcaraz.

Alcaraz nodded curtly in way of salute. "Parking area secure, sir."

"Ghouls?" Vallejo asked.

"Si."

"And the other exits?"

"Secure, sir."

"All of them?"

"Si."

"Very well," said Vallejo, confident of Alcaraz's ability and judgment. "Take up your position."

Alcaraz nodded again. His expression froze, as if the image visible of him were actually several seconds old. Then, indeed, he darkened, from the edges inward, and became again a form of pure shadow, which in turn surrendered its shape, a giant droplet of ink flowing into an inscrutable pond of black.

Vallejo raised his radio to his mouth. "Commander Bolon."

"Bolon here," crackled the response almost immediately.

"Exterior secure," Vallejo reported. "Phase two complete."

"Phase three commencing."

"Confirmed." Vallejo reattached the radio to his belt.

Now everywhere Vallejo looked, the shadows were alive with slow, methodical movement. Not figures emerging from the substance of the shadow itself, as had the commander's lieutenant, but larger shapes, vaguely humanoid—some more so than others— moved in ranks toward the museum. The shapes varied in outline, as well as number and configuration of limbs, but the figures shared an immenseness of stature. They towered over Vallejo, and he stood well over six feet tall. The impression given by this new advance was almost that the buildings of the city themselves were closing in on the High Museum.

It might just as well be so, thought Vallejo, so sure was he of the plans he followed. He had served Cardinal Monçada long enough to know that his benefactor did not lend support—much less a full squadron of legionnaires—to affairs that were chancy.

Bolon's battle ghouls—Vykos's ghouls really, just as the legionnaires' ultimate loyalty was to Monçada, not to Vallejo—continued forward unopposed and converged upon the darkness-shrouded museum, at which point they separated into patrols. One patrol headed toward the parking-area elevator. Another prepared to force entry through the main doors. Others began to scale the walls of the museum. Vallejo was amazed to see the agility of these massive creatures, but he reminded himself that they'd been created specifically for missions such as this, perhaps for this exact mission. They were masterpieces—monolithic edifices of muscle and hardened bone armor beneath a thick layer of leathery skin. Whatever mental alacrity was sacrificed in their transformations, Vallejo was assured, was more than made up in single-mindedness of purpose.

Caldwell should have been so fortunate, thought Vallejo.

But his time for spectating was at an end. There was blood to be spilled. Rich blood. And he would have some of it for his own. One final time, he checked his sidearm and the specially crafted grenades attached to his bandolier. Then, with the ease born of his Lasombra heritage, he released his physical form to join with the blackness before him, and led that blackness upward along the outside of the museum, past the ascending battle ghouls, and on to the victims waiting inside.

Tuesday, 22 June 1999, 1:04 AM
Fourth floor, the High Museum of Art
Atlanta, Georgia

"Elysium be damned, I will punish your insufferable attitude." J. Benison Hodge, Malkavian prince of Atlanta, had spoken.

Julius tested the reassuring weight and balance of the sword in his hand. He had a matching blade strapped to his back. Even though this museum was Elysium, as cried by the rightful prince, and violence here of any sort was anathema, Julius knew only too well of Benison's erratic nature, proclivities toward uncontrollable rage and violence—rules, even his own, be damned. That's what Julius had been counting on.

The gallery, a garden of statuary and black glass partitions, reminded Julius of a cemetery, only the monuments were a bit larger, and marble instead of granite. The Brujah archon was prepared—anxious, in fact—to necessitate a new headstone in the city. All he required was for the prince to try to carry through with his rash and public threat, and in the shadow of the mammoth, paneled doors, which dwarfed even the largest of the sculptures—Toreador pretension upon Toreador pretension—the prince seemed about to grant Julius's wish.

As Kindred onlookers stumbled over themselves and each other trying to scurry out of the way, Benison stalked forward, murder in his eyes. They flashed green next to his expansive auburn beard. This towering, powerfully built Kindred was one of few who could press Julius in an even fight. But Julius, sword firmly yet comfortably in hand, facing the unarmed Malkavian prince, felt no need to subject himself to an even fight.

He will attack me, and I will destroy him, Julius thought calmly.

The dispute, which reached back many years, was predicated on the prince's systematic mistreatment of members of Clan Brujah. None of whom were particularly near or dear to Julius, it was true, but appearances and the dignity of the clan must be maintained. Then, last year, a serious near-breach of the Masquerade—a leak to the press of details regarding the Blood Curse—followed by a festering revolt of the Anarchs in Atlanta, had provided Julius with sufficient cause in the eyes of his superiors in the Camarilla to apply intense scrutiny to Benison's actions, which seemed to threaten the stability so desired by the powers that be. And after last night's surface-to-air missile attack on police helicopters—a blatant violation of the Masquerade, if ever there were one!—Julius felt that any action he took against Benison would be upheld by his master, Justicar Pascek.

Mostly, however, Julius just wanted an excuse to carve up the crazed, ex-Confederate prince. Benison seemed determined to give him that excuse. Julius held his position, careful not to give away the direction of his first attack. The prince charged on, drew back one white-knuckled fist—

And darkness fell over the museum.

Julius's other senses instantly grew hyper-alert, compensating for the sudden loss of sight. Someone nearby screamed—a primeval instinct in any crowd plunged into darkness, and one which didn't die with the mortal soul—but Julius had not survived so many centuries by panicking.

He noticed everything at once: the crowd still parting nervously, even in darkness, to get away from the prince and him; Benison aborting his charge, a rare display of prudence; no one taking advantage of the darkness to move closer to either of the two combatants—so this was not some ploy by the hostess, Victoria Ash, or someone else, to get an assassin near prince or archon. At any rate, Julius doubted Victoria would attempt something so brazen. She had obviously hoped to coddle Julius into a confrontation with the prince, but she'd been caught quite off-guard by Julius's willingness, his evident intention, to pursue that course directly, without the benefit of her more subtle maneuvering and scheming. Her *modus operandi* was more a stiletto in the back, while Julius preferred to charge the lion.

After the first screams, a pregnant silence fell over the gallery. Judging by the uneasy shuffling of feet, Julius suspected that all present were surprised by the sudden blackout, but surely this was no accident....

Where are the emergency lights? he wondered, then, as he shifted his weight, he saw that there was some light from emergency units, that it was flickering—

No, the light wasn't moving. *The shadows were.*

Moving a quick step or two, Julius discerned swirling in the shadows. Patterns formed as the unnatural blackness maneuvered to surround the Kindred present. The glass dividers, black and opaque, enhanced this effect. Did Victoria, he wondered, have something to do with this after all? But then the darkness caught up with him, closed around him, and blotted out again what little light there was. Alerted to the unnatural quality of the enveloping blackness, Julius now perceived that there was weight and substance to the shadow, and it pressed against him with increasing determination. Tentacles of blackness took form, grabbed at his arms, his legs, his sword. Julius suddenly knew what he was up against.

"Lasombra!" someone shouted.

The brief silence shattered as, one after another, the emergency lights exploded. Sparks streamed through the gallery like rockets, and as they died, true darkness descended to add its influence to the preternatural shadow.

Julius struck at the tentacles. He couldn't afford to be immobilized. It was a strange sensation, his sword slicing through palpable darkness. The severed tentacles dissipated into nothingness, and the shadows drew back from him momentarily, but only to renew their assault from different directions.

Chaos took hold all around Julius. The shadows advanced and retreated menacingly; tentacles struck forceful blows that knocked Kindred to the ground. Other strands of black, proving only to be diversions, passed harmlessly through fist or sword set against them. Always, amidst it all, were the swirling shadows, sweeping through the large chamber like churning stormclouds, so that one moment Julius was standing side-by-side with a fellow Kindred, and the next, after the darkness closed in, he felt alone among the placeless expanse of black.

Julius tried to be sure of his blows. He caught a glimpse of Benison striking at a shadow but instead smashing his fist into the face of some unlucky subject. The poor girl went down in a heap.

The prince, too, seemed to be holding his own against the Lasombra attack—for what else could it be? No other creature could wield such power over shadow. Beyond keeping the tentacles at bay, however, Julius was unsure how to deal with the problem. And not all the Kindred were faring as well as he and the prince. A dozen yards away, a mass of black writhed and jerked violently on the floor. An arm emerged, clothed in a formal jacket that Julius had seen on *someone* only a few minutes ago. Now the arm, and the Kindred to whom it was attached, struggled against the relentless shadow that pressed him to the floor.

Julius's wild thoughts of what to do next—how to find the Lasombra controlling the darkness, how to stop the attack at the source—were interrupted by the discovery that his problems had just multiplied many times over.

The few remaining emergency lights produced a strobe effect through the dancing shadows, and advancing through the disorienting scene were many more shapes—large, monstrous shapes. "Sabbat!" Julius shouted, hoping to get the attention of Benison or one of the few others who might make a difference.

Julius found himself staring *up* at the creatures that seemed to be coming from every direction. The smallest was well over seven feet. Shoulder to shoulder, they blotted out what little light passed through the shadows. One pressed ahead of the others, a whirling mass of clawed appendages—six or seven—atop two sequoia legs. Julius saw eyes, blazing red with hatred and hunger, within the blur of limbs, but no other signs of a face.

Pleased for an opponent more tangible than the elusive shadow, Julius stepped forward to meet the challenge. His sword whistled through the air, and three of the creature's arms fell to the floor in a spray of bloody ichor. It shrieked and staggered back toward its mates, which were still advancing deliberately. Julius licked his lips and tasted some of the mess that had splattered across his face.

Ghoul blood. Not potent enough to belong to a full-fledged vampire.

Tzimisce blood. Julius had tasted it before. Even if he hadn't, where Lasombra roamed there were certain to be a few of their obedient fiends not far behind, like dogs waiting for scraps under the table. Add to that the presence of the freakish abominations now pressing their attack. Only a twisted Tzimisce mind could fashion something so horrid.

The battle ghouls nearest Julius hesitated for a moment, having seen what he did to their more impatient comrade. Throughout the gallery, most of the Kindred of Atlanta were going down, and quickly. Benjamin, a second-tier Ventrue, lay dazed on the floor as one ghoul beat him senseless with a leg broken from one of the statues. Nearby, a Gangrel who'd attacked rashly and unsupported was lifted off the ground by two monstrosities who used him for a wishbone. Julius didn't pause to see which one ended up with the larger piece.

Amidst the carnage and swirling shadows, one salient fact sank beneath his primed fighting instincts—this was no mere Sabbat raid, to be beaten back and shrugged off, as he'd assumed when the Lasombra darkness had first fallen; this was the most Sabbat muscle he'd seen gathered in one place. Ever.

For the Kindred to prevail over the fiends and their shadow masters would take a miracle. Soon. Very soon.

He risked another glance around as the ghouls began to close on him again. The prince was not far. He shepherded his wife, Eleanor, behind him, the two edging back closer to Julius, giving up ground in the face of the ghouls advancing from that direction.

"Benison!" Julius called.

The prince, bloodied himself—from blows given or received, Julius couldn't tell—glared at the Brujah archon. Julius whipped the second sword from its clasp on his back. Benison's eyes narrowed for a moment at perceived treachery, but then Julius reversed the weapon, took the blade in his own hand, and offered the pommel to the Malkavian.

Benison nodded gravely, then took the weapon.

From this silent exchange, a peculiar hush, a weighty gravitas that smothered speech and action, radiated to encompass almost the entire gallery; the formation of such an unlikely, even impossible, partnership between prince and archon signaled to every Kindred present what Julius, in his broader experience, had already surmised—namely that the Sabbat, though the task was not yet complete, had carried the night. The vampires of the Camarilla were doomed.

Even the battle ghouls, automaton creations of the Sabbat, seemed to sense the moment, or perhaps their hesitation was no more than a tactical pause, a gathering of forces for the final flurry of destruction. Whatever the case, the respite lasted no longer than a single mortal breath.

Glass shattered. Shards of both the black dividers and the outer windows of the museum itself exploded inward, dug into clothing and flesh alike. Julius shielded his eyes but ignored the other dozens of glass splinters that tore into him.

Bouncing into the gallery through the shattered windows were a score of fist-sized orbs the color of flesh, that smelled of blood—and for good reason. The orbs, in unison, pulsated once, then again, and on the third pulse they exploded. Bloody ichor sprayed the chamber. Kindred recoiled in shock and surprise, then for some the blood and excitement took hold of their basest instincts. The hunger of the Beast arose within them, and they fell upon one another.

At the same time, the ghouls pounced, and the shadows renewed their attacks.

The giant malformities moved with deceptive speed. Julius was hard pressed. Only the knowledge that Benison was at his back—with the prince's wife, Eleanor, huddled between them—allowed the Brujah to concentrate on the attackers to his front and flanks. His blade found many a target. Severed limbs tumbled. Julius cleaved the skull of one of the monstrosities as it staggered forward after suffering a blow to the knee. Its gargantuan corpse formed a breastwork of sorts, gaining for Julius an extra foot or two of space for maneuver.

Not far to his right, his Toreador hostess, Victoria Ash had fallen beneath one of the ghouls. Julius stepped toward her and struck at her attacker.

His distraction almost cost him dearly. He barely avoided a huge talon aimed for his head, a blow that, had it landed, would have relieved him of that portion of his anatomy. A slashing counterattack severed the talon, but there were five or six more poised to continue the attack. Julius lunged at the creature's torso, hoping for a single, killing blow, but an unexpected drag on his leg threw off his attack, and he missed badly.

The taloned creature, luckily for Julius, stumbled back, and the archon turned to hack at what he assumed was a tendril of shadow coiling around his leg. Instead, he found Thelonious, the Brujah primogen of the city, clutching him, crawling his way up Julius's leg. Thelonious's own legs were missing, ripped off above the knees. A trail of blood led back to one of his limbs. But Julius was more concerned by what he saw in his clanmate's eyes. The madness of hunger consumed him; the flesh grenades, no doubt, had plummeted him into a spiral of uncontrollable bloodlust.

Julius hesitated only a moment, then struck Thelonious with one powerful sweep of his blade. Head and body collapsed to the floor. Never mind that this was the Brujah primogen, that he was the leader of the revolt that had threatened to topple Benison. The necessities of battle did not always accommodate the demands of politics. Julius could not afford an additional threat at the moment.

As if in justification of his split-second decision, the taloned creature renewed its assault, and this time Julius struck hard and true. His sword bypassed the remaining claws and bit deeply into the ghoul's body proper. The archon twisted the blade; it did as much damage coming out as it did going in. The beast stumbled backward over its fallen comrade and collapsed for good.

But still the shadows grasped at Julius's legs and ankles, and the ghouls—their number never seeming to decrease, no matter how many he struck down—pressed the attack from all directions. The prince was down beneath a pile of the foul creatures. Eleanor, wielding a cudgel she'd scavenged from a felled ghoul, tried to help, but the weapon was too large and heavy for her tiny hands. She swung with precious little accuracy and even less effect. A great tendril of shadow smashed some poor bastard on the floor, over and over again, and then tossed him through a window. Meanwhile, Julius again waded into the fray.

Tuesday, 22 June 1999, 1:10 AM
The Firedance
Atlanta, Georgia

An explosion rocked the top story of the Atlanta chantry. Gouts of flame burst from the upper windows and fled into the night with the shriek of tormented spirits. In the front parlor, the cedarwood sarcophagus that held Hannah's remains smoldered gently amidst the conflagration.

Hands grimed with smoke, soot, and blood-sweat took hold of the unwieldy box. Ignoring both the heat and the pain, they dragged their burden roughly from the blaze.

The sound of splitting timbers cracked like gunshots in the still night. Rhodes Hall, haven of Prince J. Benison Hodge, slumped suddenly under its own weight. It disgorged a plume of golden sparks skyward.

Inside, amidst a cascade of shattering glass, badly mangled claws plucked forth the contents of the display cases. Each piece in the prince's priceless collection of Civil War-era Enfield rifles was passed admiringly from hand to hand as they traversed the few short blocks down Peachtree Street to the High Museum.

At the High Museum, the Firedance was already raging out of control. The celebrants had torn through Midtown, looting and scavenging every piece of wood that could be lifted, broken, or pried.

They heaped the fruits of their labors at the foot

of the curious sculpture that dominated the front of the museum—a huge metal mobile, sculpted by Calder. The heat from the rising flames caught at the dangling, brightly colored panels, causing the mobile to rotate slowly with an eerie, piercing creak of metal on metal.

Moved by the spirit of frenzied abandon, the Sabbat leapt heedlessly over, about and through the flames. It was an ancient ritual for steeling the nerve. The celebrants sought to outdo each other in their audacious feats of daring and agility. Each firedancer that fell victim to the grasping flames only fueled the intensity of the capering mob.

Tuesday, 22 June 1999, 1:12 AM
Parking garage, the High Museum of Art
Atlanta, Georgia

A thin line of shadow trickled through the crack around a service hatch on the outer wall. The blackness flowed to near Bolon, fearsome leader of the Tzimisce battle ghouls, and on the concrete floor the shadow took the shape of a man. It resembled a police chalk outline, except the body was more than a line; it was a solid mass of darkness. While the shadow remained on the ground, from the feet upward a mirror image of darkness formed vertically, as if the shadow cast a shadow of its own. Then the free-standing blackness took on more substance, shed its cloak of darkness, and there stood Vallejo.

"Heavy losses," spoke Monçada's legionnaire to Bolon, "but victory will be ours shortly. The prince and the Brujah archon still resist, but few others."

Bolon grunted. "If you want something done right…" He stepped over the body of the Camarilla ghoul whose bowels he'd been unraveling onto the floor. Bolon, like many of the battle ghouls of his command, stood nearly eight feet tall. He clattered when he moved, as the various plates of thick bone armor—all shaped from and directly attached to his body—grated against one another. Large spikes of bone protruded from his shoulders, elbows, knuckles, knees, and along the crest of his bone-helmeted head.

Vallejo squeezed the bridge of his nose as his senses cleared. The transition from shadow to body was sometimes a jarring shift in perspective. The allure of darkness, the unrestrained freedom of shape-lessness, not to mention the unique union between himself and the other legionnaires as they merged together to form a far-reaching blanket of shadow—enough, in fact, to reach nearly from the bottom of the museum to the top—were seductive. It was tempting simply to remain a part of that common body. Indeed, the power to join their incorporeal forms was one of the uppermost achievements in their training under Monçada, and the addictiveness of that state was the cardinal's insurance of their loyalty. Vallejo had lost not a few recruits who had been unwilling or unable to reclaim their identity from that common bond. But the strong persevered.

"Bring those barrels," Bolon shouted to a few of his nearby ghouls, and they dutifully hauled over several oil drums that had just been unloaded from a truck, and maneuvered them toward the elevator.

Vallejo was impressed by Vykos's thoroughness even more so than her ruthlessness—no eventuality had been overlooked. The tiny knot of resistance upstairs would give way shortly, and the battle would be over. It was already won.

Armed with foreknowledge of success, Vallejo released his physical form to the darkness and climbed upward once again.

Tuesday, 22 June 1999, 1:18 AM
Fourth floor, the High Museum of Art
Atlanta, Georgia

Prince Benison was free. Julius had skewered two of the prince's assailants, and even Eleanor had distracted one long enough that Benison was able to regain his feet, crush the ghoul's skull with a single blow of the Malkavian's mighty fist, and retrieve his sword. The three Kindred had also managed to battle their way closer to the main entrance of the gallery—the two sets of gargantuan bronze doors, their panels covered with friezes. One of the sets of double doors nearly touched the gallery ceiling, thirty-odd feet above. Along with the slightly shorter set, they dominated the chamber, especially now that most of the sculptures and glass partitions had been overturned or destroyed outright.

Maybe they won't expect us to break for the front door since many of them came in that way, Julius hoped. He viewed the elevator itself as more of a deathtrap than an escape route, but there were other avenues of egress in that direction. All things considered, it seemed worth a try.

Benison seemed instinctively to follow Julius's lead. Not a word passed between the two, but they covered one another's rear and flanks without fail. More than once, Julius felt the breeze of the prince's loaned sword by his ear, only to see an unwary attacker fall at his side. And Julius repaid the prince in kind. All the while, Eleanor kept to the insular eddy between the two warriors, thwacking ghouls whenever they strayed within her reach and keeping out

eric griffin

of trouble as much as she could. She was not well-versed in combat—she'd always tended toward the more subtle, though no less deadly, machinations and intrigues of Kindred society—but she was doing her best to help the two warriors, rather than letting herself become a burden.

The trio of Brujah, Malkavian, and Ventrue was at the base of the stairs directly beneath the oversized doors. Only a handful of ghouls now blocked their escape. Julius struck down one of those, his hopes beginning to rise, when he heard a strange sound, a creaking noise, the moan of metal and wood. He didn't recognize it for what it was at first; not until the giant doors, and the faux walls that held them aloft, were toppling down on him.

Julius called out as he dove from beneath the falling slabs of bronze. He landed hard on his side, but rolled and was quickly on his feet, gratified to see that Benison had escaped the trap as well. Not so for several of the battle ghouls. Two, that he could see, lay sprawled, partially pinned beneath the upended flats.

Eleanor was trapped as well.

She grimaced in agony, hundreds of pounds crushing her slight frame, and above her stood three more ghouls, the elevator closing behind them, who must have been responsible for toppling the doors. Among the newcomers—one of whom was larger than the others and wore spiked bone armor—were three oil drums.

Julius and Benison both started toward Eleanor, but the ghouls tipped the barrels, and a fiery flood was unleashed over the doors, down the steps.

Greek fire! Julius recognized—or some modern equivalent that flowed like oil and scorched like molten lead.

Before Julius or the horrified prince could respond, the liquid fire swept down over Eleanor. Her tiny body burst into flame. Her screams mingled with those of the trapped ghouls whose masters had decided worth sacrificing to squelch the final Kindred resistance.

Again, Julius could only dive out of the way. He had the presence of mind to knock Benison out of the path of the spreading inferno, and as the two climbed to their feet together, their gazes met.

Julius had thought that, over the centuries, he had seen first hand all of the horrors that war had to offer. But within the prince's eyes was a depth of pain and suffering, an anguish so fresh and pure, that goosebumps stood on the archon's skin. He turned his head—unable to hold that gaze for longer than a second—and when he turned back, the pain was gone from those green eyes. They were glazed over. Benison stared at him with a blank gaze, his face completely devoid of any emotion whatsoever. It was an expression that unsettled Julius more than the overwhelming grief of a moment before.

Julius had seen the will drain from men in battle, had seen their fury dwindle and all volition abandon them. He thought, at first, that he saw that same death of will in Benison, and knew that, alone, he himself would be able to resist for only so long.

But not for the first time, Benison surprised him. The prince raised his sword and charged at the thickest knot of ghouls in the gallery. Before, he had roared and bellowed with battle rage. This time, not a sound passed his lips. Now it was Julius who followed the Malkavian's lead.

The liquid fire had spread through the front portion of the gallery, incinerating the bodies of the dead and wounded, Sabbat and Kindred alike, but its momentum was spent. The attack had done its worst, and Julius and Benison still stood. Smoke billowed toward the ceiling, thickening the shifting darkness. A harsh alarm sounded, a piercing electronic wail that struck Julius like an arrow through the brain, and flame-retardant chemical began to spray from the sprinklers and foam as it came into contact with oxygen.

The noise and added confusion worked to Julius's and Benison's advantage. The ghouls were slow to coordinate their attacks, and one by one they fell beneath the Kindred swords. Benison slaughtered them in silence. Scarcely any of his blows failed to rend arm or leg or head from a body. Julius, too, waded into the gore. Footing became treacherous with blood and entrails ground underfoot, and the foam coating the floor.

They fought from one end of the gallery to the other, but behind the shadows, through the smoke, there were always more ghouls. They marched forward, undaunted by the annihilation of so many of their brethren, if they noticed the carnage at all. And still the shadows, which by themselves had brought down many of the Kindred, tried to distract or hinder the two Camarilla elders. It was only a matter of time, Julius knew, before a ghoul struck a telling blow, and once either he or Benison went down, the other would follow shortly.

The prince hacked mercilessly at the ghouls. He

was a dispassionate butcher; his sword taking on the aspect of cleaver, dripping blood and dispensing dismemberment to any who stood before him. So much so, in fact, that Julius made sure not to push ahead of the prince, to guard his flanks and rear instead. Benison in this state might not recognize the Brujah. Benison might simply destroy whomever or whatever moved within his sight, until he was free or dead.

They fought their way past one of the few remaining intact pieces of statuary, using it for cover of their left flank for several steps. It was a large piece, a man kneeling above his four sons, but the uppermost figure grinned disturbingly over the carnage as if he saw and heartily approved of the bloodshed around him. Indeed, Kindred and ghouls lay scattered about the base of the sculpture, some burned or mutilated beyond recognition, all caught as if frozen in the contorted throes of violent death. Final Death, for beings that might otherwise have proved immortal. Chemical foam rose like floodwater to cover their bodies.

Julius tried to shut out the noise of the fire alarm; it played on his nerves a hundredfold more than injury or thought of Final Death. In a gesture of habit, he tried to brush his dreadlocks away from his face and noticed for the first time that they were gone, burned or melted away by the fumes of the Greek fire.

The sound of shattering glass drew his attention from the two ghouls he was holding at bay. The final glass partition, a tall cubicle of sorts near the center of the gallery, toppled over and smashed into thousands of tiny black shards. The ghoul with the long, jagged spikes protruding from his body, the largest of the three who'd overturned the barrels, stalked through the wreckage. The others, showing their first attitude other than the desire to rend and kill, deferred to him. They parted before him, allowing him to wade unhindered through the sea of foam, glass, smoke, and body parts.

In the other direction, Benison drove his sword three-fourths of the way through the neck of the last ghoul that stood against him. The creature toppled with a majestic slowness so much like that of the glass cubicle that Julius expected him to shatter into pieces as well. But the ghoul rather landed with a dull thud. Behind the position he'd held stood an undulating black curtain, a fluid wall of shadow. Battle ghouls on one side, the full force of the Lasombra shadow on the other.

The prince, for the first instant since his wife had burned before his eyes, turned to face Julius. His stare was no longer blank, but his eyes were glassy, and the whites so bloodshot they seemed they might burst. "Come, my archon," said Benison, in a tone more respectful than he'd ever assumed toward Julius before. "We must withdraw into the woods."

With that, the prince turned and stepped into the shadow, disappearing from sight.

The woods? Julius, uncomprehending, stared after him. Had Benison taken *complete* leave of his senses after all? There was always that chance with a Malkavian. *The woods.* And then the prince had disappeared into the Lasombra shadow.

Julius was perplexed by both Benison's words and deeds. Nor was the Brujah enthusiastic about the prospect of charging into the blackness that had been trying to ensnare him all night—but the ghouls were closing in again, emboldened by their spiked leader, who seemed to Julius more than a ghoul, Tzimisce perhaps. The archon knew well enough that the best chance he had (if he had *any* chance) was to stay with Benison.

So Julius turned his back on the ghouls and strode forcefully into the shadow—where he was caught and held fast.

Marcus poked half-heartedly at the inert form of
the vampire that had crashed through the fourth-floor
window and landed on the street with such a resounding whomp ten or fifteen minutes ago. He could smell
the vitae leaking from the broken body. It would be
an easy thing to haul up the carcass—it looked to be
a particularly scrawny vampire—and drain the last
of its blood. But Marcus was in no mood to indulge
himself.

There was a battle going on within those walls.
Hearing the crash of broken glass, watching the body
sail through the air and then come to such an abrupt,
bone-smashing stop, had gotten his blood up. He'd
been primed for the order to join the attack, to break
bones, to rend flesh—the order that had never come.

Instead, he and Delona stood out in the street
like damned watchdogs. There weren't even any
mortals to kill or chase off. The roadblocks had
worked too well.

"Get away from that!" Marcus growled at Delona.

He'd already chased her away from the body
once. Not that there was any reason for her *not* to
help herself to that vampire's blood—only that
Marcus didn't feel like drinking it, and so he didn't
feel like watching her drink it either. Besides, he was
starting to like this business of ordering her around,
and the way she flinched at everything he said, like
she was afraid he might do to her what he'd done to
Delora.

But despite those tiny pleasures, he'd had enough of waiting in the street.

"Come on," he ordered her.

There were plenty of patrols around the museum. One less wouldn't hurt anything. Besides, Marcus suspected there would be plenty of vitae to scavenge inside. And, if he was lucky, maybe some people to kill.

Tuesday, 22 June 1999, 1:29 AM
Fourth floor, the High Museum of Art
Atlanta, Georgia

Damn Benison and his whole clan!

The tenebrous blanket of shadow smothered Julius's every attempt at movement. He might as well have been trying to lift the weight of an entire ocean. He called on the power of his blood, but he had already spent much of his strength in surviving this long. If anything, the shadow tightened about him as he struggled; it snaked down his mouth, tickled the back of his throat, held him suspended like a fly in amber. Perhaps he would become a fossil to grace the halls of the museum. More likely, he would be nothing more than a pile of ash by morning.

This is Benison's fault! Julius tried to use his anger to fuel his body where blood was not enough. *He arranged all this just to get me! Sacrificed his city, his wife—all just to get me!*

The idea was absurd. In the back of his mind, Julius knew that, but caught as he was by the Lasombra shadow, with the Tzimisce battle ghouls no doubt bearing down upon him, he grasped for any sliver of conviction that might engender enough rage within him to overcome his fatigue. His deep-seeded mistrust of the Malkavian ruler of Atlanta, who until a short while ago Julius had planned to dispatch himself and who had shouted murderous threats at him, was an easy mark—and Julius felt his color begin to rise.

But the shadow held firm.

He felt a hand on his shoulder, reaching around his neck. The ghouls were on him, were pulling him by the head, but still the shadow would not relinquish its claim to him. Enormous pressure threatened to rip his head from his shoulders. Julius added his own strength to the hands that pulled him—at least if he were free of the shadow he could go down fighting—and at last he budged.

Julius tightened his grip on his sword. He couldn't afford to leave it in the wall of shadow. His captors, if they were smart—which, with the ghouls, was a considerable *if*—would pull only his head free of the shadow, then lop it off. If he could get his sword-arm free, he'd stand a chance, however slim.

The darkness wavered for a brief moment, then his face was beyond it, his head locked in the iron grip of—

"Benison!"

The prince was pulling him free, an inch at a time, despite the greedy determination of the shadow. Somehow the Malkavian had made it through on his own. Now Julius too was out, and on the side opposite the ghouls—but only for a moment did the shadow divide them.

As Julius came free, the darkness parted, and the ghouls charged through.

The first swing of Julius's sword took off the hand and face of one. His next blow disemboweled a second.

"Archon, this is no time to dally!" called Benison from behind him.

Julius turned to see the prince slip out an emergency exit, and for the first time since the great bronze doors had toppled over and the Greek fire had poured down the steps—minutes that seemed like hours—hope took hold within Julius.

He slashed at the closest ghoul, then sprinted past one last damaged statue—a grotesque rendering of the slain Abel, now fully missing an arm that had been mostly intact earlier—and to the door. Julius threw open the emergency exit, slammed it behind himself, and was greeted by a world of madness.

Marcus opened the door to the gallery just a crack and peered through. He still hoped he would get to kill someone, but he was having second thoughts about coming in without orders. He'd hurried up the winding, circular ramp that ringed the main lobby of the museum—or, rather, he'd jumped up, bypassing the first two and a half stories, and then hurried the rest of the way.

"What do you see?" Delona nagged him from behind.

Marcus backhanded her harder than he'd meant to, and she flew backward over the railing and fell down the cylindrical well to the lobby floor, four stories below.

"Uh-oh."

But Marcus couldn't be bothered just presently. Besides, Delona was a tough little booger. She'd recover. Eventually.

Marcus eased open the door. All the activity seemed to be at the other end of the gallery, as far as he could tell. Smoke hung thick in the large, sprawling room, and some strange foam stood almost a foot deep, like there'd been a huge shaving-cream fight. A fire alarm added to the confusion. At the far end of the gallery, Bolon stood with maybe a dozen of the battle ghouls.

Where are all the others? Marcus wondered. He hadn't seen other signs of fighting on the way up, and there'd been at least four times as many ghouls before. Marcus instantly forgot his reluctance at having disobeyed orders—just as Delona was now out of sight and out of mind—and trudged over to Bolon. The commander was a fellow Tzimisce and one of the few of *anyone* as large as Marcus. With each step, Marcus's wide, flat feet crunched down through the foam and crushed whatever was beneath: glass, marble, bones.

As Marcus reached Bolon, he became confused. The wind was blowing—it *looked* like it was blowing—but he couldn't feel it. After another second, he realized that it was just a trick of the light. Shadows were swirling and whipping around violently, and it looked almost like light coming through the leaves on a windy day. Marcus looked around, but there weren't any trees inside.

"What are you doing here?" Bolon demanded.

Marcus looked at Bolon but was still confused by the puzzle of the rippling light and no wind. Several of the ghouls were pounding on a large metal door. They had ripped off the panic bar, but the door wouldn't open.

Before Marcus could think of an answer for Bolon, a strange dark shadow interposed itself between them. A second or two later, the shadow was a man, a fairly tanned vampire with black hair and a dark uniform. Marcus recognized the crest of Monçada's legionnaires above the breast pocket.

"How'd you do that?" Marcus asked, not used to seeing people materialize out of nothing.

"Commander Vallejo," said Bolon, ignoring Marcus for the moment, which suited Marcus just fine.

The smaller, darker man looked tired. The shadows he'd stepped from seemed reluctant to relinquish him. They formed deep pools in the considerable hollows of his cheeks and beneath his eyes.

"We cannot pass the door," said Vallejo, frustrated. "I've never come across anything like this—some type of seal that I can't explain."

Bolon nodded gravely. Marcus wasn't sure what they were talking about, but the mention of a seal made him think of a trip he'd taken to Sea World as a boy, and of the seals that had tossed balls back and forth without ever dropping a single one. That had been a happy time for him, but he couldn't remember it properly with all the banging on the door that was going on. Battle ghouls were like that. They didn't have much sense.

"Huh," Marcus grunted as he shoved aside the ghouls. He pressed against the door with all his weight, but it didn't budge. "Stuck pretty good." So he took three steps back and launched himself at it, using all the strength of his massive legs and the force of his considerable mass that he could muster.

The door gave way this time, almost folded in half around Marcus's head and shoulders. He stumbled through the doorway and landed in a heap, completely unprepared for what awaited him.

Tuesday, 22 June 1999, 1:36 AM
Fourth floor, the High Museum of Art
Atlanta, Georgia

Julius ignored the pounding on the door against his back. Ghouls behind him be damned, he couldn't understand what was *before* him. Every few seconds he saw what he knew he should be seeing—metal stairs going both up and down. But for the majority of those minutes he stood with his back against the door, the scene before him was of a steep, wooded mountain path—*not* of the inside of a museum in the middle of Atlanta.

The night sounds and mountain smells were ever right. And there stood Benison, partway down the path—*the stairs, dammit!*

"This way, archon," urged the prince. His emerald eyes shone with enthusiasm now, and instead of the suit he'd worn before, he was clothed in a Confederate uniform. "We'll rally the company. Sherman will never take Kennesaw!"

The sudden conviction in his voice was as baffling to Julius as all the rest. The prince seemed to have recovered from the death of his wife, or perhaps he'd plunged far more deeply into madness. But that didn't come close to explaining everything else: a mountain path, trees, outdoors where there should be indoors or at least an urban landscape.

The pounding on the door steadied Julius. He knew there were Sabbat battle ghouls on the other side—not a situation that he was pleased with, but at least it made sense. The door shouldn't have held this long. Even with Julius holding it closed, the

Sabbat should have been able to break through already. It was as if whatever madness had taken root here was determined to keep the portal closed.

Julius was not reassured when sanity reasserted itself, and the door gave way and came crashing in on top of him. It bowled him over, and very nearly knocked him down the stairs-path. An experienced warrior, he managed to hold on to his sword as well as to avoid a serious fall.

The creature that had dislodged the door and stumbled into the stairwell-wilderness was too powerful to be a ghoul. Like them, he was a veritable giant, a walking juggernaut, but he appeared at first glance more self-possessed, less deranged, as he climbed to his feet.

Apparently the mountainside surroundings caught him by surprise as well, for the juggernaut gazed around in obvious puzzlement at the trees, and the rocks, and the clear night sky. Julius took advantage of the delay. He slashed with his sword, and the behemoth's steaming entrails spilled out onto the ground. The creature dropped to his knees, but that was all Julius saw. He turned and bounded down the trail after Prince Benison.

This new, inexplicable reality, the alternating stairwell-wilderness, Julius realized, was free from the damnable Lasombra shadow. That had been true from the moment the emergency door had slammed shut behind him, but it was another phenomenon that he didn't understand. No mere door could hold back that tide of inky blackness, and there was not the remotest chance that the Lasombra didn't want to pursue him and the prince. No, something else was at work here.

Julius rushed downward around a bend in the trail and came face to face with Benison, who was waiting expectantly. The Malkavian's eyes still burned with an unnerving glee.

"Now we have them, archon! This way."

Benison turned to the steep mountainside, where Julius saw, of all things, an old metal door right in the side of the mountain. The door was set into a wooden frame, all of which was bound by together by a rusty chain and padlock. Benison tore away the entire contraption and cast it aside, then took Julius by the arm. They stepped from the mountainside into a forest glade.

Julius craned his neck around, but the mountain was gone. A cave he could have understood. At least it would have been consistent with the madness around him. But to step from a winding mountain trail directly into a level clearing was…unfathomable.

"By the gods, what is this?" Julius exclaimed.

"Why, Archon Julius," answered Benison almost playfully, "it's the 37th Georgia, a regiment of Hood's boys."

And to Julius's astonishment, truer words could not have been spoken, for double ranks of shabbily dressed Confederate soldiers were forming into a line of battle along the far edge of the clearing. Perhaps two hundred men bearing muskets waited, front rank kneeling before the second, ready to fire.

"This way, archon," said Benison, again leading Julius by the arm. "We must seek a safer vantage."

"This cannot be," Julius muttered as he let himself be led out of the line of fire.

"God willing, General Sherman will share your

sentiment shortly. He will never wrest Kennesaw Mountain from us," Benison reiterated.

"But the mountain's gone...." But Julius was unable to form any reasonable argument, as the mountain never should have been there in the first place.

The Sabbat ghouls, now edging into the serendipitous clearing, appeared to share Julius's disorientation. Their earlier relentlessness had given way to apprehension at their surroundings, the most dangerous part of which—the Confederate troops—now opened fire.

The simultaneous roar of the guns was deafening. Lead Minié balls ripped through the ghouls, tearing away limbs, shattering bones. Julius could not believe what he saw.

Before he could again assert the impossibility of the scene before him, however, another roaring filled his ears. The metal stairwell had somehow rematerialized at the far end of the clearing, and a twisting flood of pure black was pouring down it and over the field. This landscape of madness no longer held the Lasombra at bay.

The rushing shadow swept over the mutilated ghouls and on toward the line of battle. A second volley from the 37th Georgia had no effect on the darkness, which now hit the hapless soldiers like a tidal wave at landfall. It brushed them aside and swallowed their death cries. Then the darkness rose to a terrible height, only to crash down upon Benison.

The Malkavian prince disappeared beneath the tide of blackness, and simultaneously the landscape wavered, as heat rising from the earth on a summer day obscures vision. But it was the landscape itself that wrinkled, then swirled into its own tidal wave of color and sound and motion. This wave of pure force, the swirling flotsam of Benison's own dementia incarnate, smashed into the darkness, and the shadow was broken. It fled like a thousand black vipers hurled toward every point of the compass.

But the wave had not yet spent its force. It turned in on itself and, around Benison's inert form, formed a raging whirlpool. Trees, grass, boulders, sky—all hurtled past Julius's eyes, and in the center of it all Prince Benison. The whirlpool wound more and more tightly, its fury compressed into an area constantly growing smaller.

Finally, its vector shifted and it bore straight down—down with the roar of a train passing, into the depths of the earth, and it was gone. Only a dark hole remained. The mountainside, the clearing, the soldiers, Benison—all gone.

Julius stood in shock at what he'd seen. The prince's derangement had forced itself upon the world, had claimed the Sabbat ghouls…but in the end it had claimed Benison as well.

Some while passed with Julius staring down into that dark hole. Only slowly did he come to recognize it for what it was—a gaping elevator shaft, and he stood at the very edge.

He turned slowly, still stunned and astounded by the rapid shifts in perspective, by what he could only perceive as the outpouring of Malkavian madness. Again Julius was slow to recognize the reality that he faced—the eight-foot-tall juggernaut, holding in his guts, stuffed back inside him, with one hand, a look of definite consternation on his wide face. The hand not covering the gaping wound in his belly was curled into a large, meaty fist, which promptly smashed into Julius's face.

The blow shattered his jaw and lifted him off his feet, propelling him over the edge and into the elevator shaft. The fall was maybe thirty or forty feet. Julius had fallen farther before without ill effect, but he landed hard by the open hatch of the old elevator itself. The shoulder that took the brunt of the fall splintered. Shards of bone sliced through muscle and skin.

Julius had very little time to worry about that, however. The faint light that did penetrate the shaft was suddenly blotted out. Julius suspected the Lasombra shadow at first, but then the behemoth landed on him with full force, snapping the archon's spine, and all was darkness.

Tuesday, 22 June 1999, 1:51 AM
Fourth floor, the High Museum of Art
Atlanta, Georgia

The fire-retardant foam was breaking down, gathering into foul-smelling puddles with swirls of blood, like oil and water. Bolon stood amidst the carnage in the gallery, relatively unscathed himself. That was more than he could say for his battle ghouls—of the fifty he'd sent in, none remained.

Not a damn one! he thought, increasingly incredulous the more he thought about it.

Not that they couldn't be replaced. Within a week or two, Vykos and the Tailor could produce twice that number, but never had Bolon expected to lose more than half of his battalion. He wasn't even sure what exactly had happened to the last dozen. Vallejo and nine of his legionnaires had resumed physical form, but they weren't in the best of shape. They were dizzy, and puking blood—whatever had happened had taken its toll on them, even in their shadow form, and they couldn't seem to reconstruct how they'd lost three of their comrades.

But even if the Prince of Atlanta had disappeared, Bolon, consoled himself, the Malkavian's power was broken and the Brujah archon captured—that thanks to Marcus, the bulky fellow Tzimisce who'd shown up rather fortuitously in the gallery. He told a confused tale of trees in the building, and soldiers, and cyclones, but despite the vagaries of his addled mind, the idiot had defeated the Brujah archon—no small feat, that—and hauled the crushed body from an elevator shaft.

"And where is the prince's body?" Bolon asked for the fifth time.

Marcus scratched his head. "Gone."

"Taken away by the cyclone," Bolon repeated what he knew the other giant would tell him again.

"Mm-hm," Marcus nodded vigorously, glad to have someone else agree with his story. He pointed at the contorted body on the floor at his feet, the Brujah that had sliced him open. "He was the only one left." Marcus's stomach clearly pained him still, but the wound itself had healed enough that his insides were staying inside.

"I see," said Bolon. There was no point, he could tell, in questioning Marcus further. The brute had rendered a valuable service in smashing the archon; to expect more of him at this point would be to ignore his obvious limitations.

"Marcus," Bolon said, moving on to other things, "you know Commander Gregorio?"

Marcus's brow furrowed, but after a moment he nodded that he did. "The real white guy?"

"The real white guy, yes." Bolon didn't think he'd heard an albino described in that exact manner before, but Marcus's meaning was clear enough. "Go find him. Tell him that I sent you to join his force. I'm sure he'll find many uses for your particular skills."

Marcus turned away, mostly recognizing the compliment paid him. "I'll take Delona too," he said as he trudged across the gallery.

Two more matters required Bolon's immediate attention.

"Commander Vallejo."

The weary Spaniard rose to his feet from his perch on one of the larger statue fragments where he rested with his surviving legionnaires.

"Can your men see to the fire that needs to happen here?" Bolon asked. He was not surprised by Vallejo's affirmative response. For a Lasombra, the young commander struck Bolon as fairly competent.

Finally, Bolon knelt down by the crumpled body that Marcus had dutifully left behind. "Well, Brujah Archon Julius, that just leaves you."

Vykos had known this particular Camarilla dignitary—if a Brujah could be referred to as such—would be present, and Bolon had been hoping for just this sort of meeting.

The archon's body was thoroughly broken—flattened in some places, bent at impossible angles elsewhere. Bolon could easily count four kinks in Julius's spine after only a cursory examination. The Brujah's mouth hung open, as much as it could with his jaw, swollen and misshapen, wrenched around to the side. His eyes were closed. Perhaps unconsciousness had claimed him—*lucky bastard*—but as yet Final Death had not. For as severe as the damage was, these were injuries that blood could heal. How much blood, Bolon could only imagine. And without massive surgery to align properly the broken and mangled bones, the healing would cause nearly as many problems as it solved. Bones would mend, but they would knit together at peculiar angles. Julius would heal; his body might be whole, but it would be far from functional. The mighty warrior, his exploits legendary for centuries, would survive as an infirm, twisted cripple throughout eternity.

That thought carried a powerful appeal for Bolon. How satisfying it would be to see the once-deadly archon beg assistance merely to stand or sit or tie his shoe. Or Bolon could ship the Brujah to Monçada or, more usefully, to a Tzimisce benefactor who might relish the chance to perform experiments on one of Julius's stature—or former stature.

There was, however, a consideration more overwhelming than even those rewarding alternatives. *Vitae*. It was not often that an opportunity arose to possess the blood of an elder, a vampire far older than Bolon himself. With age came potency, and with potency, power. And infamy. News of such diablerie, the draining of a prominent Camarilla archon, inevitably spread like wildfire. Bolon would be known from that night forward, to friend and foe alike, as the destroyer of Julius, archon of Clan Brujah.

That made the decision easy, in the end.

Bolon lifted the limp body off the floor. "I only wish you were awake," he said to Julius, then sank his fangs into cold flesh and drank deeply till every ounce of life-sustaining vitae was his.

Tuesday, 22 June 1999, 2:03 AM
Fourth floor, the High Museum of Art
Atlanta, Georgia

Vykos stood alone at the very center of the carnage that had been the interior of the High Museum. All around her stretched a wasteland of smashed statuary, broken glass, puddles of mingled gore and ichor and fire-retardant chemicals.

She felt very much at home here.

Sighing contentedly, she surveyed the full scope of the devastation. *Impressive.* The entire fourth floor had been gutted. The elaborate labyrinth of glass partitions had been systematically shattered. Interior walls had been violently reduced to rubble. The vast entryway portals were toppled and trampled and badly scored by Greek fire.

Her gaze traveled uninterrupted around the vast empty chamber. Nothing above knee-height remained standing, save two folorn statues, and Vykos herself. To the casual observer, she too might have seemed only an overlooked piece of sculpture that had, against all odds, managed to escape the fate of its fellows.

This night, Vykos did bear more than a passing resemblance to an *objet d'art*. Her bearing was statuesque; her visage, cool as marble, sculpted without pity or remorse. Smiling at this thought, Vykos heightened the impression. Her facial structure seemed to shift disturbingly with a sound like that of ice cracking. She regarded her handiwork in a shard of mirrored glass at her feet. *Excellent.* Crushing the mirror underfoot as if grinding out a cigarette, she strode off purposefully toward the elevator.

For all practical purposes, the fighting was over. There were still a few scattered knots of resistance in the city that were being untangled even now. Already the select group of warriors that she had singled out as having distinguished themselves in this night's fighting had begun the laborious task of rounding up the surviving captives and dragging them back here for her inspection.

My carrion crows, she thought. Yes, things were shaping up nicely.

Through the high, broken windows, Vykos could see the flickering light from the dozens of fires that had been kindled in the pierced metal oilcans ringing the building. The whoops of the Firedancers, their crows of challenge, their cries of triumph, were welcome to her ears. The unmistakable signs that control of Atlanta had passed into the loving hands of the Sabbat.

Vykos, however, could not long dwell upon this night's victory. There was still far too much at stake. She collared a passing legionnaire.

"Get me Vallejo, Bolon and Caldwell, immediately."

The soldier saluted sharply and hastily turned to obey her orders.

"Soldier," she interrupted him. "Forget about Caldwell. Get me that weaselly lackey of his, you know the one. And be quick about it. We don't have the leisure to stand here all night discussing the matter. Move out." She turned away without waiting for his second salute.

"This place is far too quiet," she mused aloud.

"Where are my war ghouls? There must be *something* left to smash around here."

Vykos was distracted by the soft but unmistakable sound of stifled sobbing. She instinctively moved toward the noise, not entirely motivated by sympathy.

"Light!" she called as she picked her way forward through the debris. Her night vision was understandably keen, but her eyes were dazzled by the afterimages of great suffering that hung in the air like phantoms. In places, the lingering halos of pain were clustered so tightly together that she could not clearly make out her own footing for the glare.

Someone nearby obediently struck up a makeshift torch. Actually, it looked like more of a candelabrum. A separate flame burned atop each of the dismembered hand's four remaining fingers, giving off an oily black and unpleasant-smelling smoke.

The bold young lieutenant held his light before him. "May I escort you, my lady?"

"Not if you're planning on toting that thing around, soldier. I suspect the fire-prevention system will unleash its full fury upon you in a moment. In the meantime, find me a flashlight. Dismissed."

As the soldier hastily extinguished the flames, Vykos moved on. Picking her way over the fallen entryway doors, she discovered the source of the sobbing in the foyer.

The Little Tailor of Prague knelt amidst a heap of torn and crumpled bodies. He held one of his pitiful creations, a monstrous aberration easily three times his own size, in his arms. His eyes clamped tightly shut, the Little Tailor rocked back and forth slowly, sobbing under his breath.

"Never find all the pieces…never find all the pieces…never find…"

Vykos drew back before she was noticed. She had no desire to intrude upon the old one in his grief. She quietly retraced her steps to the gallery.

Damn it, there were altogether too many casualties here. And far too many of her forces that she could not yet account for. Where were the rest of those war ghouls?

"Bolon!" Her bellow echoed back and forth through the gutted upper story of the museum.

It was Vallejo, however, who appeared before her. He rose up suddenly from her own shadow. Vykos took a quick defensive step backward but, of course, the materializing form moved with her. It was an unsettling sensation.

To cover her unease, she barked, "Report! What the hell's going on here, Commander? I want Bolon here *now*, or I want his head on a pike. I want to know where the hell all my war ghouls have gotten to. I want the Malkavian Prince and the Brujah Archon here either in pieces or in chains. And I don't care to be kept waiting any longer. Understood?"

Vallejo weathered this storm patiently. His face was scored with fatigue and his entire form seemed to waver as if a strong wind might well tear him to tatters. Vykos was not certain what was keeping him on his feet.

He seemed to have some aversion or reluctance to meeting her gaze. "My lady," Vallejo acknowledged her orders. "I believe Commander Bolon is…coordinating activities. Near the service elevator. If you will follow me."

Vykos began to retort that she knew damned well

where the service elevator was, but she checked herself. Vallejo was near the end of his strength, that much was apparent. And she would have much need of him still this evening.

Bolon was exultant as he swaggered proudly and purposefully toward them. The mangled form of the Brujah Archon dangled from one fist, its shattered legs dragging along the ground. This awkward burden did not even seem to slow the pace of the towering Tzimisce commander.

"Lady Vykos." Bolon dropped to one knee, depositing his macabre trophy before her.

"Where is Benison, Commander? And where are your troops?"

Bolon shifted uncomfortably and did not look up. He was painfully aware that the vulnerable nape of his neck remained exposed above the interlocking bone plates of his exoskeletal armor.

"My lady, it is my unpleasant duty to inform you that the remainder of the battalion was lost in destroying the Malkavian."

"The entire battalion? Lost? Damn it, commander, I *need* those troops!"

Bolon tensed for the *coup de grâce*, but it did not fall. Slowly he raised his head and met Vykos's eyes. He forced himself to suppress his initial reaction to her fearsome visage.

"We will rebuild the company, my lady. I will see to it personally. We will be in full fighting trim within the month."

"You don't have a month," Vykos replied coolly.

"But the city is ours, my lady. Certainly there will still be some Anarchs to hunt down or convert. And there are, no doubt, a few fugitive warlocks that managed to escape the conflagration at the Chantry. But that work is best left to the resourcefulness of full-blooded Cainites."

Vallejo cut in quickly in defense of his counterpart. "Yes, it is as the commander says. The war ghouls will be required for the defense of the city, but surely there can be no reason to fear counterattack so soon, Councilor Vykos. The Camarilla was caught utterly by surprise. It will take time for them to organize their resistance. And even then…"

"Even then," Bolon picked up the dangling thread of conversation, "they have no suitable staging point to gather their strength for the counteroffensive. Charleston? Greenville, perhaps? Memphis?…"

"Savannah!" Vallejo smacked a fist into his palm. He turned hurriedly to Vykos. "My lady, they will come through…"

"Already taken care of, commander. I received confirmation just a short while ago that our forces seized control of the port earlier this evening. Exactly on schedule," she added pointedly.

Her announcement had both of her commanders clearly at a loss.

"Come, gentlemen, I have told you that this engagement was to be no simple Blood Siege—nor some mere single night's assault. This is war, gentlemen. Welcome to the Firedance."

Vykos left them there in stunned silence. After three quick paces, however, she turned back. "Commander Bolon, you have one week to reconstruct your company. You understand? One week. You have a pressing engagement that I would not care for you to miss. Do not disappoint me.

"Commander Vallejo, you are with me."

"Yes, my lady." Vallejo turned sharply on his heel and fell into step, as unshakable as her shadow.

Tuesday, 22 June 1999, 3:15 AM
Parking garage, the High Museum of Art
Atlanta, Georgia

Vykos drew up short in her inspection of the prisoners, clasping a hand to her mouth in delight.

The fallen had been arranged in neatly ordered rows, following the first organizational scheme that had suggested itself—the network of painted white lines that delineated the parking spaces. Most of the Cainites gathered here would not again stir from this final resting-place.

"Oh, will you look at this?" Vykos cooed. "Isn't she absolutely precious?"

She stooped to brush a strand of hair away from Victoria Ash's smudged face, revealing a patina of dried blood and caked ashes.

Victoria's long eyelashes fluttered open at the touch. She was faced with an apparition conjured straight from the realm of nightmare.

The face that bent over her was folded in upon itself sharply, at right angles. One eye was easily three times as large as the other and placed high on the brow. The other was small and sunken, riding low on the jaw. The nose, too, had an unsettling geometric bend to it.

The most disturbing thing about that face, however, was that it was absolutely and breathtakingly beautiful. Victoria's artistic eye, fine-tuned through intimate acquaintance with so many of the great works and artists of the past two centuries, could not be mistaken on this point. The face before her was undeniably a Picasso.

But it was no Picasso that had ever been enacted on canvas, much less in such a vivid three-dimensional medium. It was like a vision discarded by the artist, cast aside and denied life—a vision of the very face of madness and cruelty.

Victoria was certain that fever and bloodloss had taken hold of her senses. She felt herself beginning to faint. Gentle words came to her, as if from a great distance.

"My precious little rag-doll."

Victoria lost consciousness as Vykos began to wipe the grime from her cheek. She continued to scrub at the face until it shone, taking on the gleam and even the texture of finest porcelain.

Satisfied, she bent low and planted a gentle kiss upon one perfect cheek. Her lips left a small darkened mark upon that cheek, as if from a smudge of lipstick. Upon closer examination, however, the mark would be discovered to bear the unmistakable shape, etched in exacting and indelible detail, of a serpent swallowing its own tail.

Vykos gazed down with great affection at her new prize. "Bring her," she called over her shoulder.

She took three paces toward the street exit and stopped suddenly, struck by an even more delectable idea. "No..." she said, turning slowly, with one finger pressed mischievously to her lips and a look of artistic triumph in her eyes. "Take her to the Ghoulworks."

Tuesday, 22 June 1999, 5:12 AM
Thirteenth floor, Buckhead Ritz-Carlton Hotel
Atlanta, Georgia

Parmenides awoke with difficulty. He could not seem to disentangle himself from the familiar dream. He had been running, or attempting to run. To flee. Infuriatingly, no matter how he struggled, he could not seem to lift either of his feet. He was rooted to the spot and pursuit was not far behind. The "other" would soon be upon him again.

He could not even bring himself to turn to face the unknown terror that rushed headlong toward him, closing the distance at an alarming rate. The sense of panic grew to the point where it was nearly unbearable and then, suddenly, he felt the weight crash across his back, and he went down.

Flailing, Parmenides pitched forward, suppressing a scream. Arms came at him out of the darkness, caught him, steadied him. He was standing upright once again. There were soothing words being whispered very close by. He tried to turn and face his unknown benefactor, but his feet were rooted to the ground. He stumbled again and nearly fell to the floor.

The voices that came to him seemed disjointed.

"Hold still won't you?"

"There's no reason to flail about like that."

"I did not expect you to come back around so soon."

"I'm nearly finished now, though, and there's no sense putting you under again."

"You'll just have to tough out this last little bit, but we're soon finished."

"That's my brave boy."

"My young romantic."

"My *philosophe*."

It took him some moments to realize that there was but a single voice addressing him, and a while longer to piece together the flow of the monologue. It was not until a long time afterwards that he realized why he was having such difficulty with these basic cognitive functions. It was the pain.

The pain. The howling, mind-numbing, nerve-tearing pain. Somewhere nearby, someone screamed.

"Now, this won't hurt a bit," came the reassuring voice, which some distant part of his mind recognized as that of his client. Vykos.

Again the piercing scream.

"Tsk, tsk. Don't they give you even some rudimentary training in mind-over-body techniques in that mountaintop paradise of yours? No one can be expected to produce quality work under these conditions."

Another long scream. "Now you've utterly ruined the nose and I'm going to have to start it again from scratch. And if you don't hold still you might actually manage to tear one of those feet loose from the floor and do some real lasting harm."

Screaming, and more screaming, and a sharp slap striking something fleshy and nearby that might have been his cheek.

"Now, are you going to calm down or am I going to have to put you under again?" She did not have to put him under again. Consciousness fled him. The flesh became unresisting, and bent to her will.

part three:
the deception

She swallowed deeply, and the life-giving nectar washed down her throat. By the time she became conscious of this, of what she was doing, it was too late, and Victoria feared to open her eyes. But so long as she'd imbibed already, she reasoned, nothing more could be lost by continuing to feed. If the blood was tainted or was being offered under any pretext that might later damn her, then the damage was already done. Beyond that, she hated to admit, the hunger that drove her to open her throat and gulp down the stream of blood left her little real choice in the matter. For the moment at least, the hunger was stronger than she was.

But she still refused to open her eyes. Her other senses warned her that her bitter fight against the Sabbat hounds had unfortunately not resulted in her destruction. She heard movement, very close by. She smelled smoke and the unmistakable odor of burned flesh.

Nevertheless, as soon as she appeared to be feeding purposefully, the refreshment was denied. A soft, crooning voice whispered, "Don't like it too much, Toreador bitch. If you give in to that so easily, you'll be little fun for the ministrations you're meant to resist later."

The speaker moved closer to Victoria as his words purred forth. "Later," he said again, and a puff of stagnant, ruinous air breathed hot and terrible upon her face. Her captor—for this was surely no benefactor—

was so close that her skin tingled, and when she opened her eyes, her long eyelashes brushed the monster's forehead.

He—*it*—smiled.

"Did you enjoy your drink?" he asked, suddenly licking a dribble of blood from Victoria's lower lip with a thick and gristly tongue. He stared into the Toreador's eyes for a moment, but she did not meet his gaze. She dared not.

He shrugged and then stood, which made Victoria realize that she was seated. She was crudely bound, by metal bands about her wrists and ankles, to a wooden chair that might have been the throne of a fat pauper king. As the fog cleared from her mind, she registered, as well, her nakedness, and looked up at her captor.

He backed away another step and smiled as he regarded her bare form. His mouth leaked another purr. "Your polished body will not excite me as it did your Ventrue customers, Toreador whore!"

Victoria just continued her stare, however, not meeting his eyes. Her captor was a grotesque caricature of a starving mortal child. His body was impossibly emaciated, so that everywhere it seemed his flesh was stretched taut over the underlying bones. Everywhere, that is, except his stomach, which was bloated, straining the flesh, discolored with a gangrenous hue. His triangular head tapered to the small mouth, and upon a hairless pate the ugly beast possessed ridges of bone that ran in rows parallel to the width of the skull.

His legs and arms were obscenely long and folded, suggesting something like a cross between a man and a cricket. Victoria could not determine how many joints these limbs possessed, but they alternately folded and spread, and she watched the Sabbat sway back and forth as he stood before her.

Involuntarily, Victoria shuddered. She had hoped that the Sabbat hounds pursuing her would destroy her so that she might avoid just this sort of future, which was now a present she could not deny.

"Care to ring your Ventrue lover?" the Sabbat whispered, dangling Vegel's cell phone from long, skeletal fingers. "When they brought you to me, you were clutching it like a dying man's prayer."

He put the phone to his ear and mouth and feigned a woman's frightened voice, "Oh, darling, hurry, Elford has gotten hold of me and there will be nothing left of me to love but—" and here he changed his voice to a hoarse croaking, "a hollowed-out sack of scarred and burned flesh!" Cackling, he threw the phone against the wooden wall—she seemed to be in an old railroad boxcar—that Victoria's chair pressed against. Two large, clearly unusable, plastic chunks ricocheted to floor, exposing the guts of the device.

As Victoria watched one piece of the phone spin slowly to a standstill, she tried to calm herself by such degrees as well. As it slowed, so she wound to a stop, to a spot deep within herself where she might forget the terrible times in store for her now. Perhaps some night she would reawaken, some centuries hence, and this nightmare would be over.

But sharp agony jolted her body. She coughed and then choked in pain. She felt her limbs involuntarily flap like suffocating fish on the wooden chair.

"Do not seek to escape me, Victoria," Elford said pleasantly. "I told you before, you are meant to resist.

If you do, then I will make your time with me more bearable."

Victoria's insides still spasmed, though the pain had lessened—for the moment. She looked for the first time into the face of the creature who planned to torture her. To break her. But he was no longer looking at her face. She followed his gaze along the length of his arm to where his hand cupped her bare right breast. Wafting smoke obscured the details for a moment, but he blew his fetid breath and cleared the air. He chuckled as he withdrew his hand. Victoria felt twinges of pain as her seared flesh peeled away from each of Elford's fingertips.

Upon the alabaster of her pure skin were five black and shriveled marks, pressed into the firm flesh of her breast.

"Oh yes," Elford murmured, "you had best resist."

He raised a glistening, scalpel-like claw toward her mouth. Victoria's fear rose uncontrollably within her, and she vomited forth the blood she'd so recently consumed.

Wednesday, 23 June 1999, 3:52 AM
East Bay Street
Charleston, South Carolina

The not-so-distant flames danced toward the heavens, whipped themselves into a spasmodic frenzy, and from the widow's walk atop his home of more than two centuries, Davis Purrel could do no more than watch. Watch as the flames grew closer. Watch as, like a red tide, they washed across the Battery. The mortal firefighters struggled valiantly, and occasionally they managed to check the advancing firestorm. But invariably the fickle winds swept in from the bay, giving new life to the flames and howling like banshees through the eaves of Purrel's magnificent home.

If the wind were all we had to contend against, Purrel thought, *we'd have a chance*.

He'd received word of the dozen or so boats trolling into Charleston harbor several hours ago. Immediate response might have saved his city. He'd heard rumors of the attacks on Atlanta and Savannah the night before, of course, but who could have expected something of this magnitude so soon on the heels of actions a hundred miles to the south and over twice that far to the west?

As proof of his error, his city burned. He'd made so few mistakes over the years; how ironic that the consequences of this one should be so harsh. So final.

"Davis, you must come in."

At first he thought the flames were calling to him, entreating him to embrace them, as they em-

TZIMISCE

braced the heart of the city he had seen rise from colonial port to center of culture and commerce. But the voice belonged to the old man who stood half protruding from the trapdoor behind Davis.

"Davis," said the old man again, "come inside."

Davis ignored Antoine Purrel, ostensible owner of the Purrel-Turney House and most recent in a long line of descendants who had been the face of Davis Purrel's power in the kine world. The features of Davis's proud face were reflected in the older man's: distinctive, aquiline nose; sharply set brow; narrow jaw and squared, cleft chin. Antoine's face was fleshier. His skin hung loose, a milepost of time, though it was Davis who was much older, who was both progenitor and protector of both the Purrels and of Charleston.

I've been a shepherd here, thought Davis, and it was true. He had ruled the city fairly and wisely, and been surprisingly successful for a rare Toreador risen to the position of prince. From the start, he'd culled the rebellious element who would've brought instability to his city, but even in this he'd not been callous or cruel. And the city had flourished. Today, the neoclassical mansions crowded into the bastion of splendor that was the Battery, the point of land in the crook of the Ashley and Cooper Rivers, rivaled the glory of any other period, even the last antebellum years.

But now the wolves are among the flock.

The flames could not be denied. The Sabbat jackals had done what the mighty Union fleet had been unable to accomplish in that last glorious war—take the city by sea.

"Davis, do you hear me?"

"Go to bed, Antoine," said Davis with a sigh. "It's much too late for you to be up."

"By God, there's fire all around!" said Antoine defiantly. "I'm not going to burn in my bed. We should go to the house in Columbia and come back when this is taken care of."

"Go, if you wish," said Davis. Perhaps the old man could save himself, but Davis doubted it. The roads would be watched, the harbor sealed.

Davis had never bothered to tell Antoine much about the inner workings of the Kindred world. No, the old man had never possessed the proper acumen to operate among the plots of the undead as anything other than a pawn. He was capable enough to assume the public face of the family, to show himself at the country club and the Historic Foundation meetings, but little more. Antoine's son had been little better and was now banished to the West Coast, but the grandson—ah, now there was a promising lad. Jason Purrel was away at art school. He had no talent to speak of, but he possessed certain sensibilities and strengths of character that Davis admired. Enough so that Davis had planned to ghoul the boy some day. Now that would never happen.

"You shouldn't be close to these fires," Antoine scolded.

"Antoine," said Davis slowly, calmly, "I have always been truthful with you—"

"That's a damnable lie," said the old man.

Davis allowed himself a wry chuckle. "Fair enough." He leaned against the railing of the widow's walk. His head hung low, but his voice was strong and clear above the din of fire and wind and sirens. "But know that I speak truthfully now. If you do not

leave me at once, I will kill you where you stand."
Davis craned his neck to face the old man. "Do you
believe me?"

Antoine's face was grayer than before. He seemed
suddenly vulnerable to the stench of smoke that even
the gusting winds could not dissipate. He licked his
lips and, without a word, retreated back down the
stairs. Davis turned back to the city and heard the
trapdoor pulled shut behind the old man.

The flames were close now indeed. The
firefighters scurried around like ants, but for every
fire they tamed, another sprang up. Davis knew better than to believe that even the ill-timed wind was
responsible for the leaping of the flames closer and
closer to his haven. He could spy at least a dozen
historic structures already marred by fire, black swaths
across their facades like the scars of pox on the face
of a beautiful child. He could not look upon the scene
for more than a few moments before he turned away.

Perhaps if I just went out, if I gave myself to them,
he pondered, *perhaps then they would spare my city.*

Davis did not think of his fellow Toreador of
Charleston; he did not think of the other Kindred
who served him willingly or grudgingly. They could
all roast in the morning sun, for all he cared. But his
beautiful city—the fine mansions, the brick carriage
houses, the spacious gardens around his own home.
He could not watch it all destroyed, and what would
resistance do except ensure that it all burned?

Davis turned his gaze toward the faint outline of
the fort in the harbor. *Is this what you felt like, Major
Anderson?* he thought to ask the long-dead Union
hero of Sumter. *Surrounded, cut off, watching that which
you served crumble around you?*

But the only response Davis heard was a sickening crackle as the roof of one of his estate's outbuildings, the old cattle shed, burst into flames. The end was near. He considered climbing back through the trapdoor, for he longed to run his fingers along the plasterwork ornamentation within his home, to gaze upon the crystal and bronze chandeliers, to walk one last time down the grand, free-standing staircase that dominated the entry hall.

No, he steadied himself. *I will await the flames here. They will not be long.*

Wednesday, 23 June 1999, 3:59 AM
Thirteenth floor, Buckhead Ritz-Carlton
Atlanta, Georgia

Vykos waited patiently. Eventually, a ragged moan told her that her charge was clawing his way back toward consciousness. Noting the precise time, she found herself, not for the first time this evening, surprised at the Assamite's tenacity.

Another of her clan might well have immediately and obsessively fallen to recording such minutiae in some interminable experiment journal. Vykos was not in the habit, however, of leaving such revealing written records of the exact abilities and tolerances of her subjects.

The first time he had come to, last night, he had taken her unawares. The fool had fought his way back to consciousness right in the middle of the sculpting. Vykos noted that the subject had not attempted to employ even the most rudimentary of pain-control techniques—this despite the fact that a major portion of his face was, at the time, laid open to the bone.

He had screamed, of course, and the accompanying facial contortion could not have eased his discomfort. But the pain neither stopped nor slowed him. It wasn't as if the subject transcended the pain, or blocked the pain, or defied the pain. It was simply that the sensation of agony, in all its primal glory, failed to act as a deterrent.

Vykos found herself wondering if the nervous systems of these legendary killers were somehow cross-wired as part of their training and initiation? Vykos ran down the list of likely suspects: drugs, post-hypnotics, laser surgery, voodoo, neural inhibitors, fanaticism. The possibilities were intriguing, but her speculations were inconclusive.

She had experimented, of course, with disabling the pain sensors, the emitters, the receptors, the pro-cessors. But each of these efforts had inevitably produced clumsiness and led to numerous injuries to the extremities that went unnoticed by the subject until he reached the threshold of critical blood loss.

But this was something else altogether. Some-thing astounding. There was not a square inch of this subject's body that had not been battered or poked or pinched or prodded or twisted or torn or pounded or kneaded or…worse. And unless she was greatly mistaken, he was about to spring for her throat.

With a bestial howl, Parmenides sprang for her throat.

He came up several feet short and collapsed face down on the hardwood floor.

Painful, Vykos noted. *In most subjects, this would prove a strong deterrent to further attacks.*

But the subject was pushing himself back up onto hands and knees, apparently trying to regain his feet. This last endeavor was, to some extent, doomed to failure or at least frustration as the subject's legs were still fused together at the knees and ankles.

The Assamite turned a gaze upon her that was all shards and jagged edges. Ice and razors. A look full of the haunting calm and total focus of a great cat in mid-pounce.

"Enough. I have already warned you that you would only injure yourself in such foolish displays of bravado," Vykos scolded. "I have labored some hours on your behalf and I am not about to sit idly by while you recklessly undo all of my efforts."

Vykos took him by the hair, effortlessly lifting his head and chest off the floor, and pressed her face very close to his. "Now, think."

The reproach struck him like a physical blow. He reeled backwards at the very cusp of defiance— caught midway between spitting in her face and lunging forward (at the cost of a mere fistful of scalp) to tear at her face with his fangs. Vykos shook him once and pressed on before he could resolve the issue. "Think!"

He lunged.

Parmenides was expecting, *relying*, upon the fact that he would hear the sound of hair and scalp ripping free before the first wave of pain actually struck home. It would buy him a crucial fraction of a second.

He was thus utterly unprepared for what actually happened. It was over more quickly than even his adrenaline-tuned senses could follow. It was as if Vykos had suddenly loosed her grip. Or so he thought, as his face, freed of this restraint, slammed resoundingly into the floor.

Only Vykos had not loosed her grip. He was assured of this when the very next moment she yanked his head back up to face her again. For some reason, he had the hazy, pain-fogged impression that his hair had actually *stretched*—pulled out to a length of about three feet before snapping back again.

His first reaction, of course, had been one of elation. It was as if some passing spirit had granted his dying wish. His entire will had been focused on bridging the tantalizingly slight gap between his fangs and the face of his tormentor. And something within him—some previously unguessed reserve of strength or will or spirit—had risen up and answered his one defining need.

He felt hot blood welling out of his lip and streaming from a gash above one eye. He was broken in body and his legs did not respond to him. But he did not feel broken. He felt strong and whole and indomitable. He smiled broadly and savored the familiar taste of the blood trickling into his mouth. He saw the briefest look of surprise flicker across the cool, sculpted face of his adversary.

"Ah, you have seen it yourself, then," Parmenides crowed. "The righteous anger of the masters is a hammer. It thunders from distant mountaintops. It churns the intervening waters. It reaches its shadow over you and you tremble beneath it. Your blood is mine."

Her hand fell away and she backed away half a step, unbelieving. Somehow, against all expectation and in open defiance of his pitifully wracked body, Parmenides stood.

Vykos cursed softly. She could swear like a soldier when pressed. In fact, if the truth were known, she could swear like a legionnaire in perfectly conjugated Latin. She could swear like a crusader (in the vernacular). She had even been known to make the most hardened Tartar, Magyar, or Cossack blush, giving each a scourging with his own tongue.

On this occasion, however, such eloquence seemed to have deserted her. She was distracted by the ferocity of his determination, and also perhaps by the rigors of the experiment. There was no denying that this subject was unique and the effort of monitoring its responses in such minute detail was fatiguing.

She could feel the intensity of his twin passions—to survive and to kill. She could measure each of them, plot them, analyze the resulting graphs. But she resisted the temptation toward detachment. It was much more intriguing to interact with the subject directly.

She could feel his need. It rolled away from him in waves. It was as if both drives were but a single passion, one instinct, one volition—his live-kill. She immediately dismissed the clumsy term. The sentiment was more meaningful in German, but translated into English poorly. It was an instinct simultaneously toward and away from the grave. A rushing in and backing out. A frenzied dance on the edge of the precipice.

She was both surprised and delighted at the speed with which his body consumed itself.

She could not help but feel the warm glow of pride when she thought of that trick he had pulled with expanding and retracting his hair. Inspired! She would not expect such aptitude—such a seamless fusion of need and fulfillment—even in a servant many months his senior.

His desperate attack might have succeeded had she not felt the first familiar stirrings of the Gift moving within him. Even with this slight warning, however, it proved all she could do to remove herself from the direct path of his fury. She was more wary now. And he, well, the subject was about to start testing the controls of this experiment in earnest.

She thought it immensely improbable that he would be able to free his legs. She had seen to it that the bone itself had been fused, and bone was a harsh and unforgiving medium. Mastery over the hair and nails—the Inanimates—was something well within the power of a trained novice. Bending the Inanimates to the dictates of the will, however, was mere child's play compared to the true Bonesculpting—a difference like that between working in play-dough and Florentine marble.

The fact that he seemed oblivious to what should have been debilitating levels of pain was a challenge, but one which Vykos found both novel and exhilarating. Here was something that merited further examination—if the subject should survive these initial tests.

For the present, Vykos turned her critical eye back to the subject's first blind, childlike steps into the Great Art. Vykos was watching him keenly now, noting each flicker of emotion as the subject passed from the initial elation into doubt and, very soon now, into fear. These changes were but the outward symptoms of the revelation writhing within him, tearing its way toward the surface of his awareness.

"Gently, now. Do not fight it, my young romantic, my *philosophe*. Even your vengeful masters will not begrudge you this one small indulgence. It is a gift. Drink deeply and be content."

The doubt had clearly won the upper hand. He struggled to free his legs, but to no avail. "You cannot imagine that you will be suffered to…" His voice was choked with indignation, forcing him to begin again. The damage he was doing to the musculature of his legs was growing quite extensive. One small part of Vykos's mind kept a resigned tally of the hours of work wasted and the weeks of bedrest and physical therapy that he was accumulating.

Parmenides raged on. "Even if you should manage

to prevent me from feasting upon your black heart…"
He paused. The admission had cost him dearly.

Vykos could see the fight leaking out of him. He swallowed hard and rushed on. "Even so, there will be others. The masters will forge a special hell to receive you and they will not rest until they have seen you dragged, screaming and begging for your life, into the fires that burn eternally, but consume not."

Unmoved, Vykos clapped her hands slowly. As she did so, their flesh began to blacken and peel. Soon, each clap was accompanied by a small cloud of crumbling ash, gusting outward and settling gently to the floor. Parmenides could see the glaring white of bone peeking through. He heard knucklebones popping and cracking as if from extreme heat. He saw jagged blackened stubs of bone clatter and bounce noisily to the floor.

"Enough," he cried, jerking his head away from the grisly spectacle. "Enough of your infernal parlor tricks. You are not impervious to harm. The masters have had centuries to perfect their art. They will know how to accomplish your end. You may rely upon it. Do you think we have not slain your kind before? You deceive yourself, lady."

"Ah, but you, yourself, do not know the trick," she said matter-of-factly. "The wooden stake through the heart, perhaps? Immersion in running water? Garlic-flavored holy wafers?" Her hands were whole once more, all trace of the charring gone. She circled him warily. As she neared the doorway, she stooped to kneel over something on the floor, just out of his angle of vision.

He kept his gaze fixed rigidly forward as he strove to master himself. He found he was actually trembling with frustration. Through an extreme effort of will, he managed to hold his tongue, and refused to be goaded into responding to her jibes.

After a few moments he saw, out of the corner of his eye, Vykos straighten up again, righting an overturned chair. She propelled it before her, rolling it forward as she approached.

"Very shortly now," she explained, "you will collapse. Already you are pushing the point of no return—of doing irreparable damage to your legs. Will you please sit down and cease these senseless threats and posturings? There are weighty matters to discuss and time has already grown short."

He wheeled upon her, as if to lash out once more, but the effort proved too much for his maimed lower body. He went down with a sound like a canvas tent collapsing.

"This humiliation," he raged at the floorboards, unable to rise or even to turn. "It will not go unavenged. You are doomed as surely as I am." He caught a rasping breath. "Even if you were to restore me now and set me at liberty, it would be too late to buy even one additional night of your cursed unlife. Though I have fallen among fiends, it is you, my tormentor, whom I pity."

There was a long pause, during which Parmenides did nothing but suppress the racking sobs that convulsed his entire frame. But no sound of this inner struggle escaped his lips.

"My young poet," the voice was gentle, soft with affection and perhaps a touch of pride. "Be still now. It is enough. In you, I am well pleased."

It was some minutes before he felt strong hands take him firmly under each arm. He did not struggle against them. His eyes were shut tight in humiliation and defeat. Through cracked and bleeding lips, he began to spit broken prayers for the dead. He hardly noticed as he was settled into the hard, straight-backed chair. The grisly device barely registered upon his consciousness. His prayers became more fervent, as if by drowning out the sound of what was going on around him, he could deny the events themselves—shout them down, banish them.

From somewhere very far off, he heard a familiar female voice which, for a moment, he could not seem to place. It was a pleasant voice, an attractive voice, and one which seemed full of concern for him and for his well-being.

"Only in this one thing am I disappointed," the voice crooned. Parmenides pitched forward, his head nearly bouncing off his shattered knees as the chair rolled forward. "That you would, even for a moment, believe that I would be so reckless as to take you into my care without the knowledge—much less the encouragement—of your cherished masters.

"There will be no retribution, my gentle assassin, because you are a gift. A very special gift. A peace offering from the Old Man of the Mountain. You are to be a pledge between our two peoples.

"You have been given into my care. Do you understand this? You are mine completely, to do with as I will. Just think of it! The fun we shall have together."

Parmenides may have screamed. Through the haze of pain and horror, one part of his mind, a very well-disciplined part that had been rigorously trained for weeks on end to respond to just such an occasion, instinctively groped for the Words of Undoing that would preempt his suffering.

These moments of peace seemed filled with as much eternity as the hours of pain that preceded them. Victoria Ash, Toreador Primogen of Atlanta— very nearly, she felt, Prince of Atlanta—could not look at herself. It would shatter her peace, as the scent of her own blood that drenched the wooden chair nearly did. So with eyes closed, she deferred the horror of her current situation and turned to the future.

Despite Elford's worst—and it was terrible, evil and sadistic work indeed—Victoria now knew that she would survive. She would be a ruined heap, potentially for decades; the scars of this night alone would take months to repair, and there were likely to be many such nights in her future. As the cruel Sabbat had savaged her, however, Victoria had actually discovered a tiny ray of hope shining through the darkness of her torment.

At first, her fear had convinced her that she would succumb easily to such torture, that her mind would snap, and that she would cry and beg and plead and resist as Elford desired. While her vampiric flesh was indeed weak to the will of the Tzimisce flesh-crafter, Victoria's mind remained intact. More importantly, though, through Elford's wicked alterations, she was learning what made him tick, what he desired, what titillated and enthralled him. And so she resisted. She channeled the pain he inflicted. Her every groan and contortion was timed and shaped by his sadistic yearnings, which his words and deeds made clear to her; her reactions to his abrasive caresses pleasured him to distraction. Until he crawled away panting, and slammed the sliding door of the boxcar closed behind him.

How many other boxcars concealed playthings for the torturer, Victoria had no way of knowing. But surely there were others. Sometimes Elford smelled of their blood, or came to her with unidentifiable specks of their matter on his skin.

Victoria knew that her physical beauty was great enough to seduce Kindred. She had done it many times. Now she suspected that the promise of the degradation of that beauty was enough to seduce a Tzimisce. The Toreador felt that Elford would be hers—not tonight, or next week, or next month. But his desires were a scalpel in her hands, and she wielded it as expertly as he did any of his implements. Time would test her, indeed, but she would persevere, and time would bring her reward—and then her captor would pay. For everything. From the greatest malformity to the tiniest blemish.

The pain she'd endured when he had slid his hand into her chest and grasped a rib had been excruciating. His operations were filled with sexual innuendo, and that had been Victoria's first clue. The fool had spoken too much. He'd not only revealed the means of his own defeat, Elford had also given Victoria a focus for her thoughts when she'd been reaching desperately for anything to mask the pain. His intrusion within her had surrendered all significance, and from that moment onward, she'd laid her plans.

These were the marks of Elford's pleasure. In his hands, the Toreador's rib became like clay, and bent to fit his vision of how Victoria was meant to look. The former primogen could no longer resist examining herself. Her right breast, already studded with oval burns inflicted by the Tzimisce's fiery fingertips, was now impaled by one of her own ribs. Elford had bent it outward and threaded it expertly, painfully, through her body so that its tip jutted out in place of her nipple, the so-called blemish that earlier had been removed by a savage bite.

And so began a line of visible bone decorations, small horn-like protrusions that made the skin around them itch and burn unrelentingly. Her clavicle was twisted and separated into a series of outcroppings connecting those on her right arm to her bone nipple. The spurs on her arm had been massaged from her humerus and stretched until they too extended beyond her skin.

Finally, there were two more such spurs on the back of her hand, perhaps meant eventually to join with the other row.

All these wounds, these grotesque surgeries, could be healed, she thought. She *hoped*. Unless Elford bore much older blood than she imagined, or unless she was wrong in her beliefs about Tzimisce flesh-crafting—and her real knowledge of the fiends' powers, despite her present, terrifying exposure to them, was slight indeed—unless a hundred other possibilities that might leave her a scarred, misshapen monstrosity, unless just *one* of these multitudinous possibilities was true, she might eventually be able to restore her pristine form to its previous beauty. That was what she had to believe. That was the only hope she had, and she clutched it to her heart like water in a desert land. Her body was indeed her temple, and to dwell upon the damage done to it would be to surrender to despair. It would render her incapable of taking the strong, decisive actions that might eventually free her.

Victoria sank back into her chair. Her mind turned from the future to the past—either a preferable alternative to the present. She could scarcely believe the turn of events that had brought her here. Her party and plans at the High Museum had been meticulously prepared, had come so close to fruition. She had entered the gallery through the door of Heaven. Now she had descended into Hell. Assuming she did in fact survive this Hell, she would carry a valuable lesson with her, for now she knew that she was never completely safe. No matter how many tests she applied to her plans before execution, no matter how great the power she might gain, no matter how formidable the defenses she might erect—she was never safe. Even if she escaped this railcar dungeon—*when* she escaped it—she would never feel safe again.

While Victoria's confidence in eventual freedom increased by modest degrees, her short-term prospects remained monumentally grim. She possessed no desire to suffer the degradation and torture that Elford planned for her. If she could escape sooner rather than later, then so much the better.

Victoria had a multitude of ways to bend an individual's will to her whim—as both kine and Kindred, she'd always been expert in making others *want* her, passionately, desperately—but in first attempting her most potent means with Elford, she'd instantly realized that it would never work. He was too much a slave of his existing passion for his work to have an additional desire so instantly manufactured. With him, her only recourse was to ply her wiles over time. She might some night, soon or not so soon, be successful, but that was of little immediate help.

But what other options did she have? Victoria

glanced at the pieces of cellular phone on the floor. Undeniably broken, and she had no reason to believe that she could repair it, even if she could reach it. Its loss was not a cause for total despair, however, because the Toreador had other means of summoning aid. There was no guarantee of success. Far from it. But as she regained her fighting spirit—hotly pursued, as it was, by her dread of the next session with Elford—she determined to try.

Over the many years of her nocturnal existence, Victoria had come into contact with countless Kindred, and now each and every one of them was a potential savior. Even those she had not compelled consciously to adore her could not have neglected to notice her irresistible beauty and charm. Her image would be indelibly burned into their psyche. Such was the nature of the gifts that accompanied, if not compensated for, the Curse of Caine in her case. Those other Kindred, it was true, might not be predisposed to help her. Their decision, however, was not entirely one of free will. They might resist her call, and most likely those powerful enough to rescue her from this hellhole were also powerful enough to ignore her summons. But Victoria could be quite persuasive.

Though their names sounded only in her mind, she began to call them, one by one, to her side.

Her urging and urgent request would persist for the remainder of the night, no longer, so it was only worthwhile to summon those who were likely nearby. *Benison. Julius.* She concentrated on their names. These two able warriors were probably dead with the remainder of the Camarilla who had reveled at Victoria's party, but at least she would disturb their graves. She chuckled, and called *Eleanor* as well. How ironic it would be if that bitch had survived some-how and managed to save Victoria.

She tilted her chin toward the ceiling and pro-pelled more names into the ether. She would see what had become of the deserters from her party: *Vegel*. *Hannah*. *Rolph*. Perhaps their intricate plans of escape would be foiled by a return to Atlanta, assuming that's where Victoria was—for she had no way to be sure.

And others too. She had few confidants, and no one she could honestly call a true friend, no one that remained loved as the centuries passed, but any of a short list of lovers, admirers or comrades—mostly lov-ers and admirers, she admitted; she'd had precious little call for camaraderie—might come if the circumstances permitted: *Oliver*, though she thought the Brujah brute was likely in torpor; *Jan*, though she knew he was in Europe, probably bound to his Ventrue elders in ways that New World Kindred could not fathom and that he could not overcome, even if his feelings for her persisted; *Joshua*, because if anyone could sniff out her whereabouts, it was this Gangrel.

Humor was a difficult proposition, but Victoria laughed at herself as she sent her next summons: *Leopold*. The youngster had saved her once at the High. Perhaps he could do it again—unlikely, since the shad-owy tentacle had surely pounded him to pieces.

The process took a long while. By the time Victoria had mentally recited the list of names, dawn was near. Her tired, injured, violated body gave in immediately. She closed her eyes, and closed too her mind, attempting to go to that place beyond thought, where she might be free, at least until the next sun-set, of the ministrations her Tzimisce tormentor would offer.

Hardin squeezed the steering wheel so hard that his already pale knuckles turned bone-white. The truck shuddered and bucked. Discouraging sounds coughed forth from the engine. He smashed the dashboard with his fist until the plastic casing cracked and fell away.

"They'll probably take that out of your deposit," said Desmond, squished into the middle seat. On the far side of him sat Rojo, unconcerned. He picked his teeth with a fingernail—not his own; it was attached to a useful but disembodied digit.

Hardin glared at Desmond for the smaller man's attempt at humor. There had been no deposit, no fee of any kind, paid for this U-haul.

The cacophony beneath the hood grew more pronounced. Steam began to billow from the edges. Then, after a muffled explosion, the engine's labored whirring began to fade. The speedometer needle, already gyrating between 45 and 55, acknowledged the engine's death knell by plummeting toward single digits. Hardin turned the truck onto the shoulder, where it lurched to a halt.

Hardin stepped out onto the gravel. Desmond slipped past him. Rojo showed no inclination to get out of the truck. *And what good would it do?* Hardin wondered. What good would anything do?

There was not much traffic. Hardin glanced at his watch. They could spare a short break, he decided. No need to worry. Before long, someone would stop, a good Samaritan, and provide fresh transportation. And fresh blood.

Desmond, having wrapped rags around his hands, lifted the hood. After the smoke cleared, he stared for a moment at the engine. Then he stepped back, lowered his head, and made the sign of the cross.

"Gas?" asked Hardin.

Desmond nodded.

"Who put it in?"

Desmond shook his head this time. "Don't know."

"Rojo?" Hardin asked the darkly complected, red-haired passenger, who turned his malevolent gaze toward Hardin. "Who gassed the truck?" Hardin asked.

Rojo shrugged. "One of the gringos. They all look alike."

Hardin started toward the rear of the truck, but stopped and shielded his eyes against the light of the patrol car pulling over behind the U-haul.

"Break down?" asked the trooper as he stepped out of his cruiser.

At just that moment, the U-haul door, which had been closed but not fastened, slid open, and two more of Hardin's passengers hopped down onto the gravel.

A deep scowl creased the trooper's face. "You know it's not lawful to carry passengers back there." He reached for his citation pad.

"Yes," said Hardin. "I know."

The wide-bladed falchion thudded into the patrolman's neck before anyone had even seen Hardin take the weapon from the sheath under his jacket. The trooper took an unsteady step backward in disbelief, then collapsed to the ground.

"Get him out of sight before that next car passes," Hardin instructed the others. They hurried to obey, even though the other car was just cresting a hill several hundred yards away, and there was plenty of time. They lifted the body with ease, pausing only to return Hardin's knife, and carried the trooper into the underbrush beyond the shoulder. Hardin could hear them fall upon the body like vultures and claim what the police officer no longer needed. Other passengers began to climb from the back of the truck. The car sped past.

"Jacques," Hardin called to one of them.

"I am Jake."

"Jake, who the hell ever you are," snapped Hardin. "Who gassed up the truck?"

"That was Jacques."

"Tell him to come here. Then you, Lonnie, Greasy, and Amber take the police car and bring us back three more cars."

Jake did as he was told. As he and the other three were pulling away in the cruiser, Jacques ambled over to Hardin. Jacques was a short, squat man with thick hair. He never looked happy. Not that Hardin cared.

"You have diesel trucks in Montreal?" Hardin asked.

"Yeah."

"You know the difference between gasoline and diesel fuel, you stupid, asshole Canuck?"

Jacques, looking increasingly unhappy, fidgeted about, but his answer was precluded by the falchion, which again zinged through the air, seemingly of its own accord. Jacques's head fell back. A moment later, his body joined it. There was very little blood.

Hardin leaned down and wiped his blade on

Jacques's pants leg. "Nine *competent* vampires would be too much to ask for, I guess."

As Desmond dragged the body away from the road, Hardin glanced into the back of the truck. This, the smallest of the Sabbat war parties, traveled light. They'd be fine in the cars instead of a truck. Except for a few gym bags loaded with sawed-off shotguns and shells, there was no gear to speak of.

Hardin didn't count the heads as gear.

There was the Camarilla Prince of Columbia—*former* prince, that was. Then there were the three from Asheville: Prince Van de Brook—what a whiner. The young Gangrel had died better; even the Toreador, Stein, had gone with some small dignity.

Again, Hardin didn't really care. *Piss on 'em all.*

He had his itinerary, and he was on schedule. These backwater "cities" were hardly worth the trouble to clean out, in his opinion, but then again, they weren't *that* much trouble. Still, Hardin was anxious to rejoin the main forces and get in on some of the real fun. Like Atlanta. Now *that* had been worth his time—burning the Tremere chantry house to the ground. Made easier, of course, by the fact that Vykos had already taken care of the Tremere head honcho.

Head honcho. Hardin glanced at the collection of wide-eyed heads in the truck and smirked. *I'll have to remember that one for Desmond.*

Atlanta had been a blast, all right. This other puny shit was just biding time. He wouldn't have to wait too long. Winston-Salem, Roanoke, Charlottesville…and then the Big Enchilada.

Headlights again. But this time they were coming from the opposite direction, down the wrong side of the interstate. Hardin recognized the car that had passed earlier, except now Amber was behind the wheel. Hardin didn't care for her face—it was too pouty—but she had nice tits. The car screeched to a halt next to the truck.

"Move over," said Hardin, as he opened the door and shoved her aside. She bared her fangs and hissed in response to his rough treatment. "Save it, sister." He stuck his head out of the window. "Get the stuff and let's go!

"Throw the heads in the trunk," he added, to make sure they didn't get left behind.

Desmond and the other two Sabbat formed a bucket brigade of sorts and passed along the gym bags and the heads. One head got away and bounced around at bit, but Desmond scrabbled under the car to retrieve it.

"What about Jake and the others, *jefe?*" Rojo asked, as he sauntered over and got into the car.

"We'll catch up to them," said Hardin. He didn't feel like waiting any more. "If we miss them, they know where we're headed."

Thursday, 24 June 1999, 3:00 AM
Thirteenth floor, Buckhead Ritz-Carlton Hotel
Atlanta, Georgia

Parmenides awoke. A moment later, he *realized* that he had awakened and he cursed the names of some seven and forty gods before he was forced to pause his maledictions long enough to conjure up the names of further supernatural oppressors upon which to heap scorn and vitriol.

He was not dead.

Well, that wasn't technically true. He was dead, of course. A vampire, a walking corpse. But he was still, as they say, among the living. To be more precise, he was in a luxury hotel in a very exclusive neighborhood of the city of Atlanta. In short, he was among over three and a half million of the living.

More significantly, he was still among the unliving. He was a prisoner of—in order of his ascending horror and despair—the Sabbat, the Tzimisce, and one Sascha Vykos.

From the time of his Embrace, he had heard tales of the depravity of the Sabbat—their unclean and mocking rites, their predilection for drinking the blood of their sires, their insane efforts to hasten the coming of Gehenna. It was all somewhat hard to credit. Why anyone would actively seek the Final Retribution of Caine, the Dark Father, he who is called the First Murderer and the Kinslayer, it was difficult to imagine.

As a newcomer to the world of the undying, Parmenides had suspected these rumors—like so many similar stories meant to frighten childer—were nothing more than old wives' tales. In this case, those of very old wives.

He was forced to concede, however, that these accounts were no more extraordinary than the wild assertion that blood-drinking predators stalked the world by the light of neon marquees and headlights. And he no longer felt himself in a position to judge those particular claims impartially.

In later years, he had on more than one occasion been brought into close contact with the Sabbat and had found nothing that would lead him to dismiss those disturbing childhood tales out of hand. Such encounters always left him with a lingering sense of unease—one which even the blissful rewards of the mountaintop elysium could not entirely expunge from the spirit.

In dealings with the oily Lasombra, Parmenides experienced an unsettling sensation, like having a viper slide across the sleeper's thigh. He had, of course, had ample opportunity to handle snakes in the elysium. Venoms were an ancient and revered part of the profession. He knew the touch of even the deadliest cobra to be cool and smooth and not unpleasant in and of itself.

The sensation he felt in the presence of Lasombra, however, was something quite different. Something shifting, hot and glutinous—the touch of a serpent from a childhood nightmare.

And then there were the Tzimisce. Parmenides understood that in the polite circles of Kindred society—the garden parties and ice-cream socials that made up the unlife of his delicate Camarilla cousins—self-respecting vampires were embarrassed to even *think* about the Tzimisce. It would be a humiliating faux-pas, like bringing up the topic of lepers over tea. Except, of course, that lepers generally tended their own business, and that business rarely involved the torture, maiming and eventual (very eventual) death of respectable folk who would like to pretend that there was never any such deformed creature loosed on this green earth.

Parmenides had had few dealings with the Tzimisce. As a whole, the fiends tended to be withdrawn, solitary, obsessed with their disturbing experiments into the pseudo-scientific, the occult, the anatomical.

The Tzimisce were almost universally disinterested in concerns of politics, social climbing, and powermongering—those pursuits that so intrigue their brothers in the Sabbat, the Lasombra. Not surprisingly, the Tzimisce seldom found themselves in need of the kind of services that Parmenides had to offer.

This Vykos was a notable exception. First of all, she was not freakish in the manner of her clan. The Tzimisce reveled in deformity. They made an art and a passion of it.

Among the ancient brotherhood of assassins, there existed sage advice regarding the fiends. It was said: "If, in the course of your duties, you come upon a monstrosity lurking in the shadows, it is a Nosferatu. You have been seen. The victim will be warned. Depart, and submit to the scourge of the masters.

"If, however, you see a monstrosity capering in the torchlight, *that* is a Tzimisce. Go your way and do not return until three full nights have passed—and then only to confirm that your target is already dead."

Vykos was no capering monster. She was very human. And very female. Almost painfully so, Parmenides thought resignedly. She was beautiful in the same way a pouncing tigress was beautiful—all grace and inevitability.

Her other obvious departure from the predilections of her kind was her ambition. Vykos was preoccupied with the deadly game of Cainite politics—a game that slew with the same inevitability (if not always the same demanding standards of grace) as did the tiger.

While the game itself could devolve into the crude and merely bestial, Vykos maintained a reputation for an unflinching style and finesse that was rare among her clan. While most of her kinsmen were willing to leave the actual Sabbat leadership to their brethren Lasombra, Vykos had made a habit of besting them at their own game.

Parmenides knew that others of his order had been of service to Vykos in the past, and that she presently had an extensive portfolio of as-yet-unfulfilled contracts with the masters. The thought that she might jeopardize such a relationship…

He flinched away from the thought. There was something painful there, something he was not yet ready to touch, to examine in detail.

Parmenides was delighted that he could address these issues in such a rational manner. *The Sabbat, the Tzimisce, Vykos.* He repeated the words again, curious and not displeased at the utter lack of response they produced in him. He suspected that the part of his mind that was capable of registering pain and terror was otherwise occupied at present.

This revelation, however, was somewhat less than

reassuring. In addition to raising some pointed concerns about his physical well-being, this discovery seemed to conjure up more uncertainties than it dispelled. He had more than a passing curiosity as to which of his higher cognitive functions were presently under his control. He decided upon a small experiment.

He was fairly certain that emotion and pain centers were not responding in the manner to which he had grown accustomed. He further suspected the immediate cause of this shortcoming was extreme physical duress.

Other reflexive reactions seemed to have short-circuited as well. From his very early training, he knew that his autonomic functions had been specially tuned to prevent the possibility of his capture during the course of a botched mission.

He had only witnessed this fail-safe mechanism in action once. It was in Venice, now some centuries ago. But it was not something one was likely to forget. One of his brethren, in an attempt to escape the Doge's palace, was interrupted in the act of diving to the relative safety of the canal. He was hauled bodily back over the parapet and vanished under a shroud of blows—the tender ministrations of uncounted fists, heels and pikestaves.

From his vantage point at the edge of the labyrinth of narrow streets far below, Parmenides saw his brother fall beneath the throng. He started forward toward the wall. His guardian, however, put a restraining hand upon his shoulder. "Attend," he scolded. "Be vigilant now, lest you miss how our little brother accomplishes his escape."

Parmenides felt the reverberation of each buffet, fast and insistent, like a drenching rain. He was certain the downpour would drown its victim, or spill him over the parapet. But the son of the mountain, from his lofty perch high atop the wall, did not perish.

Or at least, he did not perish until after they had brought up the irons. From below Parmenides could see the flurry of activity; he could hear the metal bindings sing shut. But no sooner had the sound reached Parmenides's ears, than there also arose cries of alarm and cursing.

"Get that torch away, you fool!" someone shouted. But the torch was still held high aloft and it had never dipped down behind the crenellated wall. There was a magnesium-bright flash of light followed by a curl of oily black smoke from the pinnacle of the Doge's palace. Only then did his mentor allow the uncomprehending Parmenides to turn away, and together they melted back into the gathering crowd.

In later years, Parmenides had often wondered at the circumstances that had brought him and his master to the foot of the Doge's palace that night. He could never quite recall the exact pretext for the excursion.

His training was not accomplished, of course, amidst the decadence of the Italian city-states, caught between the excesses of the Medicis and the depravity of the Borgias. The rigors of the *khabar* demanded the unambiguously harsh necessity of desert wastes and exposed mountaintops.

Nor was it considered proper for a novice to be on hand to witness his brother's handiwork—even on a mission with a much more satisfying outcome. The presence of an apprentice introduced too many uncertainties, too many opportunities for misstep.

And yet when the Brotherhood was gathered upon some summer evening in that remote mountaintop elysium, and the long amber pipes were lit and passed from hammock to hammock by exotic creatures with shy eyes the shape of almonds and navels like perfect diamonds—then some one among them would sigh contentedly and relate a most curious story.

As the story gradually unfolded, punctuated only by generous servings of honey, dates, persimmons and ambrosia, he would relate how, on a certain unforgettable night, a much younger version of himself, accompanied by his master, had witnessed a marvel—the reciting of the fabled Words of Undoing.

He would retrace the tragic tale in its entirety, unwinding each familiar sight, sound, emotion—right up to the point that that one fortunate brother was conveyed into the heavens in a fiery chariot.

And after he had spoken, someone else would put by his pipe and speak in turn, telling his story of a night when he (a *he* that he hardly recognized across the span of years) and his master had witnessed that one forbidden something. And so it would go.

And all of their stories were one story, but whether it was because their words and memories had grown hopelessly mingled in the course of so many decades of long, slow summer evenings, or whether it was because there was really only one story that was given voice endlessly, through uncounted generations of their people—that he did not know nor could he say.

But these musings did little to reassure him. Parmenides possessed a driving curiosity and he had, of course, made discreet inquiries. The aspect of this matter which troubled him most was the fact that although, nearly without exception, all of his brethren could recount a singularly unsettling experience of witnessing the enacting of the Words of Undoing…he could never find one among them who would admit to having been a witness at any other mission, whether disastrous or not.

The situation had the unpleasant air of an object lesson. A very costly object lesson. Parmenides could not escape the thought (an irreverent and probably blasphemous thought) that these dramatic failures had been *arranged* for the edification of the neophytes.

Could the masters have foreknowledge of which missions would end in success and which were doomed to failure? No, not even the Old Man in the Mountain claimed such omnipotence.

Still, almost any of the masters would certainly have grown to be a shrewd judge of which tasks were most likely to end in destruction. Such discernment was necessary in sorting out which missions to accept and which to refuse.

But this, this smacked of something more sinister.

Parmenides shied away from this dangerously unorthodox line of thought. Who was he to question the masters, those who had ushered him into the earthly paradise? He was not sure how one might even go about repaying such a debt. The balance on his account was nothing less than one eternal life.

If the masters chose to teach him with hard lessons, to make him stronger, to forge him into a more reliable tool for their will, it was not his place to refuse them, to deny his sacred trust.

But now, it seemed, that the masters had chosen… No. The thought was too close to that place of pain and doubt which was, at present, denied him. The fiend was lying. There was nothing more to it than that. The very idea that the masters would abandon him to the clutches of the Tzimisce, it was unthinkable. It was a condemnation far worse than being chosen for some suicidal mission. In failure at least, there was glorious sacrifice and a quick end in the fires of purification.

And yet he had been unable to touch the secret place—the sheltered recess of his heart upon which were writ the Words of Undoing. He could not summon up the sacred spark to ignite the inner flame.

Parmenides doubted that even the precise neurological manipulations of the fiends could reach this inner sanctuary, much less bar the door against him. It was a place of spirit, not of the flesh, and hence not subject to their macabre arts.

How then, was the way denied him? Was it some lingering curse, some final malediction of the Tremere witch, Hannah? Had she, through some obscure and inscrutable dark magic, stolen from him his Final Death even as he ushered her to her own?

No, the execution of his mission had been precise, flawless. There was no room for error or even hesitation when stalking the Tremere. The warlocks held the uncontested honor of being the most deadly prey on the planet. None but the Brotherhood would be so foolish as even to attempt the feat. At the slightest misstep, their positions would have been dramatically and irrevocably reversed. It would have been his head decorating some trophy room of the

Atlanta Chantry.

His head… Again, Parmenides ran up against the barrier, a wall woven from screaming nerve fibers blocking this line of speculation.

But if the change was not wrought by the witch, then that would mean that the masters had, knowingly or otherwise, sent him into the very heart of the Tremere's unhallowed lair unprotected—without recourse to the ultimate escape.

He was distantly aware that his body convulsed violently, shattered knees (perceived only as a throbbing mass suspended from his legs like a dead weight) curled upwards to thump against his chest. Someone cursed and pressed his thighs down hard against the chair, lashing them in place.

Vykos. The barrier of exposed nerve endings standing between him and consciousness was rent from top to bottom.

With great effort, knowing himself alone and abandoned among fiends, Parmenides opened his eyes upon nightmare.

Thursday, 24 June 1999, 3:04 AM
CSX freight yard
Atlanta, Georgia

Victoria stifled a scream. The pain was indeed intense, but it didn't quite demand this strenuous a reaction. Elford didn't seem to notice the exaggeration, though, and he cackled with delight.

The stringy Tzimisce sat upon Victoria's lap, straddling the Toreador. His unnaturally long and slender legs stretched past Victoria's bare hips toward the wall behind the chair. She couldn't fathom how there was room for them, but they seemed to fold at any angle, so likely they were looped back beneath the chair.

Elford's arms were bent at a half dozen elbows apiece, and they found purchase on a shelf made of Victoria's bosom as the Tzimisce leaned into her and performed his work on the side of her neck.

Victoria's forehead and neck were now bonded tightly to the chair, so she was unable to move her head even a fraction of an inch. Her body was another matter, and when she felt pain, she arched her back and tried to buck the Tzimisce off her lap.

The sick bastard liked that part, so Victoria kept doing it. Except this last time, because she was applying some torture as well.

Elford suddenly stopped his work and looked into the Toreador's eyes. His own orbs were filled with blackness, though a nimbus of madness lit their edges.

With a soft, punished-child voice, Elford said, "You're not resisting."

Victoria made a show of managing a grim smile. "I'm sure I will…when it really hurts," she said, feigning determination despite what was surely already overwhelming pain.

Elford's narrow mouth split with a smile. "Maybe this…" he whispered, as he returned his attention to her neck where he was threading filaments of bone from her spine to form an exoskeleton row of needle-sharp points.

He was like a laboratory rat, Victoria thought. Or one of Pavlov's dogs, she revised, when he began to drool a gush of warm liquid that ran down her naked chest and stomach. *Perhaps he'll be mine in six months*. When he slumped against her, his fat, rounded belly slopping against her own curved frame, she revised her thoughts again. He continued to slide down her until, a moment later, he was face down on the floor.

At the moment of Elford's slow descent, the door of the boxcar slid open several feet, revealing two figures standing outside. Even during the relatively short time of her captivity—short in terms of hours, perhaps, but interminable in the face of the horrors she'd endured—Victoria had almost forgotten the sensation of fresh air against her naked body—clean air, free of the taint of her jailer's fetid breath, or the odors of blood and sweat and torture.

The two figures climbed into the boxcar cautiously, surveying the interior in silence. They moved slowly toward Victoria and seemed to take no notice of Elford's sprawled, corpulent form, as if they were satisfied that he would pose them no risk. The pair, one male, one female, edged closer still; they stared intently at Victoria and, as if they shared one expression, deep scowls crossed both of their faces. Victoria was clearly not who or what they'd expected to find.

She could return their gazes only awkwardly, as her head was bound to the chair at a slightly uplifted angle. The man was very average looking, perhaps a bit taller than the norm; in his light safari jacket, he would've blended easily into a crowd—were it not for the visible scales covering his exposed hands, face, and neck, and the forked tongue that darted from his mouth every few seconds. He stared alternately between Victoria and the compact electronic device he held. Back and forth.

The woman was nondescript, pretty but not in a striking way, though perhaps that was not a fair distinction for Victoria to draw. Her eyes were hard and demanding, offsetting what beauty she did possess. Obviously impatient with her companion's indecision, she nudged Elford's body with her foot. No response.

"Is he dead?" Victoria asked. Then, effortlessly summoning and directing the snare of her potent charm at the perplexed male, she added, "Have you rescued me?"

He looked up at her immediately and stepped forward to work at her bonds. "Of course we have," he said, all but stating that to suggest anything else would be absurd.

Victoria smiled. This one, at least, did not possess the strength of will that had insulated Elford from such supernatural influence.

The woman's face registered incredulity. She spoke to Victoria's newly won servant with scorn: "What are you doing, Orthese? Do you *know* this woman? Listen to me! We have to find Vegel and his driver first. Does the cell-phone signal lead *here*? Stop that! You can go whoring later."

Victoria immediately understood the situation, if not the full explanation of why these Setites sought Vegel. She turned her attentions to the woman, who was, in Victoria's estimation, stronger—but not much.

"Vegel's phone is there on the floor," the Toreador said. She wagged a finger toward the dark corner where Elford had kicked the pieces. "I am Victoria, a great friend of the Setite clan and a great friend of Vegel's. Free me, and lead me to safety, and you may be my friends as well," she offered magnanimously.

The woman blinked, once, twice, then was busy helping her partner free Victoria. The Setites were now convinced that her rescue was more important than their original mission, presumably the recovery of Vegel—which meant that Hesha must have sent them. Which also meant they might have useful information about Hesha and Vegel and the party; information Victoria needed if she was ever going to see her way through the entanglements of that night. She still didn't understand the game Hesha and Vegel had been playing. But *someone* had betrayed her, had used and manipulated her, and that she could not abide.

But there would be time for that later. First things first, now that she was free of her bonds.

Victoria looked at the scaled man. "Break his neck," she said, indicating Elford's body, prone upon the floor. She wasn't certain how the Tzimisce had been felled—some poisoned dart, or a Setite spell, perhaps—but she'd rather he didn't awaken before she and her new coterie were gone.

The male Setite knelt beside the motionless Sabbat and wrenched Elford's neck until it was permanently skewed at an awkward angle—as much as any physical deformity was permanent for a Tzimisce.

Victoria's back ached terribly when she stood, but this discomfort and some lesser wounds were easily repaired when each of her new friends provided several mouthfuls of badly needed vitae, after Victoria innocently suggested the idea. She was tempted to take her due in blood from Elford, but her rescuers confirmed her suspicion that there was some type of Setite poison coursing through his body, and that was better left alone.

"Give me your jacket, please," Victoria told her scaled rescuer. He did so immediately, and it was just long enough to cover her nakedness. "How did you get here?" Victoria asked the woman.

"We have a plane waiting at a private airstrip. We must get back to Baltimore, to Hesha."

"Excellent." Victoria allowed them to lead her from the boxcar nestled in the midst of radiating rail lines. How many other victims of Elford's pleasures were secreted away in the freight yard? she wondered. And what fiendish arrangements secured them from mortal discovery during the daylight hours? There was no time to answer these questions, or to search for more prisoners. Even Vegel, from what the Setites said, might be here, maybe in one of the nearby boxcars.

That's his problem, Victoria thought. She and the Setites were getting out of town as quickly as they could, no detours for anything or anyone.

"Excellent," she said again. Prince Garlotte of Baltimore was an old *acquaintance,* another of those admirers whom she could call on in her time of need, and she might need some time to recover from this ordeal before she'd be ready to deal with a Setite of Hesha's acumen.

"Of course," the woman agreed. The man nodded his assent.

But as they turned to leave, a sudden urge took hold of Victoria. "Just a moment," she told them, and climbed back into the boxcar. It wasn't easy. She suppressed her desire to flee from the place of her imprisonment and torture. *Only a few seconds,* she promised herself, as she hunted for and found a pair of pliers that Elford had used to such grim effect on her. Victoria carried scars aplenty from her time with him—open wounds that didn't seem inclined to heal, painful protrusions of bone too numerous to count. She would carry his grisly visage in her mind for many years, long after she had healed the markers he'd left on her body. *If* she managed to heal them. But in these last few seconds before her escape, Victoria claimed a memento of her own choosing.

"Awaken, my sweet young murderer. I am sorry
that I cannot allow you to remain unconscious further. It is by far the simplest buffer against the pain,
but you are at present dangerously close to delirium,
and your legs will not knit if you continue to con-
vulse so. I trust you had pleasant dreams."

Vykos's smile was innocent and her gaze intent
upon him as if expecting, nay hanging upon, his response. She looked somehow different than he
remembered from their recent confrontation. Her features had a certain fawn-like cast to them. Her eyes
larger. Her face, warmer, softer. Her ears tapering gently.

No, not *fawn-like*, he corrected himself—*faun-
like*. She seemed a wild creature stepped from some
woodland bacchanal, still spattered with dew and
over-enthusiastic libations.

He could not hold her intent gaze. "One thing
only I wish to know," he croaked, struggling to find
his voice again. "The masters, you said the masters
knew of this abduction, that it had been arranged,
approved." He hurled the words like accusations.

Vykos looked pleased. "Oh good. You do remember." She squeezed his hand affectionately. "They had
led me to believe that you would deny it, rail against
it. But there is no shame in having been given. In fact,
it is a great honor that has been lavished upon you."

Parmenides could not believe what he was hearing. If the fiend's words were to be credited, she would
have him think that he was betrayed by his beloved

masters—his wise and just mentors, his protectors, his spiritual guardians, his brothers—into the hands of devils. And furthermore that he was to be proud, to be honored by this casual betrayal by those he loved above all else.

"An honor? Is it an honor to fall unavenged among your enemies? Is it an honor to be sold into the hands of your persecutor? Is it an honor to be denied even the dignity of the final…" Parmenides broke off abruptly, fearing that in his rush of emotion he had said too much, strayed too close to revealing one of the sacred mysteries to an outsider, a barbarian, one of the unilluminated.

"I knew you would see it that way." She beamed. "Your masters spoke very highly of you. They said that you were an instrument of keen perception and one which they could ill afford to lose. That is what makes their gift all the more touching."

He laughed then. It was a barking and scornful laugh. "They would not betray me. They would not betray me and suffer me to live." He realized even as he hurled these refutations against her that the two assertions were not at all the same thing.

With every new twist of this convoluted situation, he came face to face with the same realization. "I should not be alive."

"Do not speak so, my young romantic, my *philosophe*. Can you not see that this whole complicated orchestration has been arranged so that you might yet live?"

Parmenides did not see it. He made no response, but continued to regard her with open suspicion. He was uncertain from which front this new attack would come, but he would not be taken unprepared. This time.

"Your masters would not see you fall victim to the retributions of the hated Tremere. There is no greater indignity—not only for you, but for them as well. It is within my power to help them, to help you, my dearest. But you must let me help you."

"You will help me," he said flatly. "You will shield me from the dread Tremere. You will keep me here indefinitely, confined to a wheelchair, serving as a guinea pig for your demented experiments. Here, I have no doubt, even the Tremere will not venture. Here, I am perfectly safe, my every need provided for. Shall I thank you now? Or are there other debts I owe you of which I am as yet unaware? I would not want to appear ungrateful for your hospitality."

She regarded him quizzically. "You still do not understand, I think." She walked around to the back of his chair and took hold of the handles. "Even I do not plan to be here for more than a week at the most. And I am wasting valuable time setting and resetting your legs. But I am willing to invest this time in you because you are so dear to me. I am hoping, in fact, that you will chose to accompany me when I depart."

They wheeled around and began a slow circuit of the room. Apparently the servants Vykos had alluded to in their initial meeting had returned and hastily completed their unpacking. Or perhaps not so hastily. He had no idea how long he had been unconscious.

"I do not do these things so that you will feel indebted to me. I do them for the sake of the growing friendship between our peoples. Or at least, that was the reason I initially agreed to 'recycle' you for your masters.

"After you had arrived, of course, I had the additional pleasure of doing it for the sheer pleasure of your company and for the affection I hold for you. Do not shake your head. You are a rare jewel, my sensitive young killer. All cold calculation and poetry. I find your outlook, which I must admit is quite foreign to my own, refreshing.

"We are not so different, you and I. We are joined by our common passion. Our undying enmity for the foul Tremere will be a bridge between our two peoples. You will help me by removing certain obstacles—certain sorcerous obstacles—from my path. I will help you and your people in return by rehabilitating those of your brothers who are experienced at such dangerous work but who are put in dire peril by the very fact that they have succeeded in such a mission.

"Our peoples will forge an alliance before which the entire Cainite world will tremble, and we—you and I—shall be the peace-hostages, the ambassadors of good will, the glue cementing that relationship. It is a great and terrible responsibility. You have been honored above all of your kind, young Parmenides. Your name will, no doubt, echo through the secret places of the mountain many generations after your passing."

She is deranged, Parmenides thought. He had always been told that the Tzimisce were unhinged, warped from the moment of their Becoming. Rumors of the Sabbat's dark initiation rites, of neonates being buried alive and having to claw their way out of the grave or spend eternity entombed in the earth's arms—such mind-rending torments were parceled out even to the delicate Lasombra. The forging of a Tzimisce was an ordeal made of sterner stuff.

Parmenides was no stranger to harsh discipline. The rigors of his intense physical, mental, and spiritual training had left uncounted scores of his fellow novices—every one already enhanced with the supernal strength and endurance that were the birthright of his brotherhood—dead or begging for Final Death.

Even Parmenides, however, would rather summon up the Words of Undoing than undergo a single night of a Tzimisce apprenticeship.

The fiends' reputation for both physical and emotional sadism—and their unsettling power to inflict their demented predilections not only upon their own bodies, but upon those of their neighbors—made them universally feared and shunned.

If the Tzimisce were hard on outsiders, however, they were even more fearsome to their own kind. They were fiercely proud of their clan's mastery of the physical form and delighted in demonstrating their art and mastery at every opportunity. A Tzimisce novice was literally a captive audience to such inhuman experiments.

"And if I will not cooperate with this 'alliance'?" Parmenides challenged.

Vykos paused. "Oh, I will be so disappointed. I have already invested so much in your rehabilitation. I think you will be pleased. And your masters, they are relying upon you as well. It is a grave responsibility you must bear, as well as an honor. There is no honor without responsibility."

She wheeled him around to face the large hand-carved looking glass. It was made of blackened bog-oak and stood easily seven feet high. Parmenides recoiled in apprehension.

"Oh, I know it's a bit much. Overly dramatic. But I always keep several largish mirrors about the office. It has such a disarming effect on visitors, especially when one has numerous business contacts among the Lasombra. Makes them uncomfortable. Puts them off their game.

"Oh, you must forgive me. You are unfamiliar with their ways. I assumed that such interactions with our brothers in the Sabbat are commonplace to you, but I see that is not the case. I hope you will soon have the chance to meet them. Yes, I will have to arrange it at the earliest opportunity.

"The Trojans would have appreciated this dubious honor. For them, however, it would have been sufficient to beware of Greeks bearing gifts. With the Lasombra, you must have a caution of even of those of indifferent bearing. But you will see them for yourself and then you can judge whether I have spoken rightly."

Parmenides's gaze was locked on the mirror in open incredulity. He cursed himself for a fool, knowing he should have been prepared for just such an eventuality. But still, he could not stop himself from gaping.

The face that stared back at him was not his face. *Of course it's not our face*, a distant part of his mind scolded him, *our face is still sitting on the desk—draped over that war-trophy we carried from the Tremere chantry and laid at her feet like a sacrifice, an offering.* "A peace offering," he muttered aloud.

The fact that the internal voice seemed so rational, so composed, terrified him. The face that mouthed the words *a peace offering* belonged to the ghoul. The ghoul he had struck down and strode over when first entering this foul den. What had Vykos called him? Ravenna.

Parmenides's skin was no longer the enviable true ebony that was the trademark of the Assamite line— the legacy of decades of unrelenting, moistureless, desert climate working upon a complexion devoid of the normal healthy, ruddy undertone that was the outward sign of the humble miracle of circulation.

His new complexion was not unpleasant. It was the uniform olive of a gentler Mediterranean clime. His features deceptively placed his point of origin somewhere on the Italian peninsula. Parmenides found himself thinking, uncomfortably, of Venice.

"Well, what do you think?" Vykos prompted. "You must admit that even the devilish arts of the Tremere will not be able to penetrate such a disguise. Because it's not a disguise, really, when you come right down to it."

Parmenides nodded absently. Then his gaze traveled downward. He braced himself against the first glimpse of his maimed lower legs, but a neat red woolen blanket draped across his lap spared him the worst of it. Although he could not feel his feet he noted, with some distracted gratitude, that they were no longer fused together.

Taking the arms of the chair firmly in hand, he tried to push himself to his feet. He succeeded only in unbalancing the chair, tilting it dangerously forward. But Vykos's steadying hands did not allow him to overturn.

"No, do not try to rise, my dearest. You are still bound to the chair. Your legs will not bear you up and I have not the leisure at present to dedicate the coming nights to setting things right. Great things are afoot. I am afraid you will have to remain in the chair until," she paused as if carefully considering her words. "Until you have recovered enough to stand on your own."

Parmenides did not relish the thought of spending weeks, more likely months, in such confinement.

He threw the blanket in his lap to the floor with the intention of loosing the restraints that held him to the chair.

He immediately wished he hadn't. There were no restraints. He could not tell where the grisly chair ended and his lower body began. He sat unresisting as Vykos recovered the discarded blanket and smoothed it back into place. He stared blankly straight ahead.

"There, there. Soon you will be able to walk again. You have my word on it. I will not permit you to damage yourself beyond the point where that damage can be undone. But you must control your extreme emotions. Your passion will be your undoing. You must focus your impatience, your rage, your will upon remaking your broken body. Only then will you ever be free of this...."

She made an open gesture which might have been meant to indicate this chair, this room, this situation, or even this broken shell of a body.

"In the meantime, I have important work I need for you to do. No, do not argue. This work requires no great feats of leaping and bounding. You will do quite well with your current means of locomotion. Now listen and do whatever I shall tell you."

No response.

"If you will not do it for my sake, or for the sake of your own recovery, I am instructed to tell you this: that you will do it for the sake of the one who, diving toward green waters, catches his heel. You are given to know that he is a stone dropped upward into the river of night."

Parmenides bowed his head in resignation. Nor did he stir until he had received all the words that she had to entrust to him.

222

Friday, 25 June 1999, 11:58 PM
Oregon Hill
Richmond, Virginia

Three staccato crashes cut through the night. Don Carlos immediately recognized them as gunshots. They were fired several blocks away, but he had no way of knowing who had fired them. Were the mortal drug dealers, who refused to give up this neighborhood to the young couples who had moved in and renovated block after block of the turn-of-the-century homes, settling some score? Or was the gunplay part of the grand drama that was playing out with Don Carlos at its center?

He supposed that as long as everyone assumed the former, there was no danger to him. And wasn't that the whole point of this exercise that was unlife— to accumulate as much power and wealth while subjecting himself to as little actual danger as possible?

Don Carlos marched toward one of the houses that most distinctly had *not* been renovated. Prince Thatchet was patently resistant to the concept of progress in any guise. The old fossil, Don Carlos surmised, would prefer the entire city to crumble around him. He had probably felt right at home when the Yankees had bombarded Richmond to within an inch of its life a hundred and thirty-odd years before. Don Carlos had not been around back then, not even as a mortal, but from what he'd heard and from what he could see with his own eyes, those glory days of the Confederacy had been the last hurrah for this city. Yes, it had been rebuilt, but history had passed it by.

Only constant pressure exerted by the primogen and by the prince's own clanmates, those Ventrue enmeshed within the world of corporate banking and high finance, kept the city moving forward and keeping pace—falteringly, at that—with other emerging centers of vitality in the New South, such as Atlanta and Charlotte.

Otherwise, a larger portion of the city would more closely resemble the house Don Carlos approached, the prince's primary haven. Decades had passed since ever a paintbrush had touched those walls. The roof was intact, for the most part, and several windows retained actual unbroken panes of glass. The two obviously armed men standing guard on the front porch—Don Carlos knew them to be the prince's ghouls—lent the building the air of a crackhouse, but since the police department answered to the prince's beck and call, there was no danger of harassment on that front.

But other fronts remained available.

"You are sure he is there?" the albino had asked.

"I am sure," was Don Carlos's confident response.

The albino was a profoundly disturbing creature. Perhaps it was his eyes, the palest pink, that added to his Sabbat mystique, that made him somewhat unnerving even to other undead, those who had seen enough of the unnatural and the macabre that they should long ago have ceased to be squeamish about anything. Don Carlos had observed how the albino's own followers glanced uneasily at him, how they kept a certain distance as if his touch might be poisonous. And they were anything but normal themselves. Don Carlos had, of course, heard of the Sabbat since shortly after his Embrace, but he'd always considered the tales to be the Kindred equivalent of bogeyman stories intended to frighten unruly children—or childer, in this case—toward acceptable behavior. Now, having come face to face with actual specimens of the subject of those tales, he was no longer so sure. The vampires with whom he had associated previously had been members of the Camarilla, and while many of them were certainly monstrous in their own right, there was something...*different* about the albino and the few of his followers whom Don Carlos had seen. Something more—and something less.

More menacing. Don Carlos had survived as long as he had among more powerful Kindred because he had a knack for anticipating their wants and pleasures. More than once he had performed some minor favor for an elder before she even realized that she wanted the favor done. In so displaying his own ingratiating and foppish nature, he ensured, to a degree, his safety. Not that the elders or the prince trusted him, for they rightly perceived that his fealty rose from a self-serving appreciation of their station, rather than any particular loyalty to their person. Indeed, none of them would be surprised in the least to find Don Carlos taking the side of any prevailing faction. To the victor would go the spoils. Always. The trick was twofold: to know in advance who the victor would be, and to survive long enough to enjoy the spoils. The elders, constantly locked in schemes of conquest and one-up-manship, and knowing Don Carlos's transparently opportunistic nature, did not trust him. But they trusted that they could predict his actions, and thus in their eyes he was disarmed as a threat. He reaped the benefits of their struggles as surely as any vulture on a recent field of battle.

But this albino, this creature of the Sabbat, he was a wildcard, and knowledge of his actions gave Don Carlos an advantage over even his aged brethren of the Camarilla. The albino was more menacing because he was not part of the static power structure that provided Don Carlos's security. As an unknown, the creature was more dangerous, but also potentially more useful. Either eventuality stemmed directly from the second half of the equation—the albino was less predictable. Don Carlos had been constantly weighing the advantages and disadvantages of the developing situation since he was first contacted by agents of the Sabbat months ago. Was the body half empty or half full? He had decided that the possible benefits of cooperating with the Sabbat outweighed the dangers, and despite his qualms while in the actual presence of the disturbing albino, he still believed that to be the case. For the Sabbat to establish a presence in Richmond, they would need the assistance of someone who knew the city, who knew the habits and havens of those Kindred residing there. That someone was likely to receive certain considerations in return: the disappearance of a rival, inside information that would allow him to eliminate a "threat" to the prince. There was no shortage of ways, in Don Carlos's mind, that he could help the Sabbat, and they him.

The brief meeting with the albino merely served to introduce even loftier aspirations into Don Carlos's thoughts.

"We require a demonstration of your unfettered access to the prince," the albino had said.

Now, as Don Carlos trod closer to the prince's haven, a small microphone strapped to his chest beneath his shirt, his mind was full of the possibilities revealed to him. *They want to know how to get to the prince!* The audacity of the Sabbat amazed him. Not only did they wish to strengthen their presence in Richmond, they were laying the groundwork for what could only be the assassination of the prince at some future date. Knowing what was going to happen, Don Carlos reasoned, he might be able to position himself so as to influence the selection of the next prince. Looking farther down that road, he might be able to assume that mantle himself at some point. The mere thought made him giddy. Never before in his nights of endless scheming had Don Carlos felt so completely alive, so completely aware of the pulse of his city.

As he climbed the front steps, the ghouls on the front porch returned his nod. They were expecting him. Earlier that evening, he'd sent word that he had discovered important information that he must deliver to the prince at once. Respectfully, he petitioned for an audience. "The survival of the city may hang in the balance!" Don Carlos had included at the end of his note, resorting to a level of hyperbole he normally avoided, but thereby securing timely acceptance of his request.

The porch creaked under Don Carlos's weight. *How unseemly,* he thought, *for a prince to comport himself in such a manner. I will arrange things differently.* The ghouls seemed unaware of the tight-lipped smile that Don Carlos could not quite restrain.

He quickly mastered himself and was met inside by more ghouls, at least a half dozen. They were a sorry-looking lot, rattily dressed, unshaven, foul in both odor and demeanor, unconcerned with or unschooled in the most basic facets of decorum. But they were no less lethal for their ramshackle appearance. Prince Thatchet selected them—his corps of ghouls, for he trusted his own kind so little that he would have no Kindred for his bodyguard—for their adeptness with knife or gun. Theirs was not to receive dignitaries, and they maintained no illusions in that direction.

The interior of the house was as dilapidated as the exterior and smelled of mold and urine. Don Carlos walked past the hired toughs, ignored the more obvious stairs leading to the upper floor of the rickety structure—he'd been upstairs before; the rancid quarters where the ghouls rested were unpleasant to contemplate, much less to see first-hand—and opened the door to the cellar. This door, he noticed, was reinforced and remarkably sturdy compared to the rest of the building. He descended into the dank basement, harshly illuminated by one naked bulb hanging on a wire, and was greeted by Terrence Hill, personal assistant to the prince. A ghoul, of course.

"Don Carlos, the prince is expecting you." Noticeably well-kempt among the squalor, Hill tweaked the curled ends of his moustache as he spoke. The mannerism irritated Don Carlos to no end, but he nodded deferentially. This ghoul, after all, was older than Don Carlos and many of the other Kindred in Richmond. Apparently Prince Thatchet valued Hill's abilities so much that he would not Embrace him for risk of losing the service of a most loyal servant.

How demeaning to be a servant throughout eternity, thought Don Carlos, even as he waited patiently for the ghoul to announce him.

Hill slipped through another heavily reinforced door, his fleet manner belying the speed of his movements. Don Carlos's keen ears caught the muffled introduction: "My prince, Don Carlos of Clan Toreador to see you." And then the door was open again, and Terrence was ushering Don Carlos through into another dimly lit room.

"My prince." Don Carlos bowed deeply with a flourish—so low that he could clearly see the layers of black and gray mildew covering the hard-packed, earthen floor—and maintained that position. The door clicked shut as Terrence let himself out.

"Rise, Don Carlos." The prince's words were a throaty, nearly inaudible whisper.

The ghouls in the prince's employ, to the untrained eye, were fairly indistinguishable from normal, unadulterated mortals. The prince himself, however, could certainly be mistaken for a ghoul, in the classic sense of the word. Don Carlos, as soon as he rose, averted his eyes, as was the custom insisted upon by the prince. But even the most cursory glance at the seated figure was more than enough to refresh Don Carlos's memory of that sickly, yellowed skin, so pale as to seem translucent. Thatchet's sparse, patchy head of hair was somewhat reminiscent of the spines of a Venus flytrap, and despite the impression that the years—decades, or centuries, according to some—had not been kind to the prince, Don Carlos had heard many stories confirming that the prince was as deadly to Kindred as that plant he slightly resembled was to insects.

"Don Carlos," said the prince in that whisper that his petitioner had to strain to hear.

Does he speak like that on purpose? Don Carlos wondered. *Is he trying to intimidate me? Well, it won't work.*

"What news could be so important?" asked the prince. "Why do you trouble me?"

If Thatchet's voice had failed to unnerve Don Carlos, the words the prince spoke sent a chill down his subject's spine. Don Carlos had expected a warmer reception from the prince, perhaps interest if not enthusiasm. Instead, the Toreador now felt that he was the fly noticing only belatedly the ring of spikes and the rapidly closing exit behind him. Don Carlos cleared his throat, measured his words carefully.

"I bring news of the most vital importance to the welfare of the city," he said.

"So I have heard."

A drawn-out creak of wood indicated that the prince had shifted his weight in his chair, but was he settling back to listen, or rising from his seat to strike down the impudent childe? Don Carlos, straining the limits of peripheral vision, could not tell, and the prince said nothing else.

Or did he? *Did he say something, and I missed the damned whisper?* Don Carlos wondered. Just then he heard footsteps from upstairs, someone moving above. Maybe that was also the sound of a moment ago—footsteps, not the telltale shifting of the prince. The possibility did not, however, ease Don Carlos's mind overly much.

"I have received word from reliable sources," he said at last, unable to stand the weight of silence, "that the Sabbat has plans to overrun the city."

There. He'd said it. Don Carlos had planned all along to use that bit of information as a gambit to gain access to the prince. It was an incredible exaggeration of the truth that Don Carlos had deduced, but Thatchet would thank him, perhaps even ask him to look into the matter further, which would provide cover for Don Carlos in future interactions he might undertake with the Sabbat. Also, the albino, listening in on the wire tonight and in future meetings, could gather information about the prince and his defenses, information that Don Carlos could confirm or clarify after the fact.

Ah, he congratulated himself, *playing one side against the other, while I am the true master of both—as it should be.*

"And you believe that you have access to spies beyond my reach?" asked the prince.

Hearing the words, the veiled challenge and scorn they conveyed, Don Carlos suddenly felt his confidence sucked dry until it remained little more than a desiccated corpse. The prince's icy voice soaked down into the cracks of Don Carlos's courage. Thatchet, the Toreador realized, was a master in what he left *unsaid* as well as what he said, and the unsaid was poised like an axe above Don Carlos's neck.

The prince's brief, whispered question hovered in the air, daring Don Carlos to respond. The Toreador felt his knees trembling; he prayed that his nervousness—his *fear,* fear of this aged Kindred whose mere words unnerved him—was not completely obvious. How could this interview have gone so wrong from the start? he wondered.

Perhaps there was a reason this sickly, palsied creature had been Prince of Richmond for so long. Don Carlos had seen the awed reaction of mortals faced with his own undead magnificence. All reason fled; they were prisoners of their own trepidation. Now he began to recognize the same strange power that his prince held over him. But even recognizing it, he was no more able to combat it.

Frantically, Don Carlos struggled to divine some way to salvage his plans. Then his racing mind seized upon the answer. *I will tell him everything!* Don Carlos decided. *Instead of warning him of some potential future attack, which is undoubtedly the case, I'll tell him about the albino, about the other Sabbat monsters with him. The prince will know what to do.*

But then he realized the illogic of this plan—the wire beneath his shirt; the albino would flee, and Don Carlos would look the fool. The fearful trembling that had taken hold of his knees now spread throughout his body, or so it felt to him. He closed his eyes tightly, fought for self control.

Calm yourself, he thought, and reminded himself that only seconds—not the hours that it felt like—had passed since the prince had asked his question.

Delay...but be bold about it, he chastised himself. *Answer, but give yourself time to disable the microphone.*

Don Carlos bowed his head, trying to take advantage of the fact that his eyes were already closed, in a solemn display of deference. "My prince, certainly your reach and your knowledge extend further than mine. In this case, however..." Don Carlos faltered. He was seized by the sudden fear that he'd brazenly contradicted his prince, that he was signing his own death warrant.

Spit it out, man! he thought. *You've crossed the line. Go the full mile!*

"Yes, my prince." Don Carlos swallowed hard. He hoped the gulp was not audible except in his own ears. "I believe I have access to sources that would be…" *beyond your reach,* he almost said, but the impertinence of the words choked his throat shut. "That would be hidden from one of your station."

Don Carlos sighed inwardly, congratulated himself on that tortured turn of phrase, implying as it did treachery on the part of others rather than imperfection on the prince's.

A moment passed, then stretched longer, but the prince did not respond. Don Carlos opened his eyes, but did not raise his face. From that position, he saw only the prince's foot, firmly upon the floor.

Why doesn't he say something? Damn him! The trembling was resuming, growing more pronounced. Don Carlos was sure he would be unable to control it, to hide it from his liege. The silence gnawed at the Toreador's nerves, drained the last of his patience.

I will tell him everything! he resolved. *I will throw myself on his mercy.*

Don Carlos forced open his mouth to speak, but the words he heard were not from him, nor were they from the prince.

Instead, the voice was that of a man, a large man, deep rumbling baritone, but trying to mimic a small child: "Can I play too?"

For the moment, forgetting himself and all protocol, Don Carlos whirled to see Terrence Hill's head protruding from behind the door, which was only slightly ajar. But the voice was not the ghoul's, and his expression was wrong: his eyes bulged; his mouth, hanging agape, bobbed up and down, but not in time with the words.

Then the door swung the rest of the way open, and Don Carlos saw the clenched fist around Hill's neck, and the hulking figure to whom the fist belonged. The creature had to duck to enter the room and dragged Hill like a lifeless doll, which was more or less the case. Behind the behemoth stood the albino, a stern look on his face, and behind him, others still, darting back and forth to look over his shoulders.

The fact of Sabbat vampires standing in the prince's lair was too much for Don Carlos to comprehend at first. A full three seconds passed before he thought to look to the prince. Surely the elder Kindred would strike down the intruders.

Another moment passed, however, and the prince did not move. Not when the albino pushed his way into the room, not when the behemoth threw Terrence's body to the ground, revealing that the ghoul's neck had been wrung much like an unruly gamecock's—his head looked to have made two full rotations.

Only at second glance did Don Carlos notice that the shadows enveloping his prince were too dark; they intruded where the light of the one small lamp in the room should have fallen. And though the lamp was stationary, the shadows moved. They writhed in coils around the prince's body, wriggled like snakes of pure darkness, constrictors holding Thatchet's arms and legs to his chair. A flowing band of oily black covered the lower portion of his face, but his wide eyes and the faintest of gagging sounds from his throat suggested that the shadows given life delved internally as well. For the first time in his undead existence, a vague queasiness began to rise in Don Carlos's gut.

The albino, a hacksaw in hand, stepped past him. The behemoth moved further into the room and the space, which had been quite adequate before, seemed suddenly very small. Two other Sabbat creatures followed the albino in: one, a spidery, bow-legged thing, emaciated to the point that it seemed every bone was visible, and with darkened skin, as if it had been burned to a crisp but then removed from the oven at the last second before total immolation; the other, hidden almost completely beneath a long-sleeved coat and brimmed hat pulled low, despite the summer heat.

"My prince," droned the albino, mocking the conversation upon which he'd electronically eavesdropped, "forgive the intrusion, but your assistant said that we could see you." He gestured toward Terrence's blankly staring body, then raised an eyebrow at Thatchet's nonexistent reply. "Perhaps he was mistaken," he said in the same dry tone, completely devoid of emotion. "He does seem a bit wound up. Perhaps a vacation is in order."

Don Carlos could only stand and blink, dumbfounded. The spidery creature tittered at the albino's poor joke. The behemoth seemed unaware of the attempt at humor, but laughed once because his companion did.

The ghouls? Don Carlos wondered. *Where are all the guards?*

"There will be no further intrusions," said the albino to Don Carlos, as if telepathically aware of the question.

Don Carlos glanced again at Hill. *All the guards…and no sounds of struggle.* The *coup d'etat* he had envisioned was not going to occur at some future date. It was happening now.

"You Camarilla types all have the same problem,"

the albino said matter-of-factly. He stepped to within
a foot of the captive prince. "You fear your elders too
much." He raised the hacksaw, briefly inspected the
blade in the dim light, and then placed it against
Thatchet's left arm just below the elbow. The con-
fining shadows, without freeing the prince's arm,
parted before the saw teeth.

The albino began to work the saw, forward and
back, forward and back, and it sliced neatly through
the flesh. Don Carlos looked away—he might feast
on mortal blood, but that was a far cry from this raw
butchery—but he could not hide from the nerve-
wracking sound of the hacksaw blade as it grated
against bone.

"Hmm," said the albino to himself. "Radius or
ulna? I can never remember. No matter. They'll both
have to go."

The grating sound resumed, more forcefully this
time. He finished the first bone and began the second. This time, however, the rhythmic sawing ended
with a ragged snap.

"Damn. I'm afraid I've made a mess of this one,"
the albino muttered. "But you know what they say:
practice, practice, practice."

A dull thud by Don Carlos's feet attracted his
attention. He looked down to see the prince's left
hand and forearm, a jagged splinter of bone protruding toward where the elbow should have been.

Don Carlos jumped back and, against his better
judgment, glanced at the prince, not where the albino was beginning to saw on the other arm, but at
Thatchet's face. If he'd tried to scream, the sound
had not penetrated the veil of shadow enclosing his
mouth. His eyes were wide with pain, but that was

not all. Don Carlos expected to see fear, and regret at the end of what might have been eternal existence. Instead, all that mingled with the pain in those straining eyes was hatred. Thatchet stared not at the albino, or the progressing ruin of his own right arm. He'd fixed his glare on Don Carlos, and the hatred in those eyes was as much, or more so, for the Toreador as for the beasts of the Sabbat.

"There." The albino held up the prince's right hand. "You see, my Camarilla friend. Your elders are nothing to fear once they're properly disarmed."

The spidery thing twittered again. Its laughter was like fingernails along a chalkboard. The behemoth guffawed like a giant idiot-childe, and all this time the Sabbat obscured by coat and hat stood in silence.

"Delona, fetch my toolbox, and an extension cord," said the albino. His white skin was speckled with blood, though there was little enough on the floor, all things considered. Apparently the prince had not fed recently, for little blood ran from the stumps, which were already beginning to heal over thanks to the potency of vampiric vitae.

The spider-thing loped out of the room, but the albino abruptly changed his mind and called her back. "We don't have that much time, I'm afraid."

Just as abruptly, the albino's attention and his disturbing, pink-eyed gaze shifted to Don Carlos.

Don Carlos was trying mightily to deny that which he'd seen. But the severed arms, the second of which the albino now dropped to the floor, would not go away, and the Sabbat monsters stood undeniably all about.

"You're leaving, then," Don Carlos asked, finally

finding his voice, but trying not to sound too hopeful.

The albino nodded. "There's little else to be done in Richmond. Within the hour, not one Camarilla elder will survive here."

The bold statement took a moment to sink in. *Not one Camarilla elder...*

Again, Don Carlos realized his mistake. Just as this was no covert scouting mission in preparation for a future coup, neither was it a mere surgical strike to leave the Kindred of the city leaderless.

Not one Camarilla elder will survive here.

If what the albino said was true, if every elder were destroyed, such a purge would lead those of Don Carlos's generation to take hold of the reins of leadership. He was willing to begin his ascent to power as a pawn of the Sabbat, for a pawn, in time, could be converted to a queen—or in this case, a prince.

"You will need someone to stay behind here, to keep tabs on the new leadership in the city," suggested Don Carlos. "They will be weak at first, but a contact on the inside will be invaluable in time."

And in time, Don Carlos thought, *I will squeeze you out.*

The albino didn't respond, but instead turned back to Prince Thacket, still prisoner to the shadow incarnate. Grabbing one of the wisps of hair and pulling the prince's head back, the albino placed the saw blade on the top ridge of his captive's larynx—"I'm afraid the blade is a bit more dull that it was"—and began to saw.

Slowly.

Each stroke, back and forth, sent tremors through the prince's body. His eyes bulged until Don Carlos thought they would pop from their sockets. But still the shadow held the prince functionally immobile, helpless.

Don Carlos closed his eyes, and when he opened them the albino, a pale Perseus having vanquished the gorgon, held aloft the head of the prince, his face finally free from shadow.

"I need no contact on the inside," said the triumphant albino, smiling for the first time that Don Carlos had seen. The sight struck cold into his undead heart. "For there will *be* no inside. We do not strike here and destroy the elders of your city, only to move on and allow you to continue, with only the names of the Camarilla weaklings in charge having changed.

"Tonight we stomp you out. All of you."

Don Carlos began to protest, but there was a great pressure on his neck. He was being lifted off his feet by the behemoth's hand around his throat. And already the albino had forgotten him, discarded like so much rubbish.

I can help you! Let me help you! Don Carlos wanted to say, but the voice was choked out of him.

"This should be enough to put me ahead of Hardin in our little wager," said the albino as he stared at the prince's head. Then he turned and looked thoughtfully at Don Carlos. "Maybe one more."

The Big Enchilada.

Hardin wasn't too impressed with D.C., not yet anyway. It was too quiet, too tranquil, for his tastes. There were sirens blaring in the distance, at least every ten or fifteen minutes it seemed, and though he was twenty yards from the squat little bar across the street, the bass line of some old Sammy Hagar song reverberated in his chest. Still, something was missing.

Hardin had heard that everything in Washington was either squalor or splendor, that there was no middle ground. This was a rough, working-class neighborhood, the kind that clung to the fringes around places of power. The low buildings were mostly cinderblock or old brick, and all sported either bars or metal doors to cover any glass. He suspected he'd like the splendor even less.

The handful of bystanders outside the bar didn't take much notice of Hardin as he crossed the street. With every two steps, the neon sign in the window flashed on and off:

Purgatory

Purgatory

Purgatory

How fucking cute, he thought. *Isn't that just like a Camarilla crowd?* They huddled behind their little Masquerade for protection from mortals—*Mortals! Fucking ATM machines for a blood bank*—then couldn't resist leaving nudge-nudge-wink-wink clues for those in the know.

Purgatory

Purgatory

With each step, with each flash of the sign, Hardin grew more pissed off. *They're just too stupid—too fucking cute—to live.*

There were enough motorcycles parked out front that Hardin would've pegged the place as a Brujah hangout even without the "Vampires 'R' Us" flashing sign. *At least you know what you're getting with Brujah,* he thought. *Somebody that wants to kick your ass. Maybe he's got a reason, maybe he doesn't. Doesn't really matter.*

At least the Brujah had guts. And the Anarchs, some of them had guts, the ones that weren't whiny little pissants. In fact, Hardin preferred some of the rough-and-tumble Camarilla types to his own Lasombra elders, who tended toward the high-falutin' end of the scale. The Brujah might have a chance—in general; not the ones inside the bar tonight.

Purgatory

Purgatory

"Purgatory, my hairy ass," Hardin muttered as he stepped into the crowded bar.

He stopped just inside the door. The music, loud when he was across the street, drowned out all but shouted conversations, and the smoke in the room served nearly as well as any shadows Hardin might summon. He didn't attempt to shove his way farther in. Instead, he relaxed and let his vision unfocus—distinct forms became less so, lines blurred, and the many figures before him took on quite different aspects. The scene was not completely unlike a twisting kaleidoscope; the thick smoke seemed to take on different colors and patterns, further confusing the already chaotic atmosphere, but through this clouded filter, Hardin saw what was hidden from normal sight—who was mortal, or ghoul, or Cainite. The distinctions were not always clear or precise, some requiring more interpretation than others. The colors and patterns shifted, one into another into another, and many of the patrons in the bar were moving about as well.

But Hardin didn't need exact information, just a broad impression.

The front of the bar was filled mostly with mortals, maybe a ghoul or two thrown in. Toward the rear of the establishment, amidst the densest of the smoke and shadows, were vampires. At least six or seven, maybe a couple more.

Hardin let his eyes refocus, then turned with a tight smile to one of the patrons closest to him, who might've been a ghoul, a watchdog for the Cainites toward the back, or not. Hardin wasn't sure that she was, this woman in cut-offs and half-shirt, but there was a chance. With a deft flick of his wrist, a now-open butterfly knife appeared in his hand. He placed his other hand on her shoulder, then plunged the blade into her abdomen just below the navel. Her face registered surprise at first, and above the noise and confusion, no one else in the bar seemed to realize what he had done. Even when he sliced upward with inhuman strength and speed through her belly, bra, and throat, and she collapsed to the floor, there was only confusion from other patrons, not alarm—another drunk puking or passed out. If some noticed the blood, their warnings were drowned out by the music.

Desmond and Rojo pushed past Hardin, as did Jake, Greasy, and Amber, forming a wall across the width of the bar. As one, they pulled out their sawed-off shotguns and opened fire.

The first blasts cut a huge swath through the clientele. Bodies, glass, tables exploded. The second volley had much the same effect. Hardin marveled at how quickly the front half of the establishment had emptied without anyone getting out the front door. Those customers who weren't dead were lying wounded or diving for cover.

For the first time, screams rose above the music, which had moved on to the crooning of the Righteous Brothers.

"And there's no tenderness, like before, in your fingertips."

Two howling Brujah launched themselves like missiles from the shadows in the back, but the gunmen had missed not a beat in reloading, and the concerted blast of five shotguns stopped the two Kindred and sent them hurtling in the opposite direction.

"You're trying hard not to show it, ba-by...."

Hardin's men concentrated their fire on the rear of the bar, but with the spray and rapidity of the shots, not an inch was free of the devastating fire—only behind the bar. And Hardin was ready when the bartender rose with a shotgun of his own.

"You've lost that loving feeling, whoa-oa, that loving fee-ee-ling...."

Hardin's falchion split the bartender's Adam's apple before he could pull the trigger.

"You've lost—"

Amber blew through the bar with her next three blasts, just in case, and the music stopped. From out back, more gunfire erupted. Hardin smiled. Lonnie and the others were doing their job, blocking the rear exits from outside.

A few more rounds finished it. Even those, Kindred or kine, who'd been cowering behind overturned tables were shredded. Rojo and Desmond pumped round after round in the prone bodies—no sense giving a vampire a chance. None of the Camarilla sots present, assuming they were armed, had even gotten off a shot.

A noticeable silence settled over Purgatory.

"Two minutes, boys," said Hardin. "Get what blood you can, then we're gone." He thought for a moment about collecting a few more heads, but he didn't want to stick around and fight the police. Besides, there were plenty more Kindred in D.C., and the fun was just beginning.

Sunday, 27 June 1999, 12:05 AM
The Arcanum Chapter House, Georgetown
Washington, D.C.

Chancellor Abrahm Yrul made sure that the front gate clicked securely closed, then he turned toward his car parked on the street. The security of the chapter house was no small matter. That was an issue he harped upon with some regularity with the other Arcanists.

"What about our *personal* security?" Geoffrey Truesdell had asked earlier that very night. "We should build a below-ground parking garage, so we don't have to walk along the street late at night."

It was true that the Arcanists tended to come and go at all hours of the day and night. Research, even lacking an all-too-rare breakthrough, could so easily displace one's sense of time, as Abrahm well knew. This had been a long day—three long days, in fact, since he'd left the chapter house. Some associates swore that he lived in the chapter house, and Abrahm wondered himself sometimes if they weren't correct.

But an underground parking garage was most certainly not the answer.

"Do you know how many byzantine zoning ordinances and bureaucratic offices we would have to negotiate to do something like that?" Abrahm had asked. "In addition to which, we would have to relocate the vaults, expose the chapter house to outside contractors, devise security for a *larger* access...." He'd counted off his reasons on the fingers of one hand and moved onto the second.

Of course, they were all aware of and concerned about the violence that had broken out in the southern portions of the city last night—no, that wasn't true, he realized; there were several Arcanists who were completely immersed in their studies, who had been for a number of days, and had absolutely *no* idea whatsoever about happenings in the wider world beyond the chapter house walls. But the *majority* of the Arcanists had heard about the apparently drug-related violence that had broken out down toward the waterfront and then spread like wildfire. Furthermore, there were reports that more bloodshed had erupted tonight.

Abrahm scanned the empty street. The situation was certainly one to keep abreast of, but this was Georgetown, and none of the incidents had been within five miles of the chapter house. Abrahm felt better, nonetheless, when he was safely within his Jaguar and the electric locks sank down, securing the vehicle.

The tap on his window startled him. There'd been no one else on the street, but here was a strange man patiently tapping his index finger on Abrahm's window. The man's finger was stark white, as was his face. His pink eyes loomed just beyond the glass.

How did I miss seeing him? the chancellor wondered. How indeed? The man, obviously an albino, practically glowed in the dark. Regardless, Abrahm had no desire to lower his window and speak to the man; conversely, he didn't want to appear rude. In way of compromise, Abrahm nodded politely, but then continued to insert his key in the ignition.

The white hand smashed through the window in a spray of glass and latched onto Abrahm Yrul's throat. The Jaguar's horn sounded briefly as the chancellor's knee pressed against the steering wheel.

Silence quickly returned to the empty car, the keys still in the ignition.

Barely had the plane come to rest on the tarmac than Parmenides-Ravenna and Vykos were whisked away in the waiting limousine. "A lovely evening for a tour of the monuments, don't you think?" Vykos asked, tracing a finger along the inner edge of Parmenides's knee.

She was quite proud of that knee, having constructed and reconstructed it numerous times over the past few nights. He could walk now, with some difficulty and the aid of a brass-crowned cane. Even so, the degree of his recovery had been remarkable.

"I know it's dreadfully uncomfortable, but it is your own fault," she had reminded him time and again. "I had planned for you to be completely recovered, up and about, your old self again—so to speak—by this time." His lengthy and vehement resistance to her affections, she pointed out, had "needlessly complicated matters, and caused unnecessary pain." This last she had said with a certain beatific smile playing across her features.

Parmenides had ignored those comments, and he ignored her question now about the monuments. He was well aware that it would be a lovely evening for whatever Vykos wanted it to be a lovely evening to do.

"Oh, no sulking, now." She touched his chin. "I can put a smile on your face," she said slyly.

It was true, of course. She could—and would—do anything to his physical form that she pleased. He imagined a smile would be only a slight matter, but assumed she would not take the time at present, though more than one of her passing fancies had proven (to her) worth the investment of several hours over the past nights.

Despite her playful threat, Parmenides busied himself staring out the window, ignoring not only his hostess but also the reflection in the glass, the image that was, but was not, his own. He had taken to silence, to whatever solace he could find there, since his transformation. Vykos be damned. But of course, it was Parmenides who was damned more completely, handed over to the fiend by his own. His mind was still unable, perhaps *increasingly* unable, to fathom the situation. There was no firm purchase, not even his own reflection, around which to construct a reasonable version of reality. And so he stared silently, silence being his only fortress, his only defiance— knowing full well that if his new master wished, she could with little difficulty pull down those walls as well.

They passed the Washington Monument, "a lovely mortal trinket," he heard Vykos call it. She seemed able and more than willing to carry the conversation on her own. Her voice trailed in and out of Parmenides's awareness, much as it had since that moment when he had felt her teeth at his throat. Was that really only a handful of nights ago? It seemed to him longer than the arduous years of his training, longer than the span of his mortal and undead years together. He no longer knew if the sounds he heard were words actually spoken or the echo of her voice filling the gaps of his addled mind. He tried to retreat further within, but was drawn back to her by firm pressure on his miraculous and semi-functional knee.

"*There* is a true monument," she said.

The limousine had slowed to a near crawl. Parmenides looked beyond the glass, beyond that other face, but saw only a large house gutted by fire. Vykos's admiration of the rubble puzzled him, but less so than had she been anyone else in the world. As intimate as their contact had been, he could no more unravel her thoughts than return to his mortal life.

They continued on their way, the limousine winding through narrow streets tight with parked cars on either side. Parmenides had not noticed when they'd left behind the part of the city crowded with monuments and museums—sometime before the burned building—but they were well away from it now.

Shortly, the car slowed again and then stopped. The reflection of dancing lights drew Parmenides's attention. He turned from his window to see another scene of destruction, this time, however, still ongoing. At the end of the next block, a row of brownstones burned uncontrollably. Fire engines blocked the street; sparkling arcs of water erupted into the night and fell with little effect amidst the flames. Sweating men in helmets and thick jackets busied themselves. Perhaps they would be able to contain the blaze to that block. Perhaps not.

Vykos's breast rose and fell with a deep sigh.

"The destruction of mortal architecture is a trivial thing," said Parmenides. His words, less biting than he intended, sounded vaguely pathetic. Their strength seemed blunted by the confines of the limousine, the insulated nature of the compartment that muted the sounds of the nearby inferno almost completely.

Vykos turned to him with an endearing smile.

"You do live, my *philosophe*." She gently cupped a hand to his cheek. "And your mind quite intact. I knew you were made of sterner stuff." Sterner than what, she did not say.

She returned her attention to the blazing building. "You are absolutely correct, of course. So insightful." She turned from the fire long enough to pinch his cheek. "One of the reasons you're so dear to me.

"Mortal constructs are so fleeting," she added. "But this..." she tapped the window for emphasis, "this is a *true* monument—a monument to the Ventrue prince of this city."

Her words plunged Parmenides into chaos. He had the feeling again that Vykos's words had danced through his mind without first crossing the space between them. The fire and smoke gave way to a swirling mass of colors.

Vitel.

The name rose of its own accord, as if from the hidden flames.

Vitel.

"Yes," Vykos said gently. "Marcus Vitel."

Parmenides didn't realize that he'd spoken the name aloud, but she had answered. And now he found himself with his head in her lap, a childe seeking comfort. She stroked his hair.

"This was his haven," Vykos said. "*One* of his havens."

"And the other building..."

"Yes, dearest. But don't worry yourself yet."

Her fingers massaged his temples, soothed the pounding that he'd come to accept as a part of consciousness.

Vitel. Marcus Vitel. Prince.

Parmenides opened his eyes. He was sitting upright beside Vykos. The limousine was again moving. They traveled mile after mile; residences gave way to professional buildings gave way to strip malls gave way to pawn shops and liquor stores....

Alongside the shifting external scenery, Parmenides shifted through the mileposts of his mind, trying to pin down the thoughts that had exerted themselves.

Vitel. Prince Vitel.

But there was more. Somewhere in the depths of his mind, there was more. Of this he was certain—as certain as he could be of anything anymore. The car pulled to a halt. Before Parmenides could completely separate himself from his internal landscape, Vykos opened the door, and the world beyond assaulted all his senses at once.

The limousine had been so calm, quiet, a tranquil world of its own. Beyond those confines, chaos raged. The smell of smoke demanded his notice at the same instant as did the sound of distant sirens. They had stopped at yet another burning building. *Another haven—Prince Vitel.* How many hidden lairs might the prince of such an important city have? Possibly dozens, Parmenides knew. This building, or what was left of it, appeared to be some relic of the quaint history the Americans prized so highly.

Climbing out of the limousine was neither easy nor painless, but Parmenides felt compelled to follow Vykos. There were others on the scene—all Sabbat, most notably an expressionless albino and a shorter Cainite absently twirling a knife between his fingers. They paid no attention to Parmenides, a slight at which he began to take umbrage before realizing that he was no longer a representative of Clan Assamite in their eyes—perhaps even in his own. He was Ravenna, ghoul and servant to Lady Sascha Vykos. Unacknowledged, he hobbled to her side.

"This was the stiffest resistance yet," said the albino. He handed Vykos a large sack, which was conspicuously blood-soaked. "One of the prince's bitch childer. Now you're only one up," he said to his companion with the knife.

No one seemed to be worried about witnesses. Parmenides spotted several figures darting in and out of the shadows up and down the block. Apparently, potential witnesses were being taken care of. Parmenides noted, too, that the sirens he had heard were actually receding into the distance.

"It'll be a while before police or fire crews get here," said the albino, guessing Parmenides-Ravenna's thoughts. "They've got plenty to keep them busy."

As these words were spoken, it became apparent to Parmenides that there were other fires, *many* other fires, some burning nearby and probably others spread across the city. The smoke formed an ever-shifting shroud across the sky. He could taste the ash that coated the ground like a fine dusting of snow.

Prince Vitel.

One of his havens.

"Very good," Vykos said. "Finish up here and move along." Still looking at the albino, she handed the bloody bag to Parmenides—"Come, Ravenna"— then turned back to the limousine.

Vykos barely glanced at the head in the sack.

"They're just like little kittens bringing me a trophy mouse," she said of the albino and his companion. If she'd made the same comparison of Parmenides upon their first meeting, she did not mention it now.

Since the sanctuary of the limousine had been broken, Parmenides could no longer block out what seemed to him a world of violence that faced him from just beyond the reflected visage in the window. He was accustomed to violence, of course, and death—at least he had been—but the fires, the billowing smoke, the sound of gunfire, the bodies in the street, all served to disturb him. Perhaps it was the faint but incomprehensible voice in the back of his mind, droning endlessly, that unsteadied him. Or perhaps Ravenna was not so immune to such atrocities as had been Parmenides. The miles and minutes fused hopelessly together.

Vykos sensed his unease. "It *is* only the second night of Sabbat rule," she pointed out with a dismissive flourish, as if to imply that her benevolent reign would soon restore peace and order.

When the limousine again stopped, they were back near the Mall. Vykos gazed admiringly at the Washington Monument for a moment. "I doubt I could have done better myself," she said. "Who but the Americans would erect a giant phallus in honor of the father of their country?" She shrugged and opened the door.

The street before the Presidential Hotel was a scene more normal than most of those Parmenides had seen this long night—normal at first glance. A uniformed doorman stood before the main entrance of the hotel. There was an unusual amount of activity, as every few minutes a police car or ambulance raced past, lights flashing and siren wailing. Parmenides's practiced and preternatural vision, however, picked out details that any mortal and many Cainites would have missed: a heavy shadow clung to the sides of the hotel, a coat of black in addition to the regular darkness; and near where the limousine had stopped stood another uniformed man—not the uniform of the hotel doorman, or a D.C. police officer, but the dark, battle panoply of a legionnaire of Cardinal Ambrosio Luis Monçada of Madrid.

The legionnaire bowed slightly. "Councilor Vykos." Like the others, he paid no attention to the ghoul Ravenna. "We have him trapped inside." His words were grim, and tinged with but a hint of professional pride.

"Trapped?" said Vykos with raised eyebrow. "I think not, Commander Vallejo."

Vallejo seemed taken aback by her casual dismissal of the situation as he knew it, but didn't let this sidetrack him. "We've had him cornered for just over an hour, but have not closed in—as per your orders."

"I see."

"He has requested a parley, Councilor Vykos."

Both eyebrows raised this time. "Has he now? That devil."

Vallejo clearly objected to her flippant manner. He even deigned to glance at Ravenna briefly, perhaps seeking reinforcement of the seriousness of the situation.

"Shall I give the order to terminate, Councilor?"

Vykos ran her tongue over her upper lip. "I think not yet." Then, "A parley…"

"Councilor Vykos," Vallejo said quickly, suddenly

TZIMISCE

very concerned, "you can't be considering—" He stopped in response to Vykos's pointed stare; he knew better than to tell her what she could or could not consider.

"Pull your men back, Commander. I shall face the Prince of Washington." She held up a hand to forestall Vallejo's protestations. "He has nothing to gain by killing me."

"And nothing to lose," Vallejo added, but beyond that, he did not try to dissuade her. "What do *we* have to gain?" he asked.

"*We*," Vykos said, "might gain a captive—perhaps even a cooperative—Camarilla prince, rather than another corpse, of which I believe we already have a sufficient supply."

"Ravenna," she said abruptly, "get the phones and the…trophy from the car."

Parmenides-Ravenna hurried to do her bidding, though each step was agony, and the support of the cane did nothing to relieve the stiffness of every muscle from his feet to his hips. There were, in fact, two cell phones in the limo, and the trophy he was quite familiar with already.

"Now," said Vykos, sliding one phone into a deep pocket, "I will parley with the prince. I suspect he will want to see his childe," she gestured toward the bloody sack, "one of his *daughters*, as I believe he refers to them. Hm. How quaint."

She paused and thought for a moment, then continued. "I will call down shortly. If I have ascertained certain weaknesses, I will ask for Vallejo to bring up the prince's daughter. In that case, Commander, give your legionnaires the order to advance, and we will capture him."

"Yes, Councilor."

"Otherwise," said Vykos, "if I wish to speak with him further, I will call for Ravenna to bring up the prince's daughter. Then, when we leave, you may attack and destroy him."

Vallejo nodded again.

Parmenides took a step back, a strange, rubbery feeling taking hold of his legs. Only the cane kept him from toppling over in the street. Neither Vykos nor Vallejo seemed to notice his sudden infirmity. The pounding was at his temples again, from nowhere, suddenly more painful than it had ever been.

Do you understand?

The words echoed in his mind. Or had Vykos just spoken them? Parmenides couldn't tell. He stared at the sidewalk, fearful that if he looked up, it would shift beneath his unsteady feet.

Do you understand?

He nodded his head, still not sure whether he responded to sound or memory.

Good.

Vykos was no longer by his side. She walked past the doorman, who didn't acknowledge her, who actually looked the other way as if he hadn't seen her at all. Quite possible, Parmenides knew. Not such an extraordinary trick of the undead.

Vallejo, too, had stepped away. How far, Parmenides didn't know. The world was spinning. He was doing his best merely to remain upright. And always the words, always they were telling him, calling him....

I will call for Ravenna.

Vitel. Prince Marcus Vitel.

The voice in his mind was speaking to him, was

moving to the fore. It was a familiar voice, a soothing voice.

*I will call for Ravenna, and you will kill Vitel. Prince
Marcus Vitel.*

Vykos. She had told him all this before, what
seemed so long ago. And still the words were with
him.

You will kill Vitel.

Parmenides reeled. The cane. If he could just
hold the cane tightly enough, he might not fall. His
fingers gripped the brass head, brushed over the unobtrusive latch that, if he pressed it, would spring
the spike from the ferrule. The cane would become a
three-foot oaken stake with a brass tip and, at the far
end, a brass handle to aid in driving home a blow. He
had known but not known.

You will kill him, my *philosophe.* She had touched
his face. *You will kill him for me.*

A police car rushed past. The lights shone
through Parmenides's eyelids. He didn't remember
closing his eyes. The siren's wail pierced his fog of
recollection, rattled in his ears, but could not drive
away the voice that was closer than his innermost
desire.

You will kill him for me.

Where was Vallejo? Parmenides wondered.
Could the Lasombra tell that something was wrong?
Could he tell that Parmenides was going mad? Would
the legionnaire catch Ravenna if the ghoul collapsed
to the sidewalk? *Why not him?* For a moment,
Parmenides was afraid that he had shouted the question into the night. He couldn't be completely sure
that he hadn't. *Why not the legionnaire? He could kill
Vitel.*

Vykos's playful laughter struck him like a blow—or was it another siren, an ambulance racing by, or a fire engine?

Yes, Vallejo could kill him, she agreed, *but he is the cardinal's man. The glory would go to the cardinal. If I am to reap the rewards of the city, then the telling blow must be struck by my hand—or by my assassin. My philosophe.*

Parmenides had raged against her then. Again, he'd torn his bonds, though they were crafted of his own flesh. How dare she have treated him so, and for so petty an end!

Oh, that is not the end, my young romantic. That is merely the beginning.

His heart burned. He would tear it from his breast and cast it into the fires of hell before he laid it in her hand.

But I've already held it in my hand. Hush, my Ravenna. You have tired yourself. Rest, my Ravenna.

Rest, my Ravenna.

Rest. Ravenna.

Ravenna.

"Ravenna!"

Vallejo gripped his shoulder, dug his nails into Ravenna's skin. "The phone." The Lasombra spoke firmly. There was no cruelty in his voice, in his face; he merely could not abide weakness. Neither could Parmenides…before.

"The phone, Ravenna."

The phone, indeed, was ringing. Ravenna held it before him as if revealing a murder weapon for all to see. Vallejo stared at him, waited.

Damn you. You don't know, Parmenides thought. Then strangely enough, standing there before the

hotel, buzzing phone in hand, an unfamiliar sentiment rose within him, one he had not known in
centuries—compassion. *You don't know...may you
never know.*

He looked into Vallejo's face hoping to find pity
in return for his unspoken compassion, but was
greeted by the hard expectation that duty be fulfilled.
The will drained from Parmenides-Ravenna. The
phone moved closer to his face. It was his own hand
raising it. He pressed the "talk" button, but did not,
could not, himself speak.

"Ravenna, the prince would like to see his daughter. Do bring her up."

The phone was gone. Vallejo took it from him.
Ravenna bent toward the sidewalk, his weight fully
upon the cane, and retrieved the sack. He'd set it
down at some point. It left a bloody mark on the sidewalk.

The doorman took no more notice of him than
of Vykos before. Parmenides, even in his early nights,
could have affected the mortal similarly, but tonight
there was no strength left in the Assamite-ghoul. He
moved stiffly past, each step confirming the imper-
fect alignment of ligament and bone. The hotel lobby
was deserted save for the attendant behind the front
desk, and she paid him no heed. Ravenna followed a
trail that Vykos had laid down for him, and mortal
eyes could see neither trail nor the traveler upon it.

He followed the trail past the darkened gift shop,
past the elevators of the masses, and came to a private
corridor and an elevator set apart from the rest. The
doors stood open, awaiting him. Ravenna turned the
key protruding from the console and began his ascent.
I will call for Ravenna, and you will kill Vitel.

Time stretched out before Ravenna. The hotel was not particularly tall—the sixth floor served as the penthouse—yet the light above the door seemed only grudgingly to move from G to 1 to 2. As the numbers slowly increased, so too did Ravenna's agitation. He thought of Vallejo. The Spaniard would not hesitate to kill the prince if Vykos but asked. But for the games of power, Ravenna had been bred to this task. He gripped the cane as if it were his salvation. The tiny latch was at his fingertip. He was on his way to kill—it was the art he had studied for years upon years, an act he had performed countless times. Yet that which was natural to him, that which was his purpose and passion, now filled him with dread. He recoiled from the task set before him.

Because she wants it of me, he realized.

You will kill him for me.

Vykos wanted him to do this thing, and Parmenides-Ravenna was loath to serve her whim. For what she had done to him, for what his masters had let her do, he should slit her throat, burn her black heart. His hate for her burned fiercely, almost as fiercely as his hate for himself—for he knew he would do what she asked.

You will kill him for me.

"Be strong, young Assamite."

The voice didn't startle him, didn't alarm him. It floated down, surrounded him like whispering moonlight.

"Be strong, your masters have not forgotten you."

For the second time this night, Parmenides-Ravenna was unable to speak.

The small light, so labored in its advance, moved from 4 to 5.

"I will come to you, I or my brothers."

Parmenides-Ravenna gazed toward the ceiling of the elevator. What creature lay on the other side, calling to him, speaking of his masters? Parmenides would have smashed through the hatch, demanded to face whomever accosted him so—but Ravenna's body was broken, his legs barely suitable for the simplest movement.

"Do you have news for me to give your masters?"

Parmenides-Ravenna stared blankly; he gazed at the light.

5 to 6.

"Speak, young Assamite."

The chime sounded. The doors began to open.

His lips parted but were drier than the most punishing desert of his early nights. "I am…strong," he whispered at last.

The doors stood open. With faltering step, Ravenna entered the sumptuous haven of Marcus Vitel, Prince of Washington, D.C. Vykos's deceiving smile greeted him.

You will kill him for me.

Vitel was a striking figure. The fine quality of his suit was not lost on Parmenides, nor the strong lines of his face, the wisps of gray in his hair. Parmenides looked into the prince's dark blue eyes. A confident assassin could do that—look into the eyes of even an aged Kindred elder and not give anything away—but Parmenides's confidence in the most basic foundations of his previous existence had been shaken. He froze. In the face of this Camarilla prince, this creature accustomed to commanding awe, Parmenides could not go forward. His joints gripped and would not move. It was all he could do to keep from dropping the sack he carried. The mere contemplation of such a faux pas was mortifying.

"Now look what you've done, my prince," said Vykos in the most singsong, conversational of tones. "You've frightened my poor ghoul. What if he were to drop from fear on the spot? You have no idea the lengths to which I've gone to secure good help."

"Come, Ravenna," she said, stretching out a hand to entice him closer.

Vitel watched in silence as Parmenides forced his body to move forward. Indeed, the prince's gaze locked on the sack Parmenides carried, and did not waver.

He didn't have far to where they stood—they had not proceeded into the penthouse proper to converse in comfort, as decorum might normally dictate—but with each step, under the prince's unrelenting gaze, the bag seemed to grow heavier, as if the unfortunate head had sprouted a body, and the full weight of the prince's childe now rested within.

With movement, however tortured, Parmenides thought less of the head slipping from his grasp and the sickening thud it would make against the floor. His mind raced with possibilities; his finger rested by the latch on the cane. The prince, whether he wished to acknowledge the fact or not, undoubtedly knew what was in the bloody sack. Parmenides could toss it to Vitel. Certainly the prince would instinctively catch the head of his childe, and in his moment of distraction, Parmenides could strike. Yet that scenario lacked a certain dignity. He could strike as he handed over the bag—

"Come, Ravenna," Vykos said again as he reached them.

I will call for Ravenna, and you will kill Vitel.

Her words shook him, revealed to him how easily he'd fallen into the accustomed pattern of thought when faced with the prospect of the kill. A sudden wave of doubt washed over him, and at its heart was defiance. He felt the urge, the *need*, to plunge the cane, not through the prince, but through Vykos.

She watched Vitel, observed with thinly veiled pleasure the sorrow rising in his eyes, which were rimmed with tears of blood. The bag was close enough for him to touch; he had but to reach out.

You will kill him for me.

Parmenides could not hear for the pounding at his temples. He saw in his mind Vykos smiling, staring down at her impaled breast. His heart leapt, but his hand upon the cane was stayed, as surely as had been his legs when their sinews and bones were fused one to another.

You will kill him for me.

The prince, grappling with his sorrow, sighed deeply. Parmenides pressed the latch—the spike sprung into place—and he struck. But a moment too late. Vykos howled with outrage as the prince knocked aside the blow aimed at his heart. The cane pierced his shoulder.

The back of Vitel's hand caught Parmenides across the face. The assassin-ghoul, hobbled by his infirmity, lost his footing to the powerful blow and crashed to the floor.

Vykos screeched and flung a clawed hand at the prince, but already he'd turned and thrown himself from his attackers. His body, impaled by the cane, shattered one of the large picture windows overlooking the Mall. Before Parmenides could struggle to his knees, Vitel was gone. Deathly silence reigned.

A great trembling overtook Parmenides. The weakness in his legs prevented him from standing. Vykos turned from where she'd followed the prince to the broken window, and rejoined her charge. Bloody tears flowed down his cheeks, dripped, and soaked into the luxurious carpet.

I am strong, he had said to the messenger of his masters. So strong that he could not free himself; so strong that he could not defy his new mistress; so strong that his pitiful defiance had led only to utter failure in that which was his calling.

Vykos placed a gentle hand to his face. There was no ire or recrimination in her touch. She could not know the treachery that burned in his heart still, his hatred of her...and his love.

She pulled him toward her, pressed his fevered skin to her cool belly.

"I am weak." His words were muffled against the fabric of her gown. Sobs wracked his rigid body. "I am weak."

"There, there, my *philosophe*. Have no fear." She stroked his hair, soothed the pounding at his temples. "You will redeem yourself."

Sometime later, Vallejo stood before the shattered window and reported that the prince had escaped.

Sascha Vykos sat high atop the sharply slanted roof of the Castle's sole tower. She surveyed the city below. *Her* city, she reminded herself.

The bold plan that they had devised so many months ago in Madrid had at last come to its fruition. At Monçada's urging, she had traveled to this New World. She had seized command of the Sabbat forces besieging the city of Atlanta. She had pushed forward the merciless blitzkrieg campaign, crushing all resistance along the Eastern Seaboard north to this point and driving the Camarilla before her. She had wrested control of the most powerful city on this continent from her enemies and their Antediluvian puppetmasters.

And now, at last, it was a time to rest—to rejoice in their victories, to honor their slain, to shore up their strength for the trials that lay ahead.

From below, she could hear the sound of an experimental steam-driven pipe organ—one of the curiosities of the Smithsonian's extensive collection—coughing to life. Her guests were all assembled. She had watched them arrive, singly and in small clutches.

From her lofty vantage point, they looked very small and insecure, daunted by the prospect of walking openly through the streets of what most of them still thought of as an enemy stronghold. *And perhaps, in some respects, they are correct*, Vykos thought, a wicked smile spreading across her face.

Polonia and his flunky, Costello had returned

from their 'reconnaissance mission'—to Buffalo, or Atlantic City, or wherever it was—where they had tested the mettle of the Camarilla defenses and, no doubt, found them wanting. There was no other explanation for the enthusiasm in Polonia's otherwise carefully guarded demeanor. This game of conquest and dominion was both contagious and addictive.

Borges and Sebastian had arrived separately, each from his own city. Vykos had no misgivings about the clandestine arrangement that had left Borges's protege as the Bishop of Atlanta. She had even thrown Savannah into the bargain, although she believed that, at last report, Borges still reserved the prized port city for himself.

The arrangement was expedient. The fact was that she needed to ensure that these two ambitious conspirators were kept terribly occupied and well out of the picture as the campaign pressed north of Atlanta. The last thing she needed was to have to fend off the subtle manipulations and treacheries of the Lasombra while she was engaged in pitched battle with Camarilla forces.

Even the venerable Borges, whose eyes opened not upon life but only upon its shadowy subtexts, had been quick to seize upon Vykos's proffered bargain. He had gone so far as to set his signature to the contract in his own blood. Dear old Borges.

Bolon and Vallejo, of course were already present. She seldom allowed her commanders far from her side these days. There was so much still to be done in securing the nation's capital. Perhaps in a few week's time she could spare one of them from the unrelenting labor of shoring up the bulwarks against the inevitable counterstrike.

The formidable Tremere chantry of Washington still stood defiantly, and the truth be told, Vykos's forces, as scattered and disorganized in victory as were the Camarilla in defeat, presently lacked the cohesion to face such opponents. In time, she hoped, cut off from Camarilla support, the chantry would wither on the vine. For the present, it was enough that the Tremere had not stood forth in defense of Vitel, their long-time rival.

She was toying with the idea of sending Bolon back south for a time, to rally the shattered Nomad Coalition. The group had drifted apart after the untimely death of Averros. Vykos smiled at the memory. If anyone could win the respect of the hard-fighting and fiercely independent roaming packs, it was formidable Bolon.

Vallejo, of course, was something of a gift from her patron, the cardinal. And not one she would take for granted. But having secured so much in a mere week's time—and what was a week to one such as Monçada, a manipulator so cunning that he measured out his machinations by the century?—surely he would not risk jeopardizing their gains by attempting to withdraw Vallejo to Madrid.

If it did come to such a conflict of interests between herself and the cardinal, Vykos thought, she had no delusions whatsoever about which master the seasoned veteran would obey. He would follow her orders unquestioningly, even unto certain destruction, especially after Vitel's escape. Vykos had chided Vallejo only gently, yet his fierce pride had been wounded.

He would expect *her*, however, to follow the cardinal's demands with the same unhesitating enthusiasm. She hoped she never had to disabuse him of the notion that she would.

Vykos shifted uncomfortably. This lofty perch was the only place she felt she could be assured of a reasonable measure of privacy. For the third time that evening, Vykos unfolded the letter. The unusual parchment had a disconcerting ruddy tinge to it and crinkled like dried leaves in the night breeze.

My Dearest Vykos,

How can I express the intensity of my feelings toward you at this moment? At the very thought of your nearness, I am consumed with an irresistible longing. My hands tremble in anticipation of our meeting. If I could but once caress the peerless arch of your throat, my fondest desire would be fulfilled.

But it cannot be. When I think of all you have already risked for my sake, I am both humbled and shamed. It is altogether too much to bear. Perhaps you will understand me when I say that I cannot allow you to endanger yourself further on my account. I would rather go willingly to the pyre than be the cause of your bruising even your delicate heel.

You must put this rash notion from your mind. Surely there must be diversions enough in Atlanta to occupy your thoughts for the present. Await me there and I shall come to you, I swear it—in the Autumn perhaps. Yes. I have heard such remarkable things about your Georgian scenery. I should very much like to see your Fall.

My darling, every night we are apart consumes me like the midday sun. Why must you torment me so? You know that I have given into your keeping the keys to my dark soul. There is nothing I can deny you.

TZIMISCE

*But if you must come, bringing fire and the sword
into the secret places of my heart, come quickly. Better to
yield to such arms as yours, than to fend them off.*

> "Ah, love, let us be true
> To one another! for the world, which seems
> To lie before us like a land of dreams,
> So various, so beautiful, so new,
> Hath really neither joy, nor love, nor light,
> Nor certitude, nor peace, nor help for pain…"

Neglected, the letter fluttered loosely in Vykos's hand. Her gaze was distant, staring out over the Mall at some imaginary point in the middle distance. She hardly noticed the telltale plumes of fires still burning out of control in several parts of the city. The sound of sirens and machine-gun fire and breaking glass rose up on all sides. A police riot-control helicopter banked over the White House.

> "And we are here as on a darkling plain
> Swept with confused alarms of struggle and flight,
> Where ignorant armies clash by night."

Vykos did not know she had spoken aloud until she heard someone discreetly cough behind her. A head poked through the tower window. Parmenides craned his neck to peer up at her.

"It is time, my lady, shall we go down to them?"

Vykos took one long last look over the silent city and rose. She descended the steep slope to the window.

Accepting Parmenides's arm, she allowed him to help her over the sill—although he looked to be the frailer of the two. Apprehension was evident on his face as he blocked her advance toward the tower stair.

"They will try to kill you, you know."

"I know." She leaned toward him conspiratorially. "But they do not understand that tonight I have an insurance policy."

Parmenides turned away sharply and would not meet her gaze.

"Oh, now you have gone and gotten your feelings hurt again. What is the matter, my young romantic, my *philosophe*?"

He turned upon her in anger. "You can ask that? What use can I be to you like…this?" He struck the cane against his crippled legs in frustration. Vykos winced, expecting him to go down in a heap, but Parmenides did not flinch.

"I think," she said deliberately, "that you will have to do. Do not worry, you shall not fail me."

He could not hold her gaze and his eyes fell.

"You never have."

Vykos took his arm. Together they descended the narrow spiraling stair to where the assembled Sabbat dignitaries waited to acknowledge and proclaim Sascha Vykos as Archbishop of Washington, D.C.

The cage descended into the darkness of the service shaft. Witgenstein steeled himself for the interminable journey. As many times as he had made this trip, it never got any easier.

He tried to occupy his thoughts by polishing the elaborate brass scissors-gates. The service elevator to the "dragon's lair" was a genuine relic. It had somehow managed to evade every attempt at remodeling and modernization since the '20s. Witgenstein knew that no one else would ever see, much less appreciate, the results of his handiwork, but he applied the rag with an affection usually reserved for vintage automobiles.

Three miles the shaft descended, straight into the belly of the Beast. The printing presses of the *Times* were one of the marvels of modern engineering. The thundering machines were so massive that their incidental vibrations reached near-seismic proportions. Firing up the presses would have instantly torn down not only any building they were housed in, but the surrounding buildings as well.

In the end, the presses had had to be sunk into the very bedrock of the island. The same unshakable foundation that made the city uniquely suited for its unceasing clamor skyward also concealed wonders in its deepest recesses.

Witgenstein knew the elevator was nearing the bottom of the shaft by the onset of a sudden panicked feeling of vertigo. All at once, the narrow confines of the shaft had fallen away—receding *upward* into the dim distance. As many times as he had experienced this alarming sensation, it never failed to produce in him the feeling that his brass cage was hurtling unchecked toward the unforgiving bedrock.

Witgenstein forced his eyes back open, cursing himself for a fool. Squinting into the darkness, he could make out the shadowy presence of the slumbering dragons below. They seemed to fill the vast open space. Wisps of steam rose from their bodies and coiled upwards in the chill, damp air.

Already he could tell that something was wrong. In the uncertain light of his lamp, the presses seemed to glisten wetly. Thick, slimy strands of what looked to be seaweed choked the titanic rollers. But that was impossible. Those presses would easily have ground a strong man's arms to pulp before anyone could even shut the machines down—assuming someone would be so incautious as not to accord the giants a respectful distance.

But to bring the presses grinding to a halt, those clinging strands must be as thick around as trees.

The service elevator splashed down and then continued its descent at a more leisurely pace. The rising water shorted out the electric lamp as Witgenstein clawed at the latch to the scissors-gates. Already, the lower reaches of the lattice were laced with clinging greenery, preventing their operation.

In time, the cage vanished beneath the murky surface.

Soon, even the echoes of his struggle receded, meandering back and forth between the walls of the narrow service tunnel as if trying to find their way.

Below, that which had stirred at the incessant buzzing of the presses returned to its contemplations.

About the author

Eric Griffin was initiated into the bardic mysteries at their very source, Cork, Ireland. He is currently engaged in that most ancient of Irish literary traditions—that of the writer-in-exile. He resides in Atlanta, Georgia, with his lovely wife Victoria, and his two sons, heroes-in-training both.

The Vampire Clan Novel Series..............

Clan Novel: Toreador
These artists are the most sophisticated of the Kindred.

Clan Novel: Tzimisce
Fleshcrafters, experts of the arcane, and the most cruel of Sabbat vampires.

Clan Novel: Gangrel
Feral shapeshifters distanced from the society of the Kindred.

Clan Novel: Setite
The much-loathed serpentine masters of moral and spiritual corruption.

Clan Novel: Ventrue
The most political of vampires, they lead the Camarilla.

Clan Novel: Lasombra
The leaders of the Sabbat and the most Machiavellian of all Kindred.

Clan Novel: Ravnos
These devilish gypsies are not welcomed by the Camarilla, nor tolerated by the Sabbat.

Clan Novel: Assamite
The most feared clan, for they are assassins of both vampires and mortals.

Clan Novel: Malkavian
Thought insane by other Kindred, they know that within madness lies wisdom.

Clan Novel: Brujah
Street-punks and rebels, they are aggressive and vengeful in defense of their beliefs.

Clan Novel: Giovanni
Still a respected part of the mortal world, this mercantile clan is also home to necromancers.

Clan Novel: Tremere
The most magical of the clans and the most tightly organized.

Clan Novel: Nosferatu
Horrific to behold, these sneaks know more secrets than the other clans—secrets that will only be revealed in this, the last of the **Vampire Clan Novels.**

The Toreador and Tzimisce clans are the center of attention as the Clan Novel series begins, but many other plot threads are ready for weaving. And don't expect that this is the last you've seen of many characters from the first two novels. Victoria, Vykos, and others all have greater roles to play.

Astute readers of this series will begin to put clues together as the series progresses, but everyone will note that the end date of each book is later than the end date of the prior book. In such a fashion, the series chronologically continues in **Clan Novel: Gangrel** and then **Clan Novel: Setite**. Excerpts of these two exciting novels are on the following pages.

CLAN NOVEL: GANGREL
ISBN 1-56504-803-2
WW# 11102
$5.99 U.S.

CLAN NOVEL: SETITE
ISBN 1-56504-808-3
WW# 11103
$5.99 U.S.

"Shh," Ratface cautioned her. His enlarged, rodent ears were pricked up. "That way. Someone's coming."

"You always were tough to sneak up on," said a voice from the direction Ratface was looking. A moment later, a tall man strode out of the darkness and over to Table Rock.

He was taller than Ramona and Ratface and wore sturdy hiking boots, worn jeans, and a heavy corduroy shirt, all dirty and dusty from long use but not tattered like their own clothes. The newcomer drew himself up before them. He picked a twig out of his long and unruly hair and flicked the tiny stick into the woods.

"I am Brant Edmonson," he said. "When the mortals fought among themselves for the western lands, I prowled the trails. When Alden the Cruel was lost to the Beast, I was with mighty Xaviar as we put him down."

Ratface nodded respectfully. Ramona was caught off guard by what she considered the awkwardness of the introduction.

"I am Ratface," said Ratface. "I know all the towns and cities of New York. I am smarter than the lupines, swifter than the Sabbat."

Ramona listened to the words she'd heard before. She didn't know what to say to this Brant Edmonson. Ratface seemed to have his little spiel planned already. The new guy didn't seem to be a threat. His sudden appearance hadn't alarmed Ratface, and Ratface was skittish if anything. That close, Ramona could smell that Edmonson was like them, that the blood didn't flow naturally through his body, that it was really somebody else's blood in the first place. Without thinking, she reached out and shook Brant Edmonson's hand. It seemed like the uptight, corncob-up-your-ass kind of thing that these folks might do.

"I'm Ramona," she said, then stepped back.

Brant seemed surprised and gave her a funny look, like he thought he was eating sugar but tasted salt instead. The funny look slowly faded though, and Ramona realized that his eyes weren't focused on her anymore. He was looking over her shoulder. Ratface too, she saw, was looking to the other side of Table Rock. His ears were pricked up again.

Ramona turned and saw the dark figure across the clearing.

A throaty growl rumbled through the night, but the rumble was actually words: "I am Stalker-in-the-Woods. I do not run from the mortals. I catch their bullets in my teeth. I drink their blood and grind their bones to dust."

Ramona edged away so that she wasn't the closest as the newest Gangrel stepped onto Table Rock. Stalker-in-the-Woods was hunched over, but still his shoulders were more than a foot higher than Ramona's head. His wild mane of hair covered him almost like a cloak; he wore no other clothes. He was all gaunt muscle and scars.

Edmonson stepped forward. He stood with his chin raised defiantly.

by gherbod fleming

"I am Brant Edmonson. When the mortals fought among themselves for the western lands, I prowled the trails. When Alden the Cruel was lost to the Beast, I was with mighty Xaviar as we put him down."

From where he stood, Ratface spoke his introduction as he had twice already. Stalker-in-the-Woods looked at him, and Ratface looked away, not meeting the creature's gaze.

The attention of Stalker-in-the-Woods shifted to Ramona. He stepped closer. Ramona suddenly felt her mouth as dry as if she hadn't drunk blood in a year. Stalkerin-the-Woods moved closer still. His eyes were yellowed and bloodshot, his face black with dried blood.

Ramona started to open her mouth, but no words came. She wasn't tempted to shake hands as she had with Edmonson.

"She is Ramona Tanner-childe," said Ratface, at last.

Stalker-in-the-Woods ignored Ratface and stared at Ramona until she looked away. This seemed to satisfy him. He turned and moved toward Brant until the two were only a few feet apart. Edmonson held his ground. His hands were relaxed at his sides.

Ramona almost jumped when she felt Ratface beside her. She hadn't heard him move. His hand was on her elbow and he was ushering her to the side.

"He's a mean one," Ratface whispered. "We'd do best to stay out of his way."

Edmonson didn't share all of Ratface's opinion. He stood toe-to-toe with Stalker-in-the-Woods, and to Ramona's surprise, the smaller, more human Gangrel smiled.

There was no warning of Stalker-in-the-Woods's

attack. He sprang with a ferocious snarl before Ramona even knew he was moving....

Among the Gangrel, the dominant topics of conversation were the Sabbat and lupines. Ramona didn't take part in the discussions, but she heard bits of various stories. The tales about the Sabbat were exchanged in calm tones, as any interesting news might be related. As far as she gathered, the gang, which the Gangrel opposed—although she did hear one story about a Gangrel, Korbit, who fought on the side of the Sabbat—was taking control of a great deal of territory that had belonged to the Camarilla along the East Coast. Ramona heard several cities mentioned—Atlanta, Charleston, Washington, D.C. It sounded bad, but the other Gangrel didn't seem particularly worried.

When they spoke of the lupines, however, they did so in hushed tones. They glanced occasionally over their shoulders. Probably they denied it even to themselves, but Ramona could hear the fear in their voices. Several of the Gangrel in their litany of deeds had spoken boastfully of lupines, but uncertainty, not pride, tinged their voices as they spoke of routes of safety through lupine territory or shifting hunting grounds.

It was the talk and the vague sense of fear that made Ramona begin to feel strangely detached from everything that was going on around her. The stories were all of death and dismemberment: a friend decapitated in the wilds of northern Maine; an associate crossing the Grand Tetons split open from neck to belly; another who never returned from the Everglades.

by gherbod fleming

Ramona withdrew into herself. The talk moved farther and farther away, until the voices were very small. They rang in the back of her head. Certain words echoed through her mind—*lupine… Texas… werewolf… lupine*—grew closer together, finally overlapped and merged into one disquieting mass.

I saw a lupine in Texas, Ramona said. She moved her lips, but no words emerged. She didn't remember sitting, but there she was on the ground, sifting loose dirt through her fingers.

I saw a lupine in Texas.

They had still been several hours from San Antonio. Eddie had this thing for back roads. He wouldn't drive on an interstate if he could help it, and so when they ran out of gas, they were surrounded by nothing but miles and miles of gullies, mesquite, and dust.

Jen and Darnell argued bitterly over whose fault it was that they'd run out of gas. Eddie didn't seem too upset. He claimed to have an unfailing sense of direction and saw finding a shortcut through the mesquite thickets as a challenge. Ramona asked him if his dick was a compass, but he ignored her. Too bad, they agreed, that they couldn't eat sand instead of drinking blood. Plenty of sand. No gas. No blood.

Then suddenly there was plenty of blood.

Maybe if Jen and Darnell hadn't been arguing, somebody would've heard it coming.

Lupine. The name fit the monster from Ramona's memory.

They were approaching the edge of a gully, a dry creek bed, and the lupine was there, where it hadn't been a second before.

Eddie stumbled back. The left side of his face

was gone. Ramona heard the first snarl as she was splattered with his blood. Before they could speak or scream, a claw ripped open his gut like a piñata full of shriveled intestines. Eddie's knees buckled, and then the monster slammed its jaws shut and took off the top of his head.

Eddie fell. His blood wetted down the dust.

Ramona and the others behind her stood in shock, mouths agape. She could feel the lupine's moist breath heavy on the dry, Texas air.

The first moment of decision arrived—the creature needed only reach out to take off Ramona's head, but instead it fell upon Eddie, burying its snout in his opened belly. Eddie whimpered as it tore him apart from the inside out.

The second moment of decision fell to Ramona, Jen, and Darnell. They could pounce on the lupine. It was fully consumed by its passion for carnage. They could strike back for Eddie, who no longer could for himself. The moment hung heavy in the air, bathed in blood and the staccato crack of ribs.

As one, Ramona and the others turned and ran.

They stumbled through the mesquite. Thorns dug into their flesh, but they hardly noticed. They ran and didn't stop running until the rising sun forced them to burrow into the steep bank of a dry streambed. They burrowed until the earth collapsed behind them, but they didn't need air. Only darkness.

I saw a lupine in Texas.

by gherbod fleming

Hesha woke to darkness and the silence of the tomb. He lay where he was, and did not move. Lethargy lifted from him, and he felt the last light of day leave the earth. He wondered if the face of the sun had changed in the centuries since the curse had been laid on him. He wondered if Set fled Ra's glory as he traveled the underworld, or whether the vampire-god were forced by the curse to attack his grandfather's barge every night, or if Set slept, as Hesha himself did, and fought the curse in the land of the living.

Hesha, childe in the seventh degree from Set, the son of Geb, the son of Ra, stirred in his chamber, and lights hidden in the ceiling glowed dimly at his first movement. They threw the carved walls into deep shadow; shallow relief stood forth like sculpture in the round. Farmers, fishers, hunters, artisans, scribes, priests, nobles, and royalty performed their daily tasks in the friezes. Beneath the arched body of the sky, they marked the hours with ritual, work, prayer, and pleasure. They were copies of the most beautiful art of Egypt, blended into a single masterpiece by modern hands. Hesha ran his night-black fingers over the smooth stone, and traced the outline of the cartouche in the wall to his right: a rope, bound into a loop by thinner cords, filled with the signs of Set's name and the simple title, "Lord of the Northern Skies."

Set's descendant rose and paced the walls, admiring the work. He touched his own cartouche, above the lintel of a door, and walked on. In a crooked corner of the irregular cave, he came to the only un-finished section of the work. Chisel, hammer, brush, and charcoal lay neatly in a box at the base of the stone. He picked up the stick of charcoal and drew a last cartouche on the gray stone. Within the oval, he scribed a horned viper, an open tent, a vulture, a man, and an ankh — *VGH'* — Vegel, the artist. His work was over. Hesha chiseled the rock away from the sign, and laid the tools down again. The unfinished panel would remain that way forever.

"Thompson," Hesha said into the dimness.

A small speaker among the lights clicked on. "You called, sir?"

"Conference. Half an hour. You and the Asp in person. Have Janet and the doctor call in on secure lines."

"Yes, sir."

Hesha pushed lightly on a papyrus plant carved into the rock, and a door opened to more mundane apartments. He returned clean and clad in a simple robe, the gallahbeyah of his native North Africa. The amulets that had been hidden by western garb swung freely from cords at his neck and waist.

Thompson was waiting for him. The door to the upper areas of the house swung open as he entered, and the Asp leered his way into the room. Hesha sat at the foot of the stone bench he had spent the day on, and looked up at the two of them.

"Bring in chairs, if you like. This will be rather a long session."

The two men turned uncertainly to each other. Thompson made the faintest question with his brows, and the Asp sprinted back up the stairs.

"Janet? Doctor? Are you with us?"

by Kathleen Ryan

"Yes, sir."

"I'm here, Hesha."

The Asp carried two battered folding chairs into the beautifully carved room, and he and Thompson sat nervously in them.

"Let's begin, then. Reports. Thompson?"

"The bodies of Vegel's team are all accounted for, sir. Transportation arrangements are under way; and we've made funeral provisions for their families. I'd like tomorrow and Monday afternoon free to attend services." Hesha nodded approval. "There wasn't much left of the car, but Atlanta police identified it yesterday as a wreck left in Cabbagetown early Tuesday morning. In their opinion, it was stolen for a joyride and then deliberately crashed."

"Probably true," said Hesha, "as far as it goes. Asp?"

"Six of the Family have come to the townhouse looking for shelter — three from Richmond, one each from Charleston, Atlanta, and Savannah, all separately, all in a hell of a hurry. I found them crash space here and there, and put them on field rations, per your orders. I gave them your number here; calls have been piling up, but so far they've lain low like good boys and girls."

"That won't last much longer."

"I'm afraid you're right, Hesha," said Doctor Oxenti from her office. "D.C. hospitals and the Red Cross were on our backs for rare types before the riots, and now we're low on everything. Plasma's cleaned out completely; whole blood is in short supply."

"I see." Hesha placed his hands flat on the stone beneath him.

"It's going to get worse," he began. "By now you

all have gathered that these riots are Family business. My own branch is neutral, but that won't make a difference to either faction. We support both sides against the middle, and they will take any opportunity they can to use us, to trap us into allegiances we can't afford, or to rend us in the general slaughter.

"Washington, D.C. is under assault at this moment." He drove on, ignoring the expressions on the faces before him, and the gasp — Janet's — that whistled through the speakers. "Assume, based on the war's progress so far, that Baltimore is not only a target, but the *next* target in a line north up the East Coast."

"Our open business and the townhouse are almost certain to be ransacked or firebombed. Begin removing the most valuable and portable pieces, slowly. Fake buys, arrange shoplifting, send things out for recycling, and make small shipments, but don't let it be too obvious that we're withdrawing. Warehouse the goods in the deep country — the Appalachians would be best, I think.

"I want the staff out of the buildings well before sundown every day until further notice. If we don't have more information by fall, we'll keep later morning hours as the day gets shorter.

"Janet, you're coming out of the city center. Choose whatever files and equipment you want to bring with you, but hurry. You move to new quarters at dawn tomorrow. Asp, you're moving her yourself. We'll pick a safe zone after this meeting, and the location doesn't go beyond the three of us. You understand?"

The Asp nodded, and said with a smirk, "It'll be a privilege, Mrs. Lindbergh."

by Kathleen Ryan

"I'm sure," she shot back. "But I'm driving."

"Doctor?"

"Still here, sir."

"Can you leave your research at this time?"

"No." Hesha heard the tapping of Jasmine Oxenti's long, manicured nails on the phone receiver, and then, "A week. I need a week, at least."

"We'll try to give you the week. After that, I want you to take a holiday. Janet, book passage for the Doctor to Alaska, one week from tomorrow."

"Alaska?!"

"The sun isn't setting there. I'd send you all if I could afford to do without your aid, but blood banks are particular targets, and you are particularly resistant to efforts by Thompson's people to protect you."

"But—"

"In the meantime, order the usual shipments for the next month. Have your second-in-command coordinate emergency blood drives with the Red Cross. Start at our own open offices, in fact. And put your staff on daylight hours, same as the other businesses."

"How in hell am I going to rationalize that?"

"Convincingly," Hesha frowned, "if you want to save their lives. Should the enemy take the clinic while the staff are still there, our people will be massacred. Understood?"

There was a pause. "Yes, sir."

"And all of you: Cut communications between branches of the organization to a minimum. Close what channels you can. I want our holdings concealed from onlookers as much as possible. I want the four of you speaking to each other as little as possible. Thompson has briefed you all on the emergency procedures; start using them.

"Any questions?"

Silence fell.

"Further business?"

"Yes, sir." Thompson darted up the stairs and back again, holding several plastic-wrapped bundles on a tray. He wore gloves to handle them.

"Family letters for you, and a few others that Mrs. Lindbergh had a feeling about."

"There are messages waiting on your private line, as well," said Janet. "And I show a call from Miss Dimitros's number."

The Asp snickered.

Hesha's right eyelid twitched at his lackey. "You were saying, Mr. Mercurio?" he asked, in a tone that chilled them.

"Sir." Raphael Mercurio cleared his throat. "Ah…one of your close cousins is waiting to speak with you; one of the refugees. He gave his name as Mahmoud, and said you knew him…."

"Make an appointment for three o'clock tomorrow at the townhouse." Hesha stood. "I have work to do tonight."

Thompson and the Asp left, taking the chairs with them. The door to the house swung silently to, concealed once again by the carvings. Hesha triggered open another seamless portal, entered his sanctum, and sealed the heavy stone shut behind him.

by kathleen RYan

next gangrel